MW00444314

STOLEN DREAM

BILL NASH

2B Publishing Co.

Copyright © 2015 Bill Nash
All Rights Reserved.

STOLEN DREAM

ISBN-13: 978-1508512363
ISBN-10: 1508512361

No part of this book may be reproduced or transmitted in any form or by any means, electronic or mechanical, including photocopying, scanning, recording, or by any information storage and retrieval system, without permission in writing from the copyright owner.

This book is a work of fiction. Names, characters, places and incidents either are the product of the author's imagination or are used fictitiously, and any resemblance to any actual persons, living or dead, events, or locales is entirely coincidental.

This book was printed in the United States
and published by the 2B Publishing Company.

Book Design and Layout by MIND*the*MARGINS, LLC

Special thanks to my wife, Holly, for her unwavering support and keen-eyed editing. Thanks also to Cynthia Elliott for her editing and insight, and to my son, John, for my author's photo.

CHAPTER ONE

An empty can of Diet Coke rolled out onto the dirt road as Tommy Upton opened the door of his Jeep and climbed out. He looked at the can for just a moment, wondering if it was worth the effort of picking it up. Then, with a soft grunt, bent over, grabbed the can and tossed it into the back of the Jeep where it joined five others and a collection of junk food wrappers.

He stared down the long space between two rows of plum trees at the knot of people clustered about a hundred yards down the row. Looking left and right along the road, he made a mental note of the police, fire and rescue vehicles parked along the shoulder with his Jeep. There was a story here. He wanted it. He needed it.

He inhaled deeply. It smelled good out in the orchards. Away from town. Away from everything. It smelled wholesome and pure—earth, water, tree blossoms. Smells too nice for what he knew awaited him down in the orchard.

He pulled the brim of his fedora further down over his sunglasses. The hat was light gray felt with a black satin band. The gray soiled easily but he thought it brought out the blue in his eyes. The sunlight hurt. The hat was mostly an affectation, but today it helped his eyes. They had been bloodshot and burning since he quit drinking, almost two weeks earlier.

With a small sigh he started walking toward the emergency personnel in the orchard. He knew what he was about to see. It wasn't his first crime scene, it wasn't even his first murder scene. It wasn't even his most recent murder scene. He had visited that one about a week earlier and, about five days before that, almost too drunk to stand, another one where he had seen his wife, Jen, lying in a pool of her own blood. Even that would never quite take away the initial shock of seeing a body once full of life and then suddenly empty of it. The shell of a person, the life emptied out of it by the hand of another. By the time he reached the body, the wet grass had already soaked through his running shoes and his jeans were moistened by the moisture up to his knees.

There was no yellow crime scene tape. There were no TV station satellite trucks or pretty reporters with microphones. The only photographer there worked for the Sheriff's department. Upton was the only media there and he was uninvited. It was a small-town crime scene in a secluded orchard. Regardless of who it was lying in the wet grass, there would be no film at eleven.

Sheriff Dave Miller was squatting by the body. He always went into a squat at a crime scene. He claimed it gave him a different perspective on the evidence. His deputies said it was a good thing he didn't wear spurs or he'd give himself hemorrhoid surgery. He stood as Upton approached and now towered over the crime scene. The early morning light put golden highlights in Miller's smooth, black face. At well over six feet tall, he had been a starting tight end at UCLA and he looked like he could still play.

He watched as Tommy Upton shuffled through the wet grass to the crime scene. A career in law enforcement often meant seeing people at the worst time of their lives. But he had never seen someone fall so hard, so far and so fast as Tommy Upton. He looked like he always did, a fedora hat pulled down low in front, just above black sunglasses, a flannel shirt worn open over a beige T-shirt. He wore jeans, but not the kind sold down at the farm supply store. Upton's jeans were the kind big-city people wore to night clubs. Miller knew Upton's look was carefully calculated, and it worked for him in the past, when he was the talk of the journalism world. But now, it was kind of pathetic. Like an aging actress trying to look like a starlet.

"You're up early, Tommy. Have trouble sleeping again?"

"Not again. Still. I heard the call on the scanner and, since I couldn't sleep anyway, I thought I might as well come out."

"We don't know much yet. You can stay, but no pictures."

"Deal."

Upton worked his way around the outside of the crime scene to get a better look at the body, being careful not to step on the small, numbered tent cards that marked evidence. The body itself was unremarkable. A male, maybe a teenager, lay face down in the grass. He was dressed like many of the town's teenaged boys; an unbuttoned shirt over a black T-shirt, jeans and sneakers. That stopped Upton for a moment. Except for the fedora and sunglasses, he was wearing almost the identical clothes. It might be time to grow up, he thought. There wasn't much more to see except for the black, bloody hole in the back of the boy's head. Evidence marker number 33 sat beside his right ear. Upton could see flecks of bone and brain matter in the matted blood and hair around the wound. He saw a deputy he knew with a clipboard taking notes, so he asked the obvious question.

"What happened?"

"Oh, hey Tommy. Don't know yet. Obviously shot from behind, and there's a baggie with a few meth crystals in it next to the body. Other than that, we're still trying to figure things out."

"Any chance it was self-inflicted?"

"Doubt it. Angle doesn't seem right. The Medical Examiner can help figure that out."

"What about the evidence marker?"

"What do you mean?"

"Number 33. Isn't the wound the most important piece of evidence? Shouldn't it be number one?"

"Doesn't work that way. When we arrive, we start at the outside of the crime scene and work our way in, marking evidence as we go. Same thing with the photos. We start wide and then zero in on specific pieces of evidence."

The deputy had to move around to the other side of the body, so Upton stepped away. This wasn't the first murder in Los Robles, just the most recent, but it was too many too soon in a town of their size. Jen had been the first. It was why he was here. He needed to know who had done it and why.

Upton looked at the trees surrounding him—plums, the purple life-blood of Los Robles. The town's veins had first been filled with black gold when oil was discovered in the valley and on the hillsides overlooking the valley. But as the oil dried up, the fertile soil and mild climate proved perfect for growing plums and agriculture sustained the town.

Local growers were split almost evenly into two camps. Half grew Japanese plums that were sold as fresh fruit. The other half grew European plums that were dried and sold as prunes. Although they aren't called prunes anymore. A great marketing mind somewhere decided that dried plums sounded more appealing than prunes, and the Food and Drug Administration granted the California Prune Board permission to change the name. A prune by any other name is still a prune, thought Upton.

Looking at the trees now, Upton couldn't tell what types of plums were on the trees. Most of the beautiful white blossoms had come and gone a month or so ago and the fruit had been thinned by the growers. Now it was almost time for the harvest to begin.

The harvest would begin at the south end of the valley, near the Derrick Grade where the highway ran over the hills into the next valley. As the fruit ripened, the harvest would move slowly north past Los Robles and finish around October at the north end of the valley near the town's largest packing house, Plumrite Packing. Every orchard would be picked about three times over a ten day period as the fruit ripened through the season.

Looking at the trees around the crime scene, Upton could see plums, but they didn't look like they were ready to harvest. Probably too far north in the valley, he thought.

Dave Miller stood up from his crouch near the body. Upton walked closer.

"Do you know who he is?"

"Think so. Local kid, but not a trouble-maker. Doesn't make sense."

"Doesn't the meth kind of explain things?"

"Well, I can't say that it isn't a possibility, but the kid doesn't seem like a meth-head. None of the scabs or rashes usually associated with meth use, clean, well-nourished. Not your typical druggie. Either way though, it looks like you've got another obituary to write."

"Great. I'm not really looking for that kind of work you know."

"I know."

Upton nodded a goodbye and started trudging back towards his Jeep. Miller watched him go, marveling at how far the man had fallen and wondering if he had enough spirit to pull himself back up.

As a cop, Miller had seen just about everything life could do to a man, and life seemed to have done it all to Upton. When he moved to Los Robles, Upton had been a respected investigative reporter who had just come off a successful book tour. The book had exposed corruption in the politics that brought Northern California water to farmers in Central and Southern California. Upton and his wife, Jen, had settled in Los Robles figuring the quiet, small-town lifestyle would be a perfect atmosphere for a promising new author. But success only fueled Upton's passion for alcohol and soon his trademark fedora and ever-present sunglasses hid a disheveled man with the red, teary eyes of an alcoholic. The book deals dried up and Upton survived on royalties and freelance pieces he wrote for the Los Robles Register. If it wasn't for Jen's success in local real estate, they probably would have lost their condo. At least that was what he had thought at the time. The investigation into her murder had disclosed Jen came from money and had lots of it. For a while, that had made Tommy Upton a suspect.

But his alibi had been confirmed by a dozen people drinking with him in Louie's Bar. She didn't have to sell real estate, she wanted to. And she was good at it. In fact, she was good for the whole town. She got involved and she gave both time and money. Then, Jen was murdered. When she died, Tommy inherited the fortune. Her parents weren't happy. That was the day Upton stopped drinking, but he had already lost everything he loved.

Miller watched as Upton slowly made his way up the road to his Jeep. Upton had taken his hat off and was wiping his face with his other hand. Miller could see the start of a bald spot on the back of Upton's head and noticed a slight paunch on the man's medium build. He was trying to get his life back together, but the man was in bad shape.

By the time he reached his Jeep, Upton was slightly out of breath. He put his hand on the side of the Jeep and bent over slightly to catch his breath. He glanced back down into the orchard and saw Miller striding up the row towards him.

"Jesus, Tommy. Are you OK?"

"I need to get in better shape."

Miller glanced at the wrappers in the bed of the Jeep. "Well, a diet of Slim Jims, Pringles and Diet Coke isn't going to help. What, do you drink the Diet Coke to be healthy?"

"Thanks, mom. I'm going through some things, you know?"

"Yeah, I know, Tommy. Sorry. We have a positive ID on the kid. I'm going to make the notification to his family. Do you want to come along?"

"Why would I want to do that? It sounds horrible."

"It is horrible, but you always tell me you like to make the obituaries as personal as possible. It doesn't get any more personal than this, and I thought since you were here anyway, you might gain a few insights."

Upton stared at Miller for a moment to make sure he wasn't joking. He wasn't.

"Where does . . . where did he live?"

"South of town. Park in front of the newspaper. I'll pick you up and we'll go together."

———————

Upton left his car at the curb and climbed into the front seat of Miller's patrol car. There was barely room to move on the passenger's side. The center console between the front seats was crowded with radio equipment, flashlights and office supplies—a cop's rolling desk. A short-barreled shotgun mounted barrel up pushed against Upton's left shoulder and a computer keyboard and display screen were attached to a brace that hung over his knees.

"I take it you don't have a lot of passengers."

"Not up front."

"So you give kids tickets for texting while they drive and you've got a whole keyboard and monitor in here?"

"Funny."

The grin left Upton's face as he remembered their destination.

"You do a lot of these family notifications?"

"Seems like it lately."

Miller didn't seem to be in the mood for conversation, not that Upton could blame considering the chore ahead of them. So he pulled out his pad of yellow, lined paper and looked over what Miller had already told him about the boy.

Paul Mendez shouldn't be dead. He hadn't been a spectacular student, but he was active in the campus life and, by all reports, well-liked by his classmates. He played on the basketball team, was class secretary during his senior year and had been named the student representative to the Petrolia Club, earning him a fancy lunch at the Orchard Hotel downtown every Tuesday when the service club held its weekly meeting. There was nothing to indicate he had ever experimented with drugs. After graduation he had started his own landscaping business and had done well enough that he had started apartment shopping. That all ended with him face-down in the orchard.

Miller and Upton sat in the car at the curb looking at the small house where Mendez lived with his parents.

Raul and Paula Mendez both worked at Plumrite. Raul had been there more than twenty years, Paula almost as long. Their house was just south of the downtown area, near the railroad tracks. The home was in one of the oldest neighborhoods in Los Robles, but not one of the nicest. The houses had been built just after World War II. They were small wooden boxes, usually two bedrooms, one bathroom, a kitchen and a large room that doubled as a dining room and living room. The Mendez house sat behind a freshly painted picket fence with a well-groomed lawn and a neatly painted exterior. Upton suspected the lawn was Paul's responsibility.

Miller pushed through the gate up the walk to the front door with Upton following a step behind. Upton could see the reluctance in Miller's body language as he knocked on the door.

"Mrs. Mendez? I'm Sheriff Miller and this is Tommy Upton. May we come in?"

There was fear in her face as she stepped aside to let them in. Wordlessly she gestured them toward the living room as Raul Mendez came out of the kitchen.

"Is this about Paul?" he asked.

"Let's sit down," said Miller. There was already shock showing on the faces of the Mendezes as they sat on the sofa, clutching each other's hand.

"I'm sorry, Paul is dead. He was murdered, sometime last night, we think. I'm very sorry for your loss."

Tears rolled down Paula Mendez's face, but she didn't make a sound. Raul's eyes welled up and his upper lip quivered.

"What happened?"

"We're still investigating the details, but we know he was shot."

"When can we see him?" asked Paula.

"Soon," said Miller. "After we've collected all the evidence and the medical examiner is done, we can release him to you."

She nodded and stared down at her hands, folded in her lap. Miller looked at Raul.

"When we came in, you asked if it was about Paul. Why?"

"He didn't come home last night. He's been seeing this girl, Rita Flores, sometimes they stay out late, but he always comes home. He has to go to work."

"Did your son have any trouble with drugs?"

"No. Never. He was too smart for that. Why do you ask about drugs?"

"Drugs, methamphetamine, were found next to his body."

Paula Mendez leaned forward on the sofa, eyes glaring at Miller. "They weren't his. He was a good boy. He had his own business. He didn't need drugs."

"I understand, Mrs. Mendez, but since we found drugs, I have to ask."

"Who did this to him?"

"We don't know yet. Was he having troubles with anyone? Customers, old friends, people like that?"

"No. He would have said something."

"Do you know where he was last night?"

"No. We just assumed he was with Rita." She was starting to calm down and finally took notice of Upton.

"Who are you again?"

"I'm Tommy Upton, ma'am. I work for the *Register*."

"The newspaper? What are you doing here?"

"Well, ma'am, it's my job to write about Paul, his life I mean, and I just thought I might get a better idea of what kind of young man he was if I visited his home."

She eyed him suspiciously, then the light in her eyes went out and her shoulders sagged. "You want to see what kind of boy he was, go look in his room." She nodded to a closed door across the room. "You'll see. No drugs. Clean. He was a good boy."

Holding his hat by his side, Upton stood up and walked to the door as Miller resumed his questions. Upton put his hand on the old brass door knob, turned it slowly and opened the door.

9

He stepped inside and closed the door behind him, leaving it open of a couple of inches. He didn't want Mrs. Mendez to think he was up to anything sneaky. It wasn't the room of a tweaker. It was neat, well-organized and the bedspread still had an impression where Mendez had sat to put on his shoes. A laptop computer and a few manila folders were the only things on a small corner desk. Upton carefully fanned the folders. Each was labeled with a street address. Landscaping customers, Upton assumed. The top of the dresser was equally uncluttered—a nice watch, a pocket knife and a framed photo of a pretty girl. It had to be Rita. The walls held a few sports posters, a couple of achievement certificates from the high school and, above the dresser, an 11 x 14 family portrait.

Miller stuck his head through the door.

"Well?"

"This looks like the room of a nice kid. Not the kind of kid we expect to find shot to death in an orchard."

"Let's go. I think Mrs. Mendez has had enough of me."

Both men nodded to the Mendezes on their way out and put their hats on before they reached the car.

"Drop you back at the office?"

"Yeah, I might as well get started."

CHAPTER TWO

Tommy Upton sat in front of his computer at his desk in the office of the Los Robles *Register* staring at the screen. A photo of Paul Mendez stared back. It was his high school graduation picture, now it would run with his obituary. His editor, the paper's owner, walked up behind him.

"That the Mendez kid?"

"Yeah. That's why I can't sleep at night."

"That photo?"

"All the photos, Vic. They haunt me. They float around in my head and when I close my eyes, they play like a slide show."

Vic Yanuzzi sat down on a corner of Upton's desk and stared back further into the newsroom.

"Tommy, maybe you should get some help."

"I don't need help, Vic, I need time."

Yanuzzi looked like he should have been working in a newsroom thirty years ago. He wore a white shirt with a button-down collar, the sleeves rolled half-way up his forearms and a plain black tie loosened at the neck. His hair was still jet black despite being in his sixties, and Upton didn't think it was dyed. It was combed back from his forehead and held in place by some kind of shiny hair product. A pair of half reading glasses hung from a chain around his neck and rested on a belly that strained the lower buttons on his shirt.

"You've been through a lot," he said. "Jen's murder, your battle with the bottle and everything that goes along with all that. I'm just saying maybe you should see somebody."

"Thanks, Vic. I'm doing alright. I just need some time."

Yanuzzi shook his head and walked away, giving Upton's shoulder a pat as he left.

Upton opened the drawer at his knees and pulled out a manila folder. It was labeled "Jen." It contained everything he knew about his wife Jennifer's murder.

It wasn't much. She had died brutally, her body found face-up on the sidewalk in a cul-de-sac where she had a listing. As always, she was immaculately dressed and, even in death, looked perfect and beautiful, except for the ugly halo of blood around her head on the sidewalk. There was no sign of a struggle and no apparent motive. The coroner called it blunt force trauma, but to Tommy, it was just a violation. A complete contradiction to everything she was and everything she believed in.

After they arrived in town, it hadn't taken long for Jen to become one of the top real estate agents in Los Robles. She was a petite, green-eyed blond with a no-nonsense business attitude. She was fit, trim, energetic and loved him unconditionally. Not that he made that easy.

Upton actually remembered the day they first met. It was in an early-morning English Lit class. He was seriously hung-over, she was amazingly beautiful. Yet she was attracted to him, mostly because while he had dreams of becoming a great novelist, she could only see as far as graduation. She treasured his limitless vision and dreams of success. She was already too much in love when they graduated and the reality of paying rent turned him from his novels and he found work at a newspaper, writing whatever was needed.

It wasn't until after they were married that he discovered she was an heiress. Rent wasn't the problem, she had only wanted to be sure he loved her, and he did. But by this time he was hitting his stride at the newspaper and discovering that he loved the work.

He started out writing obituaries, then moved on to mundane assignments like planning commission meetings and government hearings. But his writing was too good to languish in backwater assignments and his editors began to challenge him. He had a flair for investigative reporting and exposé after exposé led him to bigger and bigger stories and papers. Jen willingly followed. But with success came celebration, and he was celebrating a lot.

He started drinking. He never stopped. His writing suffered. The assignments dried up, but he didn't. He found himself writing progressively less important stories for less important papers. The end of his slide found him in Los Robles back to writing obituaries and he was only doing that because Vic Yanuzzi had more heart than common sense. But the drinking never even slowed down. Not until that horrible night when Dave Miller had knocked on his door. He had been asleep on the couch, drunk, the eleven o'clock news droning in the background on the TV. He had staggered to the door. Miller had guided him back to the couch and started the coffee pot. Then he told him Jen was dead. He had insisted on going to the crime scene, but he didn't remember it. His memories came from the photos of it he looked at every day.

Upton thought of her now just as he always had. Her picture in his mind was still that beautiful girl from English Lit. Her athletic body had attracted him the day they met and the attraction had never ended. She always wore her blonde hair shoulder-length, parted in the middle and her green eyes sparkled like the emeralds they resembled. Even the crime scene photos weren't enough to wipe the image from his mind.

He hadn't had a drop to drink since that night, but even he knew it was too little, too late. Jen had followed him every step of the way – all the way up the ladder of success, and for the entire slide on the way down. But while his career plummeted, hers rose, based on the strength of her personality and her skill as a Realtor. Now his life was empty. He missed Jen physically, emotionally and spiritually. The reality of her absence had somehow become a physical presence in his life. He hated being in their condo. Everywhere he looked, everything he touched reminded him of her. He walked around the condo in the dark, the only light coming from the TV and a small light over the stove in the kitchen. He didn't want to see the photos on the walls or her clothes in the closet.

He was so sick from alcohol withdrawal that he had nearly missed her funeral. If it hadn't been for Eddie Mercer, he would have.

Eddie was Upton's best friend in Los Robles. They had met at Louie's Bar the first week Upton had arrived in town. Upton knew immediately that Mercer was an alcoholic, a high-functioning one, but an alcoholic nonetheless. Mercer was a genius with numbers and worked as an accounting clerk at the Plumrite Packing house. If he wasn't so good, his drinking would have gotten him fired long ago. And if he hadn't been a drinker, he probably would have run the place. He was also Tommy Upton's biggest fan and they drank together too often and too long.

If it bothered Jen, Upton never saw it, or pretended not to. But it was Mercer who had come to the condo that morning, cleaned him up and taken him to the cemetery.

Upton had kept his fedora pulled low and he had hidden behind his ever-present sunglasses. He stood silently as the soil was shoveled on top of Jen's casket. He saw her family look at him with disgust, blaming him with their eyes for her death.

He knew at that moment he would never take another drink, knowing it wouldn't bring Jen back, but also knowing his life had changed forever.

Now, he had trouble being alone in the condo. Her presence filled every corner. Her face smiled out from the photographs and he caught her scent every time he opened a closet door. So, he kept the lights off, turning them on only when absolutely necessary. And he spent as little time in the condo as possible. He lingered at his desk at the *Register* or over coffee at the Los Robles Café. Louie's was right next door to the café, but he hadn't set foot inside since Jen died. Eddie still occasionally tried to tempt him, but Upton resisted, even after Eddie jokingly told him that Louie wouldn't be able to send his kids to college because of the drop in income.

Upton didn't believe he had caused Jen's death. He had covered enough random and senseless violence to know that bad things sometimes happened to good people. What haunted him was the realization that he had emotionally abandoned her. She adored him and he had worked and drank himself out of her life. She died alone on a sidewalk and he hadn't known or even missed her until someone sobered him up. Now she was gone and he was lost.

Worst of all, her murder remained unsolved. Los Robles wasn't very big, how could it hide his wife's murderer? And now, he wondered if it was hiding more than one. He remembered the day he had walked into Dave Miller's office with an offer to help. Dave had been cautious, maybe even skeptical, aware of his reputation as an investigative reporter, but equally aware of his relationship to bourbon. But Miller had read the pain in Upton's eyes and seen that he was drying up, or trying to.

"You're not a cop," he had said. "I can't give you anything that I don't give to everyone else. But I know you have a reputation for turning over rocks and finding things that have been hidden, so if you'll share with me, I'll do my best to share with you."

They shook hands on the deal. But before Upton could even start on Jen's case, another body had shown up—a young girl's. Lisa Erickson, nineteen years old, had been found stabbed to death. As with Jen, there was no apparent motive and no apparent suspect. The people in town had started to quietly grumble about two violent murders and no progress on either case. It was a bad time for Paul Mendez to turn up dead.

Miller and Upton had spent many hours talking over the facts of the cases, but they didn't seem related and the only similarity between all of them was the lack of a clear motive or suspect.

Upton was frustrated. He wasn't drinking, he had started concentrating on his work at the paper, but he felt like he was still letting Jen down. Miller's deputies had done all the right things, they had worked the crime scenes, knocked on doors and interviewed everyone they could think of, but nobody knew anything. Nobody had seen anything.

The first two murders remained mysteries, and now there was another one. People were dying, good people, and Miller didn't know why and neither did Upton. Upton had been frustrated enough with the lack of progress that he had even done a little digging into Miller's past. He found nothing but accolades and praise. So it wasn't a lack of expertise or talent, it was simply a lack of information. There was a murderer loose in Los Robles, maybe more than one, someone, somewhere knew something. Upton had to find that person, or be there when Miller did.

CHAPTER THREE

Alex Brewster hated his job. He stood in front of a slow-moving conveyor belt all day long at Plumrite Packing, plucking plums off the belt and sorting them into boxes. The boxes were like over-sized egg cartons, designed so the delicate fruit nestled safely into protective cardboard cups. The conveyor belts brought the fruit into the packing house after the trucks delivered picking bins from the orchards.

As the fruit was emptied from the picking bins, it went through a wash to remove debris from the field, bacteria, pesticide and any other contaminants. As the fruit came out of the wash it went into a mechanical sorter where the plums were graded by size and color, each size traveling into the packing house on a different conveyor line. The culls went down a different belt to be turned into juice. Each of the five lines had twenty people like Brewster, packing boxes. When a box was full, it was put onto a separate belt and sent to the storage and shipping rooms.

Brewster had the third position on the second line. He liked being near the front of the line because he still had a good choice of fruit. He wanted all of his boxes to look perfect—uniform color, uniform size, each plum packed stem-end up, blossom-end down. The first piece of fruit into the box was the model for the next twenty-three. Any plum that didn't match the model traveled down the line to the other packers. The precisely packed boxes were the only satisfaction Brewster got out of his job and it was little enough.

Every other packer in the plant filled more boxes than Brewster, but every one of Brewster's boxes were perfect. Nobody noticed. The supervisors never complimented him on the boxes, they only told him to pick up the pace.

He stood next to the belt on a thin, black rubber mat. The mat was supposed to make the workers more comfortable, like a half-inch of rubber really made a picnic out of standing on a concrete floor for eight hours a day. His collar-length hair, oily and unkempt, was covered by a hairnet. He was a head taller than the Mexican women who worked on either side of him so he had to stoop to reach the fruit as it came down the line. He wore a white smock that covered his grunge-band black T-shirt and faded black Levi's. Latex gloves covered his long, delicate fingers, but he knew that by lunch, his fingers and hands would be stained and dirty.

The lifts, conveyor belts and packaging equipment created enough noise that all line workers were required to wear ear protection while they worked. They had a choice between ear plugs or headsets. Brewster chose the headset. They were heavier and bulkier, but he didn't like sticking things into his ears. He liked the requirement, though. The ear protection limited conversation and allowed him plenty of time to think, a pastime he didn't believe his fellow packers did much of. It didn't matter, he was thinking enough for all of them.

He was good at thinking. He knew that because he was smart. Hadn't he proved that? He had graduated from Los Robles High School as the valedictorian. And yet, here he was in the Plumrite Packing house, making nine dollars an hour sticking plums into boxes. It wasn't fair. He worked in the same building as his ignorant mother. She stacked the empty boxes she and the others would pack onto carts for distribution throughout the plant.

Plumrite Packing had not been in his plans. Neither had Los Robles. He had planned to leave town for college after graduation and never look back. At first, he hadn't known where his college education would take him, but he knew it would be far from Los Robles. He was smart enough to become anything he wanted to be—a doctor, lawyer, maybe even a stockbroker. The world was his for the taking and he had planned to leave his mother, Los Robles and their inferior little intellects behind and he never wanted to see, smell, touch or taste another plum.

Instead, he found himself working on the packing line, his own personal hell. His hands dirty and the aroma of plums permeating his skin, his clothes, his soul.

A bell rang and the conveyor lines rattled to a stop. Time for the 10 a.m. break, a rush to the restrooms and a cup of lukewarm coffee from a Thermos and then back to the line.

He didn't have much to do with his fellow workers, nor did he want to. He believed every one of them, including his mother, was beneath him. He sat off to one side of the break room, giving his ears some relief from the constant pressure of the headset. But there was no relief, because his co-workers, mostly Hispanic women, started talking before the conveyor belts completely stopped. He was surrounded by a babel of rapid-fire Spanish, squeals and giggles as the women talked to each other. Because of the constant noise, even when the lines themselves weren't running, the conversations were always conducted at high volumes. He was relieved when the bell rang calling them back to the packing line and he could return to the relative silence of his headset.

He put his headset on as a warning buzzer sounded and the conveyor belt started moving. He mechanically sorted plums. Even his perfect boxes were no challenge for him, for his mind, so he let his mind wander. He thought about his first.

He actually thought she was quite attractive, even though she was probably old enough to be his mother. Almost. Maybe not. His mother seemed much older. His first was beautiful. Her fingernails had been perfect. They were painted fire engine red. They finished long, slender fingers circled by rings, three on each hand. Beautiful, soft hands that had never packed plums. Thinking about her caused him to momentarily fall behind on the line.

He quickly threw a full box onto the belt behind him and put and empty box in its place in front of him. The woman to his left shot him a glance, but he ignored it and returned to his thoughts.

The body. Shapely. Firm, but not hard. Curvy, but athletic. Her body was fuller than the girls his age. More womanly. More experienced, maybe.

And then there was the face. The green eyes. The lips painted to match the fingernails, all framed by golden hair.

He remembered that as he walked up the sidewalk to the house, she had smiled at him, showing him perfect rows of teeth and putting a spark of light into her eyes. She was still smiling as she turned to lead him into the house. She never saw him raise the tire iron before he hit her in the back of the head.

He didn't even need to hit her twice. She died very easily, a little too easily he thought. She spun and fell with the force of the blow and landed face up on the sidewalk. He thought she still looked beautiful, but the light was gone from her eyes.

Lost in his thoughts, time had moved on without him. Glancing left and right he saw everyone still packing, unmindful of him and, judging by the diminished stack of boxes at his feet, he had been keeping up with the pace without even being conscious of his work. There was a sheen of sweat on his forehead underneath his hairnet and he used his sleeve to try and wipe some of it away. He focused again on the plums and reminded himself to keep up appearances. If he acted the same way every day, nice and normal, he would never be suspected.

He was too smart for these people. People were dying and no one knew why. Nobody suspected the person who was killing them was so smart, so normal, such a valuable employee.

But even as he had these thoughts, his mind was slipping away, thinking about someone else. Thinking about the next one.

CHAPTER FOUR

Dave Miller threw the morning edition of the Los Robles *Register* in the general direction of the wastebasket next to his desk. He missed, but he left the paper where it landed, too disgusted to touch it.

"Everything okay, Dave?" Carol Burnside was Miller's secretary, technically his administrative specialist. She wasn't a sworn officer but, without her, he wasn't sure anything would get done. She wore the same uniform he and his deputies wore—tan shirt, green pants, black belt and shoes—but filled it much differently. Small and fit with shoulder-length auburn hair, she was what he politely called buxom. Nobody could miss seeing her badge, it led the way whenever she entered the room.

"Yeah, I'm fine. I guess I'm just getting fed up with people trying to tell me how to do my job."

"What'd the paper say?"

"Same stuff we're starting to hear from the mayor: crime's up, a rash of murders, the sheriff is incompetent. You know, the usual."

"Tommy wrote that?"

"No, no, not Tommy. That other guy, the one with the huge Adam's apple and the lisp."

"Jerry Morris?"

"Yeah, that's the one. Jerk."

"I'm not sure three murders exactly qualify as a rash, especially since they've happened all over the valley. They've come kind of close together, but statistically, we're still about average."

"Easy for you to say, you're not up for re-election in the fall."

"It sounds like Ana Espinoza's work to me. She's been mayor for six years. If she doesn't get re-elected she'll have to go out and find a real job. I don't think she can afford the cut in pay."

Miller smiled. "I appreciate your support, Carol, but the fact is, we don't seem to be making much progress. We got a little glimmer of hope with the Mendez kid. I'll update everyone at the morning briefing tomorrow, but it may be that there's something going on with our friendly local meth dealers. We found a bag of meth next to the Mendez boy's body."

"He doesn't seem like a meth-head from what I've heard about him. And Jen Upton certainly couldn't have been involved in that. What about the second one, Lisa Erickson?"

"Nothing to indicate it there, either, but we'll have to look at case again with fresh eyes after the Mendez murder."

Miller walked to his window, not really seeing his view of the City Hall parking lot.

"There's just not anything to tie these murders together; at least nothing I can see. We have a beating, a stabbing and a shooting. Random MOs, random victims, but I just can't quite buy a random rash of murders, either. There's been no other noticeable uptick in crimes. It seems like if things were escalating around here for some reason, other crimes would be on the rise too."

He picked up three, thick, red folders from the center of his desk. In his department, major crimes were separated into color-coded files for easy identification and filing. Red was for homicide. Robberies got light blue, assaults green, burglaries orange and all other felonies, yellow. Everything else was standard manila.

He fanned the three red folders, took the one from the bottom of the stack and said, "I'm going to go visit Lisa Erickson's mother, see if I can figure out anything we've missed."

The Erickson's lived on a ranch just west of town. Lars Erickson had died in a traffic accident six years earlier, but Elsa had remained on the ranch, raising Lisa and fourteen acres of plums.

The tires of Miller's squad car crunched gravel as he rolled to a stop in front of the farmhouse. There were three wooden steps up to a porch that ran along the entire front of the house. The house itself was a boxy, single story that hardly looked big enough for a family of three, although Miller was sure that Elsa Erickson felt lost in it now. The white clapboards needed paint, as did the barn just off to the left. The plum trees looked healthy, but everything else on the property seemed worn out and sad.

Elsa came through the screen door as Miller was getting out of his car. She was tall and lean, her once blonde hair now liberally streaked with gray. She wore no makeup but her blue eyes glowed from a tanned face weathered by too much time in the sun. And, despite the life in her eyes, her face and her carriage suggested nothing but sorrow and sadness.

"Do you have news, Dave?"

"Sorry, Elsa. No. I just came by to talk. I feel like I'm missing something in all of this and I'm hoping you can help me find it."

"Missing what? A clue?"

"Well, not so much a clue, but a reason, a motive. Something. I can't figure out why Lisa died."

Miller realized he'd said the wrong thing as Elsa's eyes filled with tears. He knew that no matter what he found out, Elsa would never understand why Lisa died, either.

"Tell me about Lisa," he said.

Her eyes brimmed with tears before she spoke, but they didn't fall.

"She was a wonderful girl. She wasn't the perfect daughter, but she was a typical one. We argued, mostly about boys and her chores around here." She inclined her head to indicate the ranch.

"Since Lars died, keeping the place running has been a challenge. The labor contractors are great about handling the picking and pruning, but all the day to day stuff falls—fell—to Lisa and me. We had to check drip lines, keep up on the fertilizer and the weeds and maintain the equipment. Lisa hated it. Always has. The neighbors have been great, but Lisa resented it.

"Her boyfriend, Josh, graduated and went off to Stanford in the fall. He won a scholarship and he's kind of the all-American kid, so his future was bright. Lisa wanted to be a part of that future. She wanted to go to college, too, probably not Stanford, but that dream pretty much ended when Lars died. She was a good student, but not a great one. But she was pretty and popular and all her classmates liked her."

A tear rolled out of her right eye and down her cheek. She made a small choking sound.

"I thought everybody liked her. I don't understand why this happened to her."

Miller sat down on the porch step and bent over, studying the tops of his boots and slowly turning his cowboy hat over and over in his hands. Elsa Erickson sat down beside him.

"That's the same problem I'm having, Elsa. The how of her death is obvious, I just can't find the why and, until I can figure out the why, I can't start looking for a suspect."

They both fell quiet, the sounds of the ranch and the wind in the trees were the only things breaking the silence.

"Were her and Josh still an item?"

"Yes. They were doing the whole long-distance relationship thing and it seemed to be working, at least so far. I told her that kind of relationship was difficult, but they both seemed to be working at it."

"Any trouble with other boys?"

"I don't think so. All these kids grew up with each other. They all knew Lisa and Josh were still together."

"Was she working?"

"She was looking, but she was having trouble finding anything, let alone something she could schedule around her chores here."

"Had there been any strange phone calls, e-mails, that sort of thing?"

"Nothing she mentioned."

Miller looked at her, hesitated a beat, and then asked, "What kind of relationship did you two have?"

Elsa's nostrils flared and her cheeks flushed.

"What do you mean by that?"

"I mean how well did you communicate? Did she tell you everything that was happening in her life?" Elsa looked at the ground.

"I was her mother, not her friend. I'm sure she didn't tell me everything. No teenager comes completely clean with their parents. But we talked a lot, especially after Lars died. I think if she was having trouble, she'd have said something."

The silence between them returned. Miller could hear far away traffic on the county road and a small plane was flying overhead somewhere near. The only other sound was the engine in Miller's squad car ticking as it cooled off. The day was beautiful, but the silence at the ranch was overwhelming and sad.

"I'm so sorry about all of this, Elsa. I want you to know we haven't stopped working on Lisa's case and we won't, not until we find whoever did this."

Elsa nodded, not looking up.

"Just one more question, Elsa. I'm sorry, but I have to ask it. Was Lisa doing any drugs?"

Elsa looked up and shook her head. "No. I would have known."

"Have you seen or smelled anything out in the orchards."

"You mean like a meth lab or something? No. Nothing."

Miller stood up, put his hat on and adjusted his gun belt.

"Thanks for your time, Elsa. I'll be in touch soon."

She didn't look up and she didn't move, so Miller stood up and stepped down off the porch to his car. Pausing at the driver's door he quickly surveyed the ranch.

Everything looked solid but neglected and everything needed paint. Packing bins were stacked haphazardly by the north side of the barn. The engine cover was up on the old John Deere, meaning it probably hadn't been driven since Lars died. The whole place looked pretty typical, right down to the dog sleeping in the dirt in front of the barn door. A tough life for a single woman of a certain age. He wondered how long she'd be able to hold on to the place.

Miller took off his hat, slipped behind the steering wheel, and started the car back down the gravel driveway to the road.

CHAPTER FIVE

Tommy Upton sat on a wooden-slatted bench in front of City Hall. He sat there a lot. Some of the locals even called it Tommy's Bench. It sat under an oak tree, the only one inside the city limits. Los Robles had been named for the coastal oaks that liberally dotted the hillsides that formed the valley occupied by the town and its vast orchards.

There had been fewer trees on the valley floor and now there were almost none. The earliest residents had cleared the oaks to make room for roads and oil wells and had not let the stately old trees stand in their way. The tree in front of City Hall had been painstakingly dug out of a hillside at the north end of the valley and transplanted where it stood today at the time City Hall was built. That was back when the good citizens of Los Robles thought the town would become the center of the California oil boom and, for a few brief months, it was. But bigger, and richer, oilfields were discovered elsewhere around the state and, while oil production never stopped in Los Robles, it was soon supplanted by agriculture.

Sitting on his bench, Upton's back was to City Hall. He faced the town circle, where the city's two main roads—Petro Avenue and Oakview Street—crossed. Petro Avenue is a state highway that runs north and south through the length of the valley. Oakview Street crosses it running to the valley sides. But their intersection isn't a corner, it's a circle. The city fathers constructed one of California's first traffic circles to serve as the center of Los Robles. The circle itself had originally been landscaped as a small park, but now was mostly an expanse of vibrant green lawn punctuated by a half-scale oil derrick on a pedestal in the center. A large American flag waves from the top of the ironwork derrick.

At Christmas time, the derrick is festooned with colored lights turning it into a Christmas tree. Other times, it served as a daring temptation for high school boys to climb and decorate with bras, jerseys from opposing high schools or other trophies.

Looking nearly straight ahead across the circle, Upton could see the window in front of his desk at the newspaper office. To the right of the newspaper stands the formerly grand Orchard Hotel—four stories of creaky wooden floors and dark wooden beams. During the boom its restaurant and saloon were so crowded people ate their suppers standing up. The rooms upstairs were the height of luxury and vacancies were rare. The hotel managed to stay in business, but the biggest excitement inside its walls these days was the weekly noon meeting of the Petrolia Club every Thursday.

Upton shifted his gaze in the other direction. Just to the left of the newspaper was Louie's Bar and then the Los Robles Café. He used to spend too many hours in the one, and had now substituted the other.

He sat like he always had, hat brim pulled down low above his sunglasses, face passive, the morning's edition of the *Register* folded neatly beside him. As he watched traffic slowly navigating the circle, he saw Eddie Mercer come out of Louie's and head his way.

"Hey, Up-Town."

"Nobody really calls me that anymore, Eddie."

"Yeah, I know. But you were the man, Tommy. One of these days you'll be right back on top."

"Eddie, you may be the world's greatest optimist."

"C'mon, Tommy. Your talent isn't gone, just a little rusty. You'll hit your stride again."

Upton wanted to change the subject. He didn't share Mercer's optimism but, at some level, he believed there was some truth to what he said. He wasn't completely washed up. He was still writing, even if it was mostly obituaries, and he had to admit the murder of the Mendez boy had started some juices flowing he hadn't felt in a long time.

Upton looked over at his friend and wondered if he would be able to help Eddie the way Eddie had helped him. He wasn't looking very good these day. When Upton had stopped drinking, Eddie seemed to start drinking more. He was tall, over six feet, but probably only weighed 140 pounds. He was probably heavier at some point in his life, because his belt was way too long. He had it cinched up tight to keep his pants above his bony hips and a long piece of belt was always flapping off to his side. He had jet black hair that he wore a little too long, covering his collar and tucked behind his ears. It always looked like a little shampoo would help. And his usual work uniform was a white, long-sleeved shirt with a button-down collar, buttoned at the neck with no tie. His eyes were as sad-looking as a Bassett hound's, but redder. Still, it was Eddie offering comfort to Upton.

"I hate to see you sitting here like this every day," he said.

"I kind of like it. I watch the town go by and think. It's relaxing."

"It's not relaxing, it's sad. Why don't you come back over to Louie's with me? The whole gang's there."

"You know I can't do that, Eddie. I can't go back down that road. I can't do that to Jen."

Mercer's eyes glistened as he looked at his friend.

"Jen's not here, Tommy. You've got to think about yourself."

"I am thinking about myself, Eddie, and about a promise I made to her and me. I won't do that to myself again and I won't do it to her memory."

Both men were silent, staring off into space when Dave Miller pulled his squad car up to the curb and called to Upton. Upton got up from the bench, leaving Eddie watching, and leaned into the passenger side window of the car.

"I'm going to see Mary Ellen, she's doing the autopsy on the Mendez kid. You wanna come along?"

Upton turned, waved to Mercer and climbed into the passenger seat without another word.

CHAPTER
SIX

Mary Ellen Driscoll was standing over a shiny metal table in a clean, tiny room behind the emergency room at Los Robles Community Hospital. She was in full surgical scrubs except for a face mask, unnecessary under the circumstances.

The blue hair cover she wore hid her close-cropped blond hair and the matching blue scrubs rendered her shapeless. Petite in every way, she stood just over five feet tall and while not curvy, she had an athletic build that turned heads when not camouflaged by her scrubs. Muscles showed in her forearms and she moved with an athlete's grace. Green eyes above a spray of freckles across the bridge of her nose greeted Miller and Upton as they came through the swinging door.

Miller introduced Upton as Driscoll eyed him carefully.

"Is he allowed to be here?" she asked, as if Upton wasn't in the room.

Miller smiled, "It's okay, Mary Ellen, he's been working with me on this one. I've needed someone to bounce some ideas off and he's had some good insights."

She looked skeptical but nodded in understanding and she looked Upton straight in the eyes.

"Is this your first autopsy?"

"Not my first dead body but, yes, my first autopsy."

"Don't throw up on the evidence. If you think you're going to lose it, use the sink." She indicated a stainless steel sink with a nod of her head. It was located just to the left of four square doors set into the wall opposite from where they had just entered the room. Upton knew without being told what was behind the four doors. They opened to refrigerated body drawers.

"What makes you think I'm going to throw up?"

"It's your first autopsy and you look like a puker."

"Sheriff, isn't that profiling?"

"She's allowed, I'm not. See if you can prove her wrong."

The body on the table was Paul Mendez. Driscoll had already washed it and now it laid on the autopsy table, covered to the waist by a surgical drape. His arms were tanned up to where his shirt sleeves would have ended and, even in death, his face and neck showed the tan gained from hours working in the sun. His chest was so pale it seemed almost translucent.

"He looks so young," Upton said.

Driscoll looked up, mildly annoyed, then softened.

"Well, he *is* young, but when we die, all the muscles in the body relax. Lines, creases and wrinkles smooth out and that helps make any face look more youthful."

Driscoll had the bedside manner of a family practitioner, not a medical examiner. She had a family practice located right behind City Hall but, at Miller's urging, had accepted the city's part-time medical examiner's job because her services wouldn't be needed very often and the city paid her almost a thousand dollars a month whether someone died or not. Lately, she'd been earning her money.

Driscoll adjusted the large surgical light over the table until it was centered on the body's chest. Then, with no preliminaries, she picked up a scalpel from the instrument table and made a large Y-incision in the chest. She started a cut near each shoulder moving diagonally to the center of the chest. Then, from where those lines met, she made another incision, a single straight line down to about the waistline.

Upton said nothing, felt nothing. It didn't seem real. There was only a slight trickle of blood from the incisions, no machines electronically measuring pulse and respirations, no hovering surgical team. Just a boy's body, stark and white, the smooth chest now violated by a silently moving scalpel.

Driscoll looked up at Miller and Upton. "The cause of death here is obvious, but I can't just call it a gunshot wound and close the case. If I get called to testify, I have to be able to speak to his entire physical condition."

She slowly flayed the skin and muscle tissue back from the Y-incision, exposing the rib cage. Upton gagged slightly as she reached for a bone saw. Driscoll looked at Upton with some sympathy.

"Why don't you guys go grab some coffee in the cafeteria," she said, glancing up at a wall clock. "I should be done with all the preliminaries in about forty-five minutes. Then I'll move on to the head wound. Come back then and bring me a cup of black, two sugars."

An hour later Driscoll was wearing a new pair of gloves and standing at the head of the autopsy table. Miller had donned gloves as well. Driscoll had carefully shaved Mendez's head around the bullet wound and taken close-up photos of the point of entry.

"It's pretty clear-cut," she said. "We have single entrance wound, no exit. That's usually indicative of a relatively small bullet—a .22 or .38. He appears to have been shot at close range. There's stippling around the wound from burning gunpowder. I'm not really an expert in this, but the shooter had to be close to produce stippling, five feet or less."

"Our working theory is that this is some kind of a drug deal gone bad," said Miller. "We found a bag of meth next to the body."

"I don't think so. It's more consistent with an execution. I'll have to do a little more work to be sure."

"An execution?" Upton had been standing slightly behind Miller, reluctant to get too close to the autopsy table. "You're saying there's someone running around who thinks he had a reason to execute a hard-working teenager?"

"I'm not saying any of that, at least not yet. What I'm saying is, if there had been a fight, I would expect to see evidence of some kind of a struggle. But I don't see that. He doesn't have any recent scratches or bruises and no defensive wounds of any kind. There's not even anything to suggest he was hit on the head or something and then executed."

Miller looked frustrated. "So what's your theory on how this went down then? The suspect couldn't just sneak up on him in an orchard and shoot him in the back of the head."

"I'm just guessing, Jim, you'll have to look at your other evidence but, from what I can see now, the bullet entered the back of the head at a downward angle. So, either the assailant was quite tall, or Paul here was kneeling." She pulled back the blue sheet covering the body. "There are slight abrasions on both knees. He could have easily done that at work—I imagine landscapers are on their knees a lot—but with everything else I've seen, I think the killer made him kneel and then shot him."

"If that's what happened, how does the bag of meth fit in?" asked Upton.

Miller was staring at the boy's knees, like he could read something there. "It doesn't. The meth doesn't fit. Not with Paul and not with this MO Meth dealers don't use .22s or .38s. They like nines or .45s. And the whole execution thing doesn't fit either. When a dealer wants to make a statement, they do it publicly. And they don't mess around, they just shoot. And they sure as hell don't leave a bag of saleable product behind."

Everyone thought about that for a minute.

"If he was executed," said Upton, "what was his crime?"

Miller and Upton left the hospital in silence, each lost in his own thoughts. At the patrol car, Miller said, "Mary Ellen will recover the bullet and explore the trajectory when she takes a look at his brain."

Upton was glad they hadn't stayed for that part of the autopsy and he suddenly felt a little nauseous as he realized that Jen must have suffered the same indignities. "What's that going to tell us that we don't already know?"

"Nothing really, it's just a matter of confirmation. And if the trajectory confirms her theory, it means that mine is no good and I have to come up with something new. Fast."

Miller slammed his door while Upton maneuvered around the electronics and the passenger side and finally got his closed.

"Where do you want me to drop you off? Back at your bench?"

"Nah. The paper. I've got to finish Paul's obit. How 'bout you? What's your next step?"

"The office. I've got to try and make some sense out of this mess."

CHAPTER
SEVEN

Tommy Upton liked that there was a window right behind his computer monitor. His desk at the *Register* was an old industrial model, probably obtained as government surplus. It was gun-metal gray with three drawers on the left side and two drawers and a file drawer on the right side. Until recently, he had used the file drawer mainly as a liquor cabinet. Now it contained a large bag of Doritos, a bag of beef jerky he bought at a gas station and about a dozen reporter's pads, all completely full.

Anywhere else in the building, his work space would have been miserable. But his window afforded him a view across the traffic circle, roughly opposite from his bench at City Hall. He enjoyed the view almost as much from the paper as he did from City Hall but, unlike the time spent on his bench, the time at his desk was generally productive.

At the moment though, he wasn't enjoying the view and he wasn't being productive. He was too distracted by the view on his monitor. The Mendez obit was there, half-finished, and he could hear Vic Yanuzzi, his editor and the owner of the *Register*, stomping down the aisle toward him.

Vic Yanuzzi was about as subtle as a brick through a plate glass window. He never had an unexpressed emotion and he always expressed them as if he was trying to talk over the noise of a printing press. He was wearing his usual white button-down collar dress shirt and a black tie. Upton sometimes wondered if he had a whole closet full of white shirts and black ties, or if he wore the same ones every day. He never buttoned the top button of his shirt and his tie was always loosely knotted. He combed his hair straight back from his forehead and kept a pair of reading glasses balanced on the end of his nose.

"You got the obit on that Mendez kid, Tommy?"

"Workin' on it, Vic."

"We're on deadline. What's the deal?"

"The deal is I saw his body in the orchard and I listened to his mother cry. I can't just pound this one out."

Upton hated writing obits but he was too much of a professional to write anything badly. Having fallen into his career cellar, he was determined to fight his way back. The murders might be his ticket to both redemption and respect but, right now, the obits were paying the bills.

"I need you to jump on it, Tommy."

"I know. But Vic, you know as well as I do I have to get this right. Most people only get their name in the paper twice; when they're born, and when they die. Maybe when they get married. The least we can do is give them a good send-off. Jesus, this kid barely lived. Let me do it right."

Yanuzzi had been in the business longer than Upton, but he knew Tommy was right. More than that, he knew a small town newspaper couldn't afford to lose any subscribers; they were becoming harder and harder to come by in the Internet age. And, although he had never mentioned it to Upton, his obituaries were so well-written, people were actually reading them out loud at funeral services. He was somewhat disgusted—and shocked—by what had happened to Upton, so much talent wasted, but he couldn't deny Upton's capabilities or re-discovered drive. And, he had to admit, at least to himself, giving Upton a shot at redemption working for the *Register* was also a little bit of "there but by the grace of God go I."

"Close of business, Tommy. Close of business."

Upton turned back to his monitor. He had written two paragraphs. He didn't need to look at them, he could already recite them from memory, just like every obituary he had written since Jen died. It was a weird talent and one he had never had until that day. It was like death had invaded his mind, forcing him to remember.

The words he had written so far weren't bad, they just weren't enough. He had answers to all of the standard obit questions—name, age, address, occupation, cause of death, education, survivors, funeral information—all of the answers to all of the questions except the big one: Why?

Of course, people have been asking that question for as long as people have been dying, but Upton sensed the question was more important with Paul Mendez. Why him? Why now? Why there?

The more he thought about it, the more he wondered if the same questions didn't apply to Jen and Lisa Erickson. The three lives seemed to have nothing in common, but all of them were dead. Violently dead, with no apparent motive. They were murdered by different methods, in different places at different times. Why? What was the common denominator?

He forced himself to concentrate on the obit. Slowly at first, then more rapidly, words appeared on the screen, summarizing in about six column inches what had been the short life and times of Paul Mendez.

From a purely professional standpoint, Upton knew it was a good obit. He was a good writer and the talent showed, but he didn't feel a sense of accomplishment over the piece. In fact, he felt the opposite. Writing obituaries is never particularly challenging or uplifting, that's why the task is usually assigned to the newest reporters, but this felt like unfinished business to Upton.

With his murder unsolved, Mendez' obituary felt incomplete, wrong somehow.

Looking back at his monitor, Upton saved the document and sent it to Yanuzzi for final editing. Yanuzzi rarely changed his copy but, because it was his newspaper, Vic reserved the right to look at everything before it went to press. Actually, he gave Vic a lot of credit. When other papers wouldn't even return his calls, Vic let him write and even gave him a desk. What he really gave him was a chance. He had fallen so far he feared he would never recover, but Vic Yanuzzi had given him the first rung of the ladder. After that, it was up to Tommy to climb. Upton tried to repay Vic by giving him a quality product, even if it was just an obituary. Dave Miller was giving him a chance, too. By allowing him some access to the murder investigations, Upton had a chance at a big story. He knew he could write it, but he needed to figure out what was happening. But nothing was getting any clearer, the mystery only deepened.

He shut down his computer and straightened the few papers on his desk. He hated this time of the day. Quitting time. It used to be the hour he looked forward to. He'd meet Eddie at Louie's and the bourbon and stories would flow. Then it was home to Jen. Beautiful, loving, caring Jen. Now he didn't go to Louie's and he didn't want to go home. Everything in the condo reminded him of Jen. It was better to get home after dark.

He made his way around the town circle to the Los Robles Café. It was located right next to Louie's but, lately, he had overcome the urge to walk past the restaurant to the bar. Small towns were bad places for temptation. Everything is close to everything else and everyone knows everyone. It seems like there are no secrets in a small town, and yet there were three murders and no clues. He shook his head to clear it. He looked at the neon tube that spelled out "Louie's" over the door to the bar and was relieved to not feel an urge to push his way through that familiar swinging door. Denying himself the liquid comforts of Louie's and the painful memories in the condo had made the café one of his usual hangouts. Anyone looking for Tommy Upton had only to check the bench in front of City Hall, his desk at the newspaper or his regular booth at the café.

He pulled open the right side of a set of glass doors and saw Eddie

Mercer waiting for him in the booth. Upton always sat facing the door and Eddie had considerately taken the opposite side of the booth.

Eddie was sitting in the center of the bench seat, both hands wrapped around a thick, white ceramic mug filled to the brim with steaming black coffee.

"Your hands cold?" said Upton as he slid into the booth.

"No, just kind of stiff. Lotta typing today, the warmth feels good."

Upton took off his hat and put it on the bench next to him, brim up.

"Busy at the plant?"

"Yeah. Harvest is starting so we've got both shifts going and orders are starting to pour in."

"Prices good?"

"The best. Weather's been good so the crop is a little early. We're beating everyone to the market."

They stopped talking as Francine Lewis slid a glass of ice water in front of Upton. Francine had been a beautiful woman when she had started waitressing at the café, but that was fifteen years and two husbands ago. The years and the work hadn't been kind to her. She was still tall and trim with an attractive figure, but her features were now lined and her eyes dull. Upton remembered seeing her at Louie's and having a few liquor-induced impure thoughts, but now in the diner, he was pretty sure it had been the bourbon talking, or maybe the dim lights. Maybe both.

"What's it going to be tonight, Tommy?"

"I don't know Frannie, is there anything I haven't tried yet?"

"I don't think so. Well, you've never tried the fish, but nobody orders that twice, so I'd recommend the meatloaf. It's good tonight and the gravy's fresh."

"Bring it on, and a cup of coffee while you're at it, please."

"You got it."

Upton watched her walk back toward the kitchen and thought maybe the attraction hadn't been just the bourbon. She had a way of moving that made men look.

"It was a lot more fun when we used to get together next door," said Mercer.

Upton broke off his observation of Frannie's backside and looked over at Eddie. "Yeah, I know Eddie. Good times. But those times are over for me."

"So you're going to quit forever, not just take a break for a while?"

"I'm done, Eddie. I've got to get my life back together. I can't go down that road again."

"Together how? You gonna write another book?"

"Maybe, but not until I get some other things wrapped up."

Frannie was back and slid a cup of coffee in front of Tommy. "The meatloaf will be right up."

"Thanks, Frannie." Upton looked across the table at his friend. Mercer was twisting a spoon over and over in his hands and staring at it like it was the most fascinating thing he had ever seen.

"Eddie, is there something bothering you?" Mercer stopped twisting the spoon and looked over at Upton.

"Do you think I drink too much?"

"Yes."

"You do?"

"Yes, I do, Eddie. It takes one to know one. I'm not judging you, I'm just telling you what I see."

"Do you think I should quit?"

"Yes. Don't end up like me, Eddie. I lost everything, you don't have to. It's not too late."

They looked at each other across the table, neither one speaking. The spell was broken when Upton's meatloaf arrived.

"You sure you don't want to eat, Eddie?"

"Nah. I'm going to go next door and think about this quitting thing for a while."

Frannie watched him head for the door. "Do you think he'll quit?"

"Nope. But I've decided I need to be honest with the people in my life, including me."

The meatloaf was good, just the right amount of meat, bread, onions and ketchup. It came with a mound of mashed potatoes covered in gravy and a pile of French-cut green beans. Upton unwrapped two pads of butter and put them on top of the beans and then mixed the beans in with the potatoes.

He ate mechanically, his mind occupied by murder. Jen, Lisa Erickson and Paul Mendez. He could recall every word of their obituaries. Writing Jen's had been one of the hardest things he had ever done, but he felt he owed her that much. Their obits had been sanitary, ordered descriptions of their lives. There was no ugliness. No mention of how they died, only their accomplishments while they lived. There was no blood. No blank, staring eyes clouded by death. No tears or cries of despair from their families. Just black ink on white newsprint, their final entry in the world of the still-living.

And there wasn't even anything to connect them in death. Except for the fact that they were each murdered, nothing seemed to tie their lives or the crimes together. They had been killed using different methods in different parts of town. By all the evidence, what little of it there was, they looked like separate crimes, but Upton didn't believe that and he didn't think Dave Miller did, either.

Upton's plate was clean and his coffee cup empty. Frannie hadn't been back to fill it in some time and now she was fussing by the cash register, wiping down the lunch counter over and over. He looked around and saw he was the only one left in the café. She was ready to close, but too polite to push him out the door.

He slid a five under his plate and then paid Frannie at the register. "Night, Tommy. See you tomorrow?"

"Most likely," he said as he pushed through the door.

He heard comforting sounds coming from Louie's—a mix of music, voices and the clinking of glasses—but he turned the other way and trudged home.

CHAPTER EIGHT

Dave Miller leaned back in his desk chair and clasped his hands behind his head. His close-cropped hair still held the indentation made by his cowboy hat. The white, tightly-woven straw hat now hung on an old-fashioned hat and coat rack that stood next to his office door. His Sam Browne leather gun and equipment belt hung just below the hat.

Miller's office had all of the characteristics of a busy, but organized, man. His desk was clean and neat, but not empty. His in-box was about half-full and there was a file folder laying in the exact center of his desk blotter labeled "For Your Signature." He knew his assistant, Carol Burnside, wouldn't let him leave for the day until he had signed whatever was in there. In the upper left-hand corner of his desk was a neat stack of three red file folders. They all held more paper than the other folders on his desk and each one was labeled with a single name: Upton, Erickson and Mendez.

Miller sat down into his chair which issued an audible squeak as his weight settled. He reached for the stack of folders, centered them neatly on top of the one Carol had left for him, and then leaned back again. Just picking them up had seemed to drain the energy out of him.

He looked around his office. Decorated was probably too nice a term for the way his office looked, but he had filled it with important memories from his life. His blue and gold number 88 UCLA football jersey was in a frame on the wall opposite his desk. Behind his desk was a large frame displaying uniform patches from police departments around the world. Another frame held his badges from every rank he had achieved as he climbed the promotion ladder to Sheriff of Los Robles. There was an autographed football on a stand, a photo of him shaking hands with the governor and numerous awards and certificates. And, on the right-hand corner of his desk, a cheap frame covered in glued-on macaroni held an 8 x 10 photo of his kids. The oldest, at eleven, was his son, Marcus. A handsome boy, Miller used to joke that Marcus had his mother's features and his father's fixtures. His daughter, Elena, was nine and already too pretty for her own good.

He saw them most weekends, now. Lorraine had taken them and moved back down to Los Angeles shortly after he became sheriff. To this day Miller didn't know if she had gotten tired of him, his job or Los Robles. Maybe it was all three. But one day she announced that they were through and she and the kids were gone before he knew what happened.

There was no animosity. They still got along, even had dinner from time to time, but the marriage was over, for good, and she made sure he knew that.

His attention returned to the folders on his desk blotter. He laid them out side by side without opening them. His fingers drummed the desk as he faced the blank red covers. His mind was racing but his thoughts had no destination. It was like he had both too much information and not enough. He just couldn't find a way into the maze.

"You okay, boss?" Miller jumped as Carol Burnside appeared next to him. He hadn't even been aware of her presence and Carol Burnside was hard to miss.

With a body that even a Sheriff's department uniform couldn't disguise, Burnside was the main reason people wanted to meet with him in his office. Since everyone who saw him saw her first, the law-abiding males of Los Robles looked for excuses to drop by the Sheriff's office. She didn't have any law enforcement duties, her job was strictly administrative, so she didn't carry a weapon. But she did wear a badge. Miller remembered her badge ceremony well. He had broken into a sweat pinning it on and he had felt Lorraine's anger from across the room where she was seated in the audience. But Burnside was a professional. Obviously aware of her physical gifts she never flaunted them and she was the hardest worker on the department. She was extremely organized and had an almost photographic memory for dates and names. Today, her hair was swept up into a bun at the back of her head, held there by a claw-like hair clip. She looked slightly flushed, her cheeks naturally rouged by the heat. He knew she had been reorganizing files in the outer office and he realized she must have been tackling the project with her customary enthusiasm.

"I'm fine, Carol. I just can't seem to get my mind around these murders."

She backed up a step, cocked her head slightly to the side and crossed her arms under her breasts, causing her badge to go almost horizontal and point towards the ceiling.

"So, what are you going to do about it?" Miller looked at her, surprised.

"Are you mad at me?"

"I'm not mad at you. I'm mad that people are getting killed in my town. People I know. Jen sold my house. She was such a huge booster for Los Robles. She was going to be a force here." Burnside's eyes had welled with tears, but not spilled over. Miller nodded. Jennifer Upton had made that same impression on lots of people in town.

"Maybe I'm just too caught up in the individual cases, Carol. I'm not seeing the big picture. Would you help me move that big white board from the squad room in here?"

Together they wheeled the board into his office. While Miller positioned the board across from his desk, Burnside briefly disappeared and came back with a fresh box of colored markers and a new eraser.

"What's your plan?"

"Plan? I don't have a plan. As a matter of fact, I'm feeling kind of silly right now. I thought I'd try what they do in all those TV cop shows. I'll put their names up on the board and start listing facts from the cases. Maybe something will pop out at me and I can start connecting the dots. I'm looking for a common thread or something. Anything."

Burnside left to answer a phone and Miller started his project. He began by writing the three names across the top of the board: Upton, Erickson and Mendez. He used a different color for each and then drew vertical lines between the names, dividing the board into thirds. He took the tape dispenser from his desk and taped a photo of each victim beneath their name. Jen's photo was the professional head shot she used in all her real estate advertising. Mendez' photo was his senior photo from high school. Erickson's was an autopsy photo. He made a mental note to ask her mother for a different photo, he didn't think he'd want to stare at that one every day.

Intimidated by the amount of white space on the board, he began writing in details from each case. The date, time and cause of death. The crime scene location, witness names, even the clothing they were wearing when they died—anything that might start to shed light on the darkness beginning to overwhelm Los Robles.

He created timelines for each victim, detailing how they had spent the last day of their life. Wherever there was a gap, Miller made a note. He would assign deputies to fill in the blanks.

When he was done he sat back down behind his desk. His chair was sturdy, covered in brown leather. He swiveled it absent-mindedly, his eyes never leaving the white board. Slowly, he started rocking, starting the wheels of his mind turning, trying to get up to speed, like a locomotive leaving the station.

He stared at the three photos, and they stared back. He had known Jen, not well, but well enough to be on a first-name basis. She was a go-getter, so if there was a function or event in town, she was usually there. As the sheriff, so was he, either as a dignitary or in his official capacity. She was active in every aspect of the community. Much of that was done to promote her business, but anyone who spent time with Jen Upton quickly realized that she had come to love her adopted town.

He just couldn't come up with a motive for her death. She hadn't been sexually assaulted and when they found her body, she was still wearing all of her jewelry. Her purse was right next to her with her cell phone clipped to the handle. Someone had simply struck a savage blow across the back of her head and walked away.

It was a terrifying murder in a small town. A popular victim and no apparent motive had started rumblings that a monster was loose in Los Robles. Then came Lisa Erickson and Paul Mendez. Suddenly front doors were being locked, people hurried to and from their cars and the streets seemed deserted after dark.

There were times Dave Miller thought he knew every person in Los Robles, but he realized he hadn't known either Lisa Erickson or Paul Mendez. They didn't even look familiar to him. He knew them only in death. Somehow this made him feel guilty and sad. He wondered if he knew their murderer. Nobody expected him to know everyone, but he felt badly that he didn't have the same personal connection to the kids that he did to Jen. He silently vowed to compensate for that by finding their killers. Miller swiveled his chair to face his office door.

"Carol, is Bert around?" he called.

She poked her head into his doorway. "I just saw him down in the squad room."

"Would you ask him to come in please?"

Humberto Vega was a third generation Los Robles native. His grandparents had moved to town hoping to make their fortune in oil, but had instead found work in the orchards as agriculture began overtaking the oil industry. Their oldest son, Tomas, had worked hard in the fields, but in school too, and now was a manager at Plum Valley Produce, Plumrite's main competitor. Tomas' position had allowed his son, Humberto, to leave the fields and, eventually Los Robles, when he went south to Cal State Bakersfield and received his degree in Criminal Justice.

After he graduated, Bert had come home and applied for a position as a deputy. Over the years he had risen through the ranks to captain, Miller's second in command.

"What's up, boss?" Vega entered Miller's office the way he did everything else, with quiet confidence. He was just under six feet tall, lean and sinewy. Still in terrific shape, he was as comfortable out on the streets as he was behind his desk.

"Nothing. That's the problem. We've made zero headway on these murders."

"Is that what the board is all about?"

"I thought if I laid everything out it might show me something—similarities, common denominators—something."

"And?"

"Nothing."

Vega walked over and stood in front of the white board.

"We found meth by the Mendez boy, it could be a drug thing," he said.

Miller shook his head. "I don't know. It just doesn't feel right. There's nothing to indicate a drug connection with either Jen Upton or Lisa Erickson and nothing we've turned up in the Mendez investigation so far has drug overtones. That bag of meth seems like an anomaly, or maybe even a red herring."

"But you want to do something."

"Yes, and right now. Are drugs all we've got?"

"Seems like it. No robbery, no sexual assault, no obvious motive for any of the three."

"Well, if drugs is what we've got, then let's climb all over it. If nothing else, maybe we can eliminate the meth angle."

"I'll put the troops on it. We can rattle some cages and see if we can spook someone."

"Let's start with Mike Zepeda. I'll talk to him myself; see if I can put a little fear of God into him. Paul Mendez was found at his end of the valley. Maybe we can finally get the guy on something."

"We might, but I don't think it will be this. The guy's a Class-A crankhead, but I don't see him pulling off anything like these murders. He's not that neat. Or that smart. If Zepeda was involved, I think things would have been a lot messier and I think we would have heard some kind of a buzz on the street. These killings haven't even caused a blip on the bad guy's radar screens. If there was a connection, we'd be hearing something. On top of that, we don't have anything near what we need for a search warrant on Zepeda, so all we can do is poke him a little and see if he roars."

"I know, Bert, but I can't just sit around waiting for another body. We don't even know if there are three murderers out there, or one serial killer. I've got the mayor already making political noises and Tommy Upton has started nosing around, too."

"So which one is the bigger problem?"

"The mayor, for sure. Her agenda is strictly political and she'd love to have a reason to publicly rip me a new one. I'm not sure Tommy is even in it for a story. He's got a guilt thing going on with Jen's death. He's not objective, but he's committed. If he's digging, he might even be a help to us."

"Yeah, as long as his digging around doesn't get himself killed. We don't know the first thing about the person—or people—behind these killings. He starts pushing the wrong buttons, he could end up as part of the story."

"I hadn't thought about that, but you could be right. We won't be able to get him to quit looking, so I'll keep him close and maybe his perspective will open some new doors."

"I'll get the troops shaking the trees and we'll see what falls out."

"That works for me. I want an update every day by five. We can meet more often if we need to."

Vega left the office and Miller got up and walked around his desk to the white board. They needed a break. He didn't think he could sit at his desk every day with Jen's face staring back at him.

CHAPTER NINE

Alex Brewster softly turned the button on his bedroom door, locking it. His mother had a rule about not locking doors, but he knew he really didn't have to worry. She was in the living room watching TV with the sound up so loud that he could hear the laugh track through the door.

He surveyed his room and was pleased with what he saw. Everything was exactly where he left it, nothing out of place. That was important because he believed that everything had its own place. That was how you kept organized. To be successful you had to be organized and he was meticulously organized and, therefore, very successful.

The added benefit to the organized room, of course, was his ability to instantly see if his mother had been going through his things. She hadn't done that for a while now, but it didn't hurt to be careful. Especially lately. Usually, she just wanted money, but he didn't like her going through his belongings or moving things around. He couldn't keep the door locked while he was at work, but the door was locked whenever he was in his room.

He crossed the room to his desk and opened the center drawer. Nothing had been touched. Two twenty-dollar bills were stacked along the left-hand side of the drawer. He kept them there so his mother would find them quickly and not feel the need to search any further. Next to the bills were two pens, lined up as straight as goal posts. Next came three yellow pencils, identical in length, each sharpened to a precision point. Finally, by itself, was a multi-tool Swiss army knife. He took the red knife from the drawer and opened the screwdriver blade. He carried his desk chair back across the room to the door and stood on it. He used the screwdriver blade to carefully unscrew the four screws holding the heater vent cover on the wall above the door. He lined up the screws on his desk, followed by the cover. Returning to the chair, he reached into the vent and carefully removed a small cardboard box.

He carried the box to his desk and took off the lid as if the contents might explode if he were careless. The box contained only three items. The first was a composition book. It had a stiff cardboard cover, printed to resemble black marble. The white paper inside was printed with college-ruled light blue lines. The books could be bought for about a dollar at any office supply store. Students used them for note-taking or writing projects. He used this one for something else.

The second item gave the box its weight. It was a .38 short-barreled revolver. The pistol was a dull gray-black with checkered wooden hand grips. He kept it wrapped in a soft cotton rag. The gun was the only thing he owned that had belonged to his father.

The third item was a box of .38 shells. The box was full except for seven shells. Six were in the revolver. The seventh was in the back of Paul Mendez' head.

He re-wrapped the gun and placed it and the shells back inside the cardboard box. Then he retrieved his chair and placed it precisely in front of his desk. He sat down, his back straight and both feet on the floor, and opened the composition book.

Slowly, he began turning the pages. They were full of precise block lettering so neat it could have been typed. When he came to a blank page, he began to write. He wrote only on the front of each page. When he wrote, he pressed so hard with his pen that it nearly cut through page. Leaving indentations on the following page. He wrote slowly, methodically, never rushing, never pausing to think of the right word, never crossing a wrong word out.

At this session, he started by describing an orchard. He wrote down every emotion he felt, every word he said, and every move he made, right up to where he pulled the trigger and Paul Mendez fell face-first into the grass.

Mendez hadn't died like a man. He cried. He begged. He had known Brewster just well enough in high school to jump into the battered pickup truck when Brewster told him he knew a guy looking for a landscaper. Brewster had promised it would be a lucrative commercial account. By the time Mendez figured out something was wrong, Brewster already had the ugly little pistol pointed at Mendez. At the orchard, Mendez didn't want to get out of the truck. Brewster threatened to shoot him then and there. Brewster got out and went around the truck and literally pulled Mendez out. Paul Mendez was both bigger and in better shape than Brewster, but the gun was more than enough to make up the difference.

As they walked between the trees, Mendez began to cry.

"Alex, I don't understand. What are you doing?"

"Just keep walking."

"Where are we going? What do you want from me?"

Brewster grabbed Mendez by the collar of his shirt and spun him around so they faced each other. "What do I want from you? I want my future. That's what I want. Now walk." He pushed Mendez ahead.

"Your future? I don't understand."

"No, I'm sure you don't. And you never will. Get on your knees."

"Alex, please."

Brewster took that as an invitation and pulled the trigger. Back at his truck he carefully wiped down every surface, inside and out. If he didn't eliminate all the fingerprints, he was certain that he had at least rendered them unusable by smearing them. Then he wrapped the pistol and tucked it under the driver's seat.

He put his pen down on the page and placed both hands palm-down on the desk. He could feel his pulse racing and he was breathing rapidly. He consciously slowed his breathing and began to bring himself back under control. Finally, breathing normally, he picked up his pen and turned to the first page of the composition book. The only writing on the page was a list of names. Two of the names were crossed out. Slowly he drew a line through the name of Paul Mendez.

A smile came to his face as he completed the line. Another step in the journey, he thought. Another step towards redemption. Another step towards . . . what? Justice? He wasn't sure. But he knew it was the right thing to do. Just as he knew the composition book was the wrong thing to do.

Brewster knew the book—and its hiding place—were mistakes, but he simply couldn't help himself. The story of what he was doing had to be recorded. It was historical in its own way. And, since he really couldn't tell anyone else his story, he wrote it for himself. For posterity.

He knew his mother would never find the book, but the cops would—if he ever gave them a reason to look. They'd probably find it in seconds if they searched his room. So, obviously, he had to make sure that never happened.

He glanced at the time displayed on his cell phone. His mom's television show would be ending soon. When it did, she'd want something to eat and come looking for him to thaw something from the freezer or go for take-out.

He took the time to re-read what he called the first two chapters of his manuscript, the ones titled "Jennifer Upton" and "Lisa Erickson" and then turned back to the first page. He scanned the list of names, selected one, then made a small check mark next to it.

He put the book back into the cardboard box and the box back into the heating vent. The vent cover went back on easily and, just as he was placing his chair back at the desk, he heard his mother call his name.

CHAPTER TEN

Carol Burnside rapped three times on the doorjamb of Miller's office and poked her head through.

"Tommy Upton is here to see you."

Miller closed the file he was reading and said, "Send him back."

Upton came into the room, immediately noticing the white board across from Miller's desk. Miller waved him to a chair and the two men sat facing each other, neither saying anything. Upton finally broke the silence.

"I can't stop thinking about Paul Mendez," he said.

"Maybe it's not such a good idea for you to go to crime scenes, or autopsies. You're dealing with a lot right now."

"No, no. It's not that. It's just that there's something that doesn't make sense about all of this and I can't get my mind around it. I feel like we're missing something. Like there's a clue somewhere that we're just not seeing."

"Tommy, murder never makes sense. But this isn't a TV crime drama, either. There isn't some kind of criminal mastermind roaming the streets of Los Robles."

"I know, but there is a killer—or killers—out there and, master-mind or not, three people are dead."

"You're not the first person to mention that to me."

"Sorry, I didn't mean to imply anything."

"I know, but the mayor did, and so did some of the other people I've talked to around town. I can hardly show my face at the café these days. And it's not just here, either. Some of the regional papers are starting to talk about Los Robles as some kind of rural murder capital."

"Yeah, I saw the editorial in the Bakersfield *Californian*. But they all seem to think it's meth-related and I'm just not getting that vibe."

"Vibe? I don't think they taught us that at the police academy."

"C'mon, you know what I mean, and I don't believe you think meth has anything to do with it either. You wouldn't have that big board in here to stare at all day if you did."

"Okay, you're right, I don't believe there's a meth connection, but the mayor is already pressuring me to bring in the FBI, so I asked Bert Vega to have some of the guys go out and shake the trees to see if a meth dealer falls out."

"So, has your board given you any insights?"

"Not one. We have three murders, three different MOs and nothing in common with any of them. Well, that's not exactly true, but the commonalities don't help. That's the problem with a small town. Everyone knows each other, they all shop at the same stores, go to the same schools, belong to the same clubs. Anyone could be a suspect, anyone could be a victim."

"So what's your plan?"

"For now, I don't have many choices. We keep doing good police work running down every lead to see if something pops, and, I guess I have to pursue the whole meth angle. I told Bert I'd go out to see Mike Zepeda myself. We know he's hooked up in the meth world, but we've never been able to make anything stick against him. I doubt he's got anything to do with the murders, but maybe a little visit will loosen his tongue up about what he's hearing on the street. He lives in a piece of crap trailer north of town. You want to go meet your first meth dealer?"

"Absolutely."

The drive to Zepeda's trailer took about twenty minutes. They drove north through town on Petro Avenue, past the café on the circle, through some light industrial and commercial areas, then past the sprawling Plumrite packing house on the west side of the street and finally out into the orchards. Miller slowed the squad car about four miles out of town and made a left off the two-lane paved road and onto a rutted single-lane dirt road.

The trees on both sides were dropping flower petals as the blossoms turned into immature fruit. The petals made the grass beneath the trees look like it had been dusted with a light snowfall. In front of them, the orchard opened up into a clearing. The ground was littered with trash and junk around an old travel trailer. A gray Chevy Silverado pickup truck was parked in front of the trailer. It looked like it could probably tow the trailer, but it was obvious the trailer hadn't moved in a long time. The trailer looked like, at some time in the past, a green stripe had run down its length, but now, most of the green had flaked off. Upton could see that two of the four tires were flat and the window screens had holes large enough to let crows in. The predominant color scheme of the truck and trailer combination was rust.

All four truck tires had air in them and the windshield wipers had recently swiped several layers of grime off the windshield so, presumably, the truck ran. Upton couldn't see into the cab, but the bed contained an odd assortment of junk and trash. Upton could see a gas can, dried and cracked rubber tubing, old rubber gloves and about a dozen miscellaneous cans, jugs and bottles. Miller noticed him surveying the truck bed.

"It kind of looks like the back of your Jeep."

"Funny."

"It's all meth lab components."

"Is it safe?"

"Oh yeah, they're just components, there's no lab here. Zepeda is smart enough not to have the lab where he lives. He's barely smart enough, but I guess that's about as smart as a tweaker needs to be."

"If you know all this is meth lab stuff, why can't you arrest him? Wouldn't there be traces of meth on everything?"

"Nope. There'd be traces of meth *components* on everything, and none of the components are illegal."

They were standing at the edge of the clearing watching the trailer. When they weren't talking, the only sound was the clicking of the squad car's engine as it cooled.

"It's hard to believe he actually lives in this dump."

"He has all the comforts of home. He steals water off the irrigation system and taps power from the line running through the orchard. I don't even want to think what he does about sewage, but it's all rent-free because the family that owns these trees is too afraid to try and kick him off the property."

The two men stopped talking and stood quietly for a few more moments, just watching. Upton broke the silence.

"I guess no one's home."

"Oh, he's home alright. He's watching us watch him. He's hoping we'll go away."

Upton noticed Miller reach down and casually unsnap the flap on his holster and start walking toward the trailer. Upton followed a couple of steps behind and, after a bit of reflection, slightly off to the side. About halfway across the clearing, Miller called out to the trailer.

"Sheriff's Department. Zepeda, come out of there." Miller waited a moment and then shouted again. "Now, Zepeda. I've got probable cause and if I have to come in and get you, you'll be leaving with me."

Upton saw the trailer shake from movement inside and then the door opened about a foot.

"What do you want? I haven't done anything wrong."

"You've done everything wrong, Mikey. Your whole life. Now get out here."

Zepeda pushed the door open the rest of the way and awkwardly stepped down from the trailer. The trailer's metal step was missing and it had been replaced by a cinder block sitting unevenly on the ground.

Zepeda looked terrible. His skin was so pale it was almost translucent. There was almost no flesh on his skeletal frame and Upton could see rashes and sores on his arms, neck and face. A sheen of sweat covered his forehead.

Miller was also busy sizing up Zepeda as he emerged from the trailer. "You don't look so good, Mikey. You been sampling the inventory?"

"I don't have an inventory. And don't call me Mikey. I hate that."

"Well that's too damn bad *Mikey* because I have a dead kid who was found with a bag of crystal right next to his body."

"So what? Lots of kids OD."

"He didn't OD, Mikey. He was shot in the back of the head." Miller glanced back at the trailer. "Is there anyone else in the trailer? If there is, tell them to come out right now."

Upton unconsciously took a step backwards. This was starting to sound like trouble.

"There's no one in there, I swear."

Upton was studying Zepeda. He didn't think it would have been possible, but Zepeda seemed to have gone even paler when he heard the news about the shooting. He didn't think you could fake that.

Zepeda started pacing and started waving his arms like he was trying to signal a tow truck on the highway. "I didn't shoot anybody. You can't hang that on me."

"Really? Then help me out. Where were you the night before last? Be careful what you say, because I'm going to check."

"I . . . let me think, let me think. Yeah, I was here. Just hangin' out, you know?"

"Just hanging out. Anyone else here? Somebody that can verify that? I told you I was going to check, if someone says you were somewhere else, you're in a world of hurt. Hanging out alone? A guy like you needs a better alibi than that, Mikey."

"I don't need an alibi at all and you know it. You're just turnin' on lights hopin' to find a roach. One of your deputies has already been by here. If you had something on me I'd be sitting in the back of your car."

Miller smiled.

"You've been watching *Law and Order*, huh, Mikey?"

"Hey, I know my rights."

"You should, they've been read to you enough. Well, if you're innocent, why don't you tell me what you know about all this."

"I don't know nothin'."

"C'mon, Mikey, a guy like you hears things."

"Yeah, sometimes I do. But I ain't heard nothin' on this. Who was it?"

"A kid named Paul Mendez."

"Never heard of him."

Miller gave Zepeda a long, hard look, then changed his posture, taking a less aggressive stance.

"This is serious shit, Mike. You don't want any part of it. If you hear something, you call me. I'll remember that you did me a favor."

"I've got plenty of my own trouble; don't need any of anyone else's. I'll call you if I hear any talk, but you'll owe me."

Zepeda spun and climbed back inside the trailer. Miller and Upton watched him go. He slammed both the screen door and the trailer door. Then they saw him peek through a curtain at them. Miller nodded at Upton.

"Let's go."

"Was that productive?" Upton asked as they turned to walk away.

"Well, it's really just a gut feeling, but I don't think he was involved, so at least we've eliminated a suspect. But I don't think it's moved us along very far."

The men stopped in the orchard, about halfway back to the car. Zepeda's trailer was no longer visible, neither was Miller's squad car. They were surrounded by the stillness of the orchard. A light breeze rustled leaves and birds made small sounds from the branches. The calm took the tension out of both men. They had walked in just in case they could surprise Zepeda doing something he shouldn't have been. Now Upton realized he had been tense from head to toe the entire time.

He stuffed his hands into his front pants pockets and idly kicked some pebbles in the dirt tire ruts. "It doesn't seem right, Dave. I know bad things happen everywhere, even in Los Robles, but these murders feel different to me, and it's not just because of Jen. I'll never believe Jen had anything to do with a guy like Zepeda, and from what I know about Lisa Erickson and Paul Mendez, they didn't seem like the type, either."

Miller sighed. "I know what you're saying, believe me. I've circled around this thing a hundred times and I still can't decide if we're looking for one guy or three."

"Are you getting pressure?"

"Big time. Elections are in the fall and the posturing has already started."

"So, where do we go from here?"

"It's just business as usual, Tommy. I ignore the politicians and just do my job. And sometimes, that's not fast enough for them, but it's all I can do. They all watch TV and think murders are solved in an hour. Meanwhile, I have to keep shaking trees and turning over rocks until something turns up. And it always does, eventually. No matter how smart criminals think they are, eventually they make a mistake. When that happens in these murders, I'll be there and I'll be ready."

CHAPTER ELEVEN

"Do you want something to eat?

"No, I'm not hungry." Brewster couldn't figure out how his mother always seemed to beat him home from the packing house. She couldn't sneak out early because she had to punch the time clock like everyone else. He was sure she was doing something sneaky. After his current mission was finished, he'd have to pay some attention to his mother's activities. She wasn't intelligent enough to outsmart him and, when he found out her secret, he was sure he would be able to use it to his own advantage.

She was standing in the kitchen at the stove, her back to him, stirring something from a can. It could have been soup, or maybe chili, he couldn't tell. She had the burner up too high and he could hear the stuff scorching on the bottom of the pan. There was a slight smell of burned tomatoes, but his mother didn't seem to care. Seeing her in front of the stove, he realized how small she was. He had never noticed. There was no way she weighed a hundred pounds, but her arms were wiry and sinewy from her work at the packing house. She had short black hair, now streaked with gray and Brewster suspected she cut it herself with the kitchen scissors.

She reached for a coffee cup to the left of the stove and he knew it was about even odds whether it was full of coffee or vodka. Those were the only two things he ever saw her drink. Her fingers looked like she'd been dyeing Easter eggs—they were stained yellow and purple from cigarettes and plums.

She turned and looked at him, capturing his eyes with her milky blue ones. Her face was heavily lined and her jaw seemed perpetually set. Her voice was rough and gravelly from the cigarettes, but strong, probably from shouting over the machinery at the packing house.

"You sure you don't want something? There's plenty. You should eat."

"No, I'm fine. Maybe I'll have something later."

She turned back to the stove without saying anything. Brewster couldn't quite suppress a smile, geez she was a tough old broad. He turned away from the kitchen and went back down the short hall to his room. He carefully locked the door behind him.

Quiet as a cat burglar he removed the box from its hiding place and centered it on his desk. He lifted off the lid and laid it down behind the box, corners precisely squared to the box in front of it. Using both hands, he took out the composition book and put it down on the desk in front of him. He stared at the cover a long time without opening the book. Hands folded in his lap, back straight and head bowed, he appeared to be in prayer. But he wasn't. He was in a barely suppressed state of excitement that was almost sexual.

Finally, he opened the book. He turned pages until he reached the one with the list of names. He looked at the name with the checkmark next to it and smiled. Three other names also had checkmarks next to them—Jennifer Upton, Lisa Erickson and Paul Mendez—but those names now had a single, neat line running through them. Soon, so would the next name, Sandra Gibson.

For a brief time, Sandra Gibson had been the most important person in his life. As the guidance counselor at the high school it was her job to encourage promising students to consider continuing their education at the college level. With his standing in the class, Gibson had encouraged him to swing for the fence and apply to the top tier colleges. She found financial aid to pay for the applications and told him that, with his grades, he was a lock for several scholarships she knew about.

For weeks, after the last bell, he'd hurry to her office, a converted classroom, where she would help him with the paperwork. Looking back, he realized he'd probably had a little bit of a crush on her. She was tall, for a woman, but not as tall as him, and slender. Her hair was a tangled mess of blonde and brown curls, naturally curly, he thought. She dressed in clothes from the women's department at Walmart. They didn't look bad on her, but they made her look a little older than she really was. He didn't think she wore makeup, not much anyway, and she was pretty in a wholesome, natural kind of way. Even with all that, he didn't think he'd have any trouble killing her.

The question was, how? Brewster had a good thing going and he needed to make sure he kept his standards high and his thoughts and actions focused.

He knew he was too smart to be caught by the local cops, and too smart to do the things that might bring in state or federal authorities. He'd watched enough TV crime shows to know not to leave evidence. He wore gloves—latex gloves were everywhere around the packing house—and he made sure he didn't leave anything at the scene. He did not leave taunting little clues like the villains on TV did and he didn't send anonymous messages to the media. Besides, the Los Robles *Register* wasn't exactly CNN. He did have a little fun with Mendez. He thought the bag of meth was brilliant. That would send the Sheriff and his minions off in a million directions, none of which would lead to him.

Mostly though, he knew the best plan he had made was one he had decided on early, he would use a different method to kill each victim. The Sheriff would never figure out there was only one killer if the victims all died by different methods. He'd think it was a crime wave.

But all of that left him with the question of what to do with Sandra Gibson. It's not like there are that many ways to kill someone, he thought. They're all sort of variations on a theme. He'd already bludgeoned one victim, stabbed another and shot a third. He didn't want to repeat himself, but there weren't really a lot of methods open to him. Poison was a possibility, but it was slow and a quick medical response might save her. He could blow up her car or something like that, but he'd have to do a lot of research for that. Not that research was such a big problem. He was sure everything he needed could be found on the Internet and, with his intellect, a little chemistry wouldn't slow him down. Still, a bomb could be problematic. A bomb that caused a death would probably bring in the Feds. That wouldn't be good. The local yokels would never catch him, but he wasn't sure he wanted the FBI or the ATF on his tail. Besides, a bomb wasn't very personal, and he was taking this matter very personally. It was the same thing with fire. He could set her apartment on fire and simply walk away. Low risk, high probability of success, but not much satisfaction.

Strangulation. Now that was personal. She could look into his eyes while she died and he could calmly explain why he was killing her. Strangulation. That was an idea with some merit. But not with his hands on her throat. That was too brutish, too common. No, he'd use a garrote. That would be elegant. A garroting would require some planning, some careful planning. He would have to use his brain for this one, and he would prove to Sandra Gibson that his brain was very good. Good enough for Harvard.

In fact, he'd make it a point to tell her that specifically. If she happened to ask why he was still in Los Robles—quite an accomplishment while your larynx is being crushed—he'd casually mention that none of the scholarships she had practically guaranteed him had come through. And, just to be sure she understood, just before she died, he would tell her about the Petrolia Club scholarship, the one that would have sent him to Harvard. The one that was awarded to a God-damned football player who thought he was smart enough for Stanford. Stanford. Harvard's pathetic West coast cousin suffering from delusions of grandeur. A refuge for those not smart enough for Harvard. A school best-known for a subversive marching band and a color as a mascot. Stanford. The word tasted vile in his mouth.

Gibson had said, with his grades, the scholarship was a lock. And he knew that scholarship was the key to the doors of Harvard for him. His dream was in sight. He could feel it, almost touch it. He had gone online to plan his first-semester classes and arrange his housing. He even mail-ordered a Harvard sweatshirt. And then, as he sat at the front table of the Petrolia Club's scholarship banquet, he heard the club president read the name of Josh Slater. A jock. A guy who thought being the class president was something worth aspiring to. A blonde, grinning pretty-boy was awarded the scholarship that Sandra Gibson has promised to him.

So, if she asked why he was still in Los Robles, that is what he would tell her. And then he would watch her die.

CHAPTER TWELVE

Sandra Gibson sat in a wooden swivel chair behind an industrial model teacher's desk in a classroom that had been converted into her office. But her mind was somewhere else—on a sunny, sandy beach, enjoying an exotic vacation she knew she could never take. For the moment, she had blocked out the Armed Forces recruitment posters covering the walls, the shelves lined with college catalogs and the large, round tables that she hoped would soon be occupied by college hopefuls in the fall researching colleges. The florescent light fixtures hanging by chains from the ceiling became the tropical sun in her mind and she lifted her face to their light.

She came back to reality as the ancient air-conditioner in the window rattled to life. She wasn't sure how it stayed there. It was held in place by an ill-fitting piece of plywood. The air-conditioner did little to cool the room in the spring and summer and the gaps between it and the plywood allowed frigid air to enter during the winter.

Her day was almost over, but the last hour, from the final bell at three o'clock until about four, was the most important hour of her day. It's when she saw the serious kids, the ones with aspirations for college educations or a career in the military. The kids who saw more in their future than a minimum wage job on the Plumrite packing line. Her office was their ticket out of Los Robles. The three o'clock kids didn't come to her office because their parents or a guidance counselor forced them, they came to work. They pored over college catalogs and websites and completed application after application. They needed help and they asked questions, and she had the answers. For the last hour of her work days she felt needed and appreciated. She couldn't help them all, of course. She knew that and so did they. But that was the way the system worked. The kids worked hard, got good, no, great grades. They joined clubs and participated in campus and community activities. They wrote compelling essays, all with an eye towards improving their chances of acceptance by the college of their choice and a chance for the limited scholarships still available in a struggling economy.

But one of the lessons learned in her office was that life is not always fair. It seemed like every year there was at least one promising student who had his or her dreams dashed against the rocks of academic competition. Most of them re-grouped and went to a back-up college, or commuted to the community college over the grade in Bakersfield for a year to complete some of their required courses so they could re-apply as transfer students the next fall. But others gave up. After working hard through twelve years of school, they quit. They hung their heads and took jobs at Plumrite or the supermarket. There was nothing wrong with these jobs, they just weren't the level these kids had worked so hard for. She saw these former students around town all the time. They would never leave Los Robles. They'd grow up, marry someone they knew in high school, have a couple of babies and start the cycle over.

Today, business was slow. She was busiest late in the winter when the college application season was in full-swing. Springtime was a time for waiting. The students scanned their mailboxes looking for the thick envelopes from the colleges. The thick envelopes were the acceptance letters. They came stuffed with information on housing and financial aid. The thin envelopes were the rejections. Once the letters started arriving, good or bad, her business picked up.

Come to think of it, the kids didn't get many letters anymore. They got emails. She wondered if there was anything worse or more impersonal than a rejection delivered by email.

And it wasn't just the email. More and more of the communication was electronic. Even the long application forms were now done mostly online. She had shelves of printed college catalogs, but many of them were more than five years old. The students did their research on the Internet. But that didn't mean they could do everything by themselves.

Kids would still come to her for help with scholarships or to make desperate attempts at getting into colleges that had been further down on their lists.

Today though, the room was still. No clicking keyboards or scratching pens, whispered conversations or the buzzing of cell phones on the vibrate setting. Today there was just the rattle of the air conditioner and the series of clicks from the industrial clock on the wall as the minutes slowly ticked by.

For all she knew, the campus was deserted and, from her standpoint, it pretty much was. If there weren't college-bound students headed her way, then there weren't any students at all around at this end of the school. Her office was in the oldest building on campus. Over the years the school had grown in the opposite direction, leaving her classroom nearly isolated, blocked from view on Oakview Street by the bulk of the school and far away from whatever activities were underway on the athletic fields at the far end of the campus.

When students were headed toward her office, she could usually hear them coming. The emptiness at this end of the school seemed to amplify their footsteps and voices and, as a result, she often knew who was about to walk in before they even opened the door. Today there was just the quiet. She checked the clock again. It didn't seem to be making much progress toward four o'clock. Usually, if the kids didn't come shortly after the last bell, they weren't going to come at all and she thought that seemed to be the case today.

She could just lock up the room and leave and, most likely, nobody would know or care. But she told the kids she would always be there until four, so she stayed.

She went around the room straightening catalogs that were already alphabetized by college name and precisely aligned on the shelves. None were out of order. She taped down the uncooperative corner of an Army recruiting poster and shuffled the files on her desk.

Finally, the clock ticked over to four. She crossed the room and turned off the air-conditioner. She made sure the windows were latched and the computers were shut down. At her desk she put a couple of folders into the large, white shoulder bag that doubled as her briefcase and purse, walked to the door where she turned off the lights and stepped outside. Pulling the door closed behind her and checking to be sure it was locked, she paused for a moment to savor the afternoon.

The school was quiet and the pleasant spring afternoon was still warm. She thought a Cobb salad and a glass of Chardonnay might be nice for dinner. She hoisted the bag up onto her shoulder and started for the small parking lot at the end of the row of classrooms. The lot only had room for about six cars and that was usually three or four spaces more than were needed. By this time of day, her bright orange Volkswagen beetle was often the only car left in the lot. She could see it, shining in the sun, just past the dumpster. She was already thinking about the glass of wine. The only sound was the clicking of her heels against the concrete.

CHAPTER THIRTEEN

Brewster looked at the time display on his cell phone and smiled in approval. Right on time. He'd been watching her for more than a week and her schedule hadn't varied by more than five minutes during that period.

She's about to regret that, he thought.

He had planned this operation with care. His hiding place was perfect. He was crouched behind a hedge that ran along the edge of the parking lot and he was hidden from view by anyone at the school by the dumpster in the corner. Miss Gibson had parked her little pumpkin-looking car in the same spot every day. A creature of habit. She would walk right past him to reach her car. This had all been so easy. In fact, the hardest part about the whole plan had been devising the garrote.

Not that a garrote is such a complicated thing. At its most basic, it's just a short piece of wire with a handle at both ends. To use it, all he had to do was come up behind her, cross his arms as he passed the wire over her head to her throat, and then pull on the ends to strangle her. Simple. What wasn't quite so simple were the specifics of the device. If the wire was too long, he wouldn't have enough leverage to pull it tight. If it was too short, the handles would prevent him from completely crushing her esophagus. It seemed odd to him that he couldn't find a source that told him the optimum length for the wire. He thought you could find anything on Google, but none of the thousands of posts on garrotes had included how long the wire should be. There was, however, plenty of information on the wire itself.

It was important to use the right gauge of wire. If it was too fine, he could end up slicing her head off, although that would be an acceptable result. If the gauge was too thick, the wire wouldn't be flexible enough. It was like Goldilocks and the Three Bears, he thought. He needed to find the mama bear wire. Just right.

And, of course, there was the question of the handles. Strictly speaking, the handles were optional equipment. But he knew she would struggle, in fact he was counting on it, so he needed something the help with his grip. They had to be something he could grasp firmly. If he should happen to let go of a handle, she might be able to scream for help, or even escape.

In the end, he had chosen simple, hard to trace items for the garrote and found them easily available at Plumrite. He used two six-inch pieces of broom stick for the handles and baling wire for the garrote. He drilled a hole through each handle, passed the wire through it and made several passes around the broom handle. He thought that would be enough to keep the wire from pulling out. Then he wrapped both handles in athletic tape to give him a good grip, just like baseball players wrapped their bat handles.

He discovered that there was a certain amount of skill required to effectively use a garrote, but he hadn't been able to figure out a good way to practice the technique. He spent a lot of time in his room crossing his arms in the air and pulling on the handles as he tried to visualize the wire passing over Gibson's head. But, since there was no actual neck involved, he wasn't certain he had the move down perfectly. On the other hand, he was bigger than Gibson and he'd have the element of surprise in his favor, so he thought he probably had enough of an edge to overcome any flaws in his technique. Mostly, he just needed to be sure he got the wire below her chin and onto her neck. After that, it was all about brute strength.

While he waited, he rehearsed his speech in his mind. He would explain to her exactly why she was about to die and she would die slowly enough to look into his face, see the hatred there, and then understand her fate.

His timing had been perfect for Sandra Gibson, although she probably wouldn't think so. Plumrite had shifted some of its line hours to meet some East Coast shipping deadlines, and that had given Brewster the opportunity to scout Gibson's daytime habits before his overnight shift at the plant started.

He had originally planned to attack her at home, but after following her there one day, he discovered she lived in a garden apartment where at least five of her neighbors could watch her every move from the time she parked her car to the time she walked through her front door. So, he had started watching her at school.

He had never realized how isolated her classroom was while he was a student. But he was seeing things differently now. For the last four days he had been crouching behind the hedge, watching her, timing her, studying her. He had to admit that he still found her attractive and he enjoyed watching her as she came down the walk from her classroom and then across the parking lot to her car. When he had been applying to Harvard, spending hours in her classroom, he had often wondered how she would feel in his arms. Well, today he would find out, but not in the way he had imagined back then.

Brewster cocked his head to one side, listening carefully. He was amazed how quiet it was. School had only been out for about an hour and the school was just a block and a half from the center of town, but all he could hear were birds in the trees above him and a slight buzz from the traffic out on Oakview Street. Then he heard something else. He heard the classroom door close, followed closely by the sound of her heels on the concrete.

He tugged at the latex gloves—they were snug and secure on his hands. He held both handles of the garrote in his left hand as he checked the .38 in his back pocket. He was ready. He had almost left the revolver at home but decided at the last minute to bring it along—just in case. It was his insurance, his backup plan. If Miss Gibson had thought to counsel him about backup plans, she might not be about to die.

As her footsteps grew closer, his pulse quickened. A sheen of sweat coated his forehead. He could see her feet beneath the dumpster and he silently moved from behind the hedge to the side of the dumpster. As she passed he stepped in behind her and quickly looped the wire over her head, around her neck, and pulled on the handles.

Reflexively, Sandra Gibson reached for her throat, trying to grasp the wire that was choking her. She bucked violently, trying to throw off her attacker and, at least once, managed to stomp her foot down onto his instep. He had grunted in pain, so she knew she had hurt him. But he was hurting her, too. She could feel the wire cutting into her flesh and it was making it hard for her to breath. She tried to scream, but the constriction of her throat and the lack of oxygen prevented any sound from escaping. So she simply continued to struggle, fighting for her life.

Brewster knew he was in trouble almost instantly. The wire was too long. He couldn't get the leverage to pull the wire tight enough around her neck and she was fighting like a wild thing.

She kept reaching up, trying to pull at the wire. She threw her elbows at his ribs and kicked his shins repeatedly. And then she stomped on his instep. That infuriated him and he tried to pull harder on the handles. As he did, he spun her half way around so she could see him.

"You bitch. This is your fault. I should be at Harvard right now." He was speaking through clenched teeth, his breathing ragged from the struggle. He was mad at her and with himself. He wasn't giving the speech he had planned so carefully. He was enraged seeing her face and in pain from her stomp on his foot.

As she turned, he could see recognition on her face. Her mouth tried to form his name, but no sound came out. Good, he thought. But now, aware of who he was, her struggles increased. She was making desperate squeaking sounds as she tried to scream and she reached out and scratched his face. Brewster wanted to cry. His foot hurt, but the pain from the scratch was intense as sweat poured into the wound. He felt Gibson's struggles ease momentarily, and then his world went white with pain. She had brought her knee up into his groin and connected solidly. He gasped and as he started to bend over in agony, he lost the handle out of his right hand.

Gibson continued to fight and he could tell she believed she was about to escape. He wasn't going to let that happen. As she pulled against the wire still wrapped around her throat he reached into the back pocket of his jeans, pulled out the small revolver and fired without aiming.

A small red stain slowly started to spread across the front of Gibson's blouse. Her eyes opened wide in shock and she fell to the pavement on her back. He was breathing hard from exertion, she hardly seemed to breathe at all. She looked up at him with a question in her eyes.

"You stole my dream," he shouted at her. She opened her mouth as if to reply as he fired a second shot into her chest. And then another.

Suddenly, he was aware of the silence. He could hear himself breathing, rapid and raspy. He could smell sweat, and blood and gunpowder. This was not how it was supposed to have gone. It was too loud. There was too much blood—his and hers. All of his careful planning had not taken into account the fact that she might fight back. He had wanted it to be personal, but he had never imagined she could fight with such intensity.

He knew someone would have heard the shots. He had to go. He jumped the fence into the neighboring middle school and, after a dash across the softball field, jumped another fence into a yard on Orchard Street. He was only a few blocks from home, but he was limping and bleeding. He had to arrive home before his mother and not attract any attention along the way.

He forced himself to walk instead of run and dabbed at the scratch on his face with his shirt sleeve. It didn't seem to be bleeding as much. There were scratches on his hands, too, but they hardly bled at all. They were just deep furrows of missing skin. He tried to calm his breathing and his heart rate, but the combination of adrenaline and physical exertion was making it difficult.

The walk home was surreal. He could hear sirens in the distance and he felt like someone was staring at him from every window along the way, but he reached his apartment building without incident. Everything was quiet around the complex. He took the stairs two at a time up to the front door. He let himself in and leaned back against the front door, safe for the moment.

His mother wasn't home yet so he quickly stripped and got into the shower. He'd sneak his bloody clothes out to the dumpster later. He lathered and scrubbed and saw the water at his feet turn pink. He toweled off and had just finished getting dressed when he heard the front door open.

"Hi, Mom."

"Jesus. What the hell happened to you?"

"Little accident at work. I tripped and fell into a pallet of boxes, right at the corner. They tore me up."

She looked at him and shook her head as she gazed at the deep scratch running down his cheek. He wasn't convinced she believed his story.

"When did you go back on days?"

"I haven't yet. Rosie called in sick so I took part of her shift."

"I didn't hear anything about you falling."

"It was no big deal, Mom. A little clean-up and I was right back on the line. Rico said I didn't even have to fill out an accident report since I didn't miss any time."

"Are you still working your regular shift tonight?"

"Yeah. I go in at six."

"Well, you better have something to eat and get moving."

"I will, Mom. Thanks."

He shut his bedroom door, his heart racing again. He could hear her open the cabinet and the clinking of glass as she pulled out the vodka bottle and a tumbler. He thought she'd finally bought his story, but it wouldn't hold up if she started asking around. But there was a lot of vodka between now and her next shift, so he thought his odds were pretty good.

He looked around to see if his room needed straightening up. It didn't. The only thing out of place was the pile of bloody clothes behind his closet door. He stuffed them into a trash bag he had grabbed from a box under the sink in the kitchen, picked up the keys to his truck and peeked out into the hallway. His mother's bedroom door was closed.

He walked into the living room and shouted, "Bye, Mom!" and closed the front door without waiting for a reply.

He hurled the trash bag into the dumpster at the end of the carport and climbed into his battered old white Ford 150 pickup. It had seen better days, much better days, but it still ran good. But what he liked most about it was its anonymity. The valley was full of white pickups. It seemed like every farm had at least one and so did most of the oil guys. He didn't know why, but it was true. Maybe it was cheaper for Chevy and Ford to make white pickups. He didn't know, but driving one made him almost invisible.

As he made his way to his position on the packing line he noticed some of his coworkers checking his appearance. This incensed him for some reason. He had a scratch on his face and some scratches on his hands. So what? They acted like they'd never seen a guy wearing a Band-Aid. And what business was it of theirs anyway?

He pulled on his latex gloves and placed his headset over his ears just as the bell rang and the conveyor line started. He reached behind him, grabbed a carton and started inspecting plums for the one he would use as his example for the box. As he moved into the familiar routine, his mind settled and his heartbeat slowed.

It hadn't gone perfectly, he thought, but he could draw a line through another name in his book.

CHAPTER FOURTEEN

A squad car sped past his window at the *Register*, the roar of its Interceptor engine rattling the glass as the car went by. Upton stood, leaned over his desk and peered to the right as the car made its way around the circle and turned right onto Oakview Street. The car had its blue lights on, but not the siren. It couldn't be going far. As he watched, two more sheriff's units, a fire engine and an ambulance made the same turn.

Upton grabbed his fedora by the crown and settled it on his head. He picked up a pen and his yellow pad and left the office. He had flipped through the pages of the pad so many times the edges were starting to curl. Coming in on Petro Avenue the squad car had to go almost completely around the traffic circle to reach Oakview Street. Tommy simply went left from the paper's front door, walked the few feet to the corner and he could see the emergency vehicles turning into the high school's driveway on the far east end of the campus.

Upton crossed the street and walked the length of the school to reach the driveway. Rounding the corner of the building he almost collided with a deputy unspooling a roll of yellow crime scene tape across the driveway.

"Stay back, sir."

"I'm press."

"Press is already here, sir."

"I'm more press," Upton said and flashed the deputy his *Register* identification pass.

"Fine. Go on back, just don't get in the way."

"Is it bad?"

"As bad as it gets."

Upton started down the driveway and could see the collection of emergency vehicles clustered in a small parking lot at the end. He heard tires on the pavement and stepped aside as Mary Ellen Driscoll drove by in a metallic-blue Prius. She nodded as she went by, her mouth set in a grim line.

Upton saw two emergency medical technicians sitting on the back bumper of their ambulance. Between Mary Ellen's presence and the inactivity of the two EMTs, it didn't take much of an investigative reporter to know that meant whoever was laying inside the circle of sheriff's deputies no longer needed medical attention. Dave Miller had assumed his customary crime scene pose, squatting next to the body.

As he approached the scrum of deputies, a hand grabbed his right bicep and spun him around.

"This isn't your story, Upton."

One of the *Register's* three full-time reporters, Jerry Morris, had a hold of his arm and wasn't letting it go. He was younger than Upton, and considerably less talented according to everyone at the paper. But he was sober and reliable, so he had tried to fill Upton's shoes when Tommy finally fell from grace.

His face was perpetually flushed, even more so now because he was upset. His short-cropped sandy hair contrasted with his ruddy face, making him always appear slightly embarrassed. He was a couple of sizes heavier than his belt size, so his buckle was pushed below his belly and faced nearly straight down at the ground. He was sweating in the late-afternoon sun.

His prominent Adam's apple bobbed as he talked and because he had a slight lisp, a fine spray of saliva caught the late afternoon sun.

"I've got this, Tommy. You can head on back to the office, or stop by Louie's."

Upton let the insult slide, but not the suggestion. "I think I'll just poke around a little and see what I can find out."

Morris gave him a one-handed push to the chest. "It's not your story."

Upton gestured toward the body on the asphalt. "If that person's dead it is," he said. "Unless you're writing my obits now, too."

Morris was stunned speechless and Upton shouldered his way past him. He could see the body now. It was a woman.

Dave Miller looked up and saw him. He called him over by gesturing with his chin. He was wearing latex gloves and holding a large purse.

As Upton walked toward the body, he glanced over his shoulder. A deputy now stood in front of Morris, blocking him from advancing any further. Morris' face was glowing a bright red.

"Watch your step, Tommy. We're still tagging evidence," Miller said.

"My God, what happened to her?"

Mary Ellen Driscoll was on the other side of the body, using her gloved hands to gently turn the head right and left. Upton leaned into look.

"It's too early to say for sure," she said, "but my working theory is that someone tried to strangle her, couldn't, so he shot her."

"This is her purse," said Miller. "It looks intact. Her wallet is in here, with plenty of cash. So are her cell phone and car keys. Nothing to indicate anything was taken, or even gone through. We could be looking at another pure murder."

Upton stood up and put his hands on his hips. He felt short of breath. He looked behind him. Jerry Morris was being restrained by a very large deputy. He kept gesturing at Tommy, but the deputy was having none of it. Morris was red-faced and gave Tommy the finger. Tommy smiled at him and then turned back around toward the body. His gaze wandered the surroundings and he felt out of place.

"What was she doing way back here? I've never even seen this part of the campus."

"The classroom she used as an office is right over there," said Miller, then pointing at the Volkswagen said, "and this is her car. I think she was done for the day and walking to her car when this happened."

"She was a teacher?"

"Guidance counselor."

Upton looked at the body again. The face was so contorted by pain and fear he could barely recognize it as human.

"Is there more than one guidance counselor here? Jen worked with one last year when she was on the committee for the Petrolia Club scholarship award."

"I don't know. We'll check."

"Dave, I need to roll her over," said Driscoll.

With Miller pulling and Driscoll pushing, they rolled Gibson's body onto the right side. Driscoll stared intently, tugging at Gibson's blouse with a large pair of tweezers and scrutinizing the asphalt under the body.

"Look here, Dave." She pointed to two pockmarks in the asphalt. "It looks like she was shot three times, at close range. I'm looking at these depressions in the asphalt and they seem to correspond to two of the wounds. I think she was shot twice after she was already down. The bullets are probably buried in the asphalt. She must have been looking right at him when he shot her."

"Why do you say 'him'," Upton asked.

"Well, you're right. I really don't know yet. But, based on the way the ligature marks on her neck run up towards the corners of her jaw, I think her assailant had to be taller and stronger than her, so I'm assuming a male."

A female deputy taking photos of the scene came by and circled the bullet marks in the asphalt with yellow chalk and then placed one of the numbered evidence markers next to them. For the next couple of minutes she took shot after shot from every angle. Technicians would come back after the body was removed to see if they could recover the bullets from inside the holes.

Miller remained in his squat, watching his deputy work. Driscoll had stood up and was making notes on a sheaf of papers held on a clipboard. Upton used the time to take in the scene.

"This one's different," he said.

Both Miller and Driscoll looked at him.

"Different how?" said Miller.

"The other crime scenes—and bodies—were neat, almost staged. Jen was on her back, hands at her sides, almost peaceful." His voice broke slightly and he cleared his throat before resuming.

"Paul Mendez simply fell forward. The grass was hardly disturbed. And with Lisa, there was more blood, but she looked like she had just laid down, too.

"This one's different," he repeated. "Her clothes are disheveled. There are marks around her neck, but they clearly didn't kill her, the bullets did."

"Thanks, doctor," said Driscoll.

Upton allowed himself a slight smile and nodded at Driscoll. "Sorry, but you know what I mean. There's just a different feel here. A lack of control. It's messy. Could this be a different killer?"

"Could be," said Miller. "We really won't know until we get a closer look at the evidence. It could also mean that we're looking at a screw-up. Our guy from the first three murders—assuming it's one guy—was methodical, like you said. He obviously planned well. This crime scene shows plenty of advance planning, too.

"First, one of my deputies found a spot behind that hedge where it looked like someone may have been watching or waiting. Maybe both. We're trying to take some shoe impressions from the dirt. And then there's the time. This place is like a ghost town. She's the only one here. When the 911 calls came in for shots fired, the deputies looked all over the place for the source. We might not have even looked back here except a deputy caught a glimpse of her car. The bright orange color caught his eye.

"And there's the murder itself. There was an obvious attempt at mechanical strangulation, but she was also shot. I'm with Mary Ellen, my gut says he planned to strangle her, but things didn't go right so he shot her."

A lanky deputy called out to the sheriff and walked up. He nodded at Upton and actually tipped his hat to Driscoll. Tommy was pretty sure Jen had sold a house to the deputy and his wife.

"We found this over by the fence," he said, holding up a plastic evidence bag containing a short length of wire with a piece of wood attached to one end. Miller took the bag and looked at the contents.

"Good work. This could be one of the weapons."

"There's more, sir. The Techies found blood on the fence. No way to know if it's our suspect's at this point, but we're collecting samples. He may have escaped over the fence, so we've got guys going around to the other side to see if we can pick up a trail."

Miller thanked the deputy and turned back to the body.

"You almost wrapped up, Mary Ellen?"

"Yep. Not much more I can do with her here. I need to get her back to my place and start looking for the small stuff. If your guys have all the shots they need, I'll have the medics bag her and transport her to the office."

Miller nodded and Driscoll waved in the medics. She closely supervised their handling of the body to make sure no evidence was compromised.

Miller and Upton watched as the unwieldy black bag was lifted onto a gurney and wheeled away.

"Does she have relatives in town?"

"None that we know of," said Miller. "We're checking for a next of kin, but we may not know until tomorrow. The school office is already closed and that's where all their personnel files are. We'll try to get in there today, but, who knows. To be honest, I hope her family is somewhere else, I'm not sure I can handle another family notification right now."

The remark was uncharacteristic for Miller and Upton looked over at him. He looked tired—mentally and physically. His shoulders were slumped, there were bags under his eyes and, Upton wasn't sure, but he thought Miller might have lost a little weight.

Three technicians remained at the scene taking measurements. Everyone else had left. Miller and Upton watched them stretching tape measures and taking photos.

"I was thinking about walking over to the café for a bite of dinner. Care to join me?"

Miller paused for a moment, then said, "I could eat. We'll need to go through Gibson's office, but that can wait until tomorrow."

———

Upton pushed through the café door first and nodded to Frannie. Miller followed him back to his usual booth.

"You eat here a lot?"

"Almost every night."

"What's good?"

"Nothing."

Miller looked up from the menu and laughed.

"Thanks for that, Tommy. I haven't laughed much lately. I'm feeling kind of lost on this thing."

"I know it goes against your grain, but is it time to ask for outside help?"

Miller shrugged.

"Maybe. But I'm not sure what I'd have to tell anyone. All I've got is a growing stack of dead bodies with nothing to indicate whether we're talking about one murderer or four." Miller stopped and looked at Upton. "I didn't mean any disrespect, Tommy."

"I know, none taken. I also understand exactly what you're saying. The murders are all different, but it doesn't feel like different murderers."

"Exactly. But it's highly unusual for a serial killer to vary so much in his methodology. They usually find something they like and stick with it. But if it is a serial killer, maybe I should call in the FBI. They might be able to see something I don't and profile this guy."

"Maybe it's not a serial killer in the true sense of the term," said Tommy. "As I understand it, a serial killer usually murders people to satisfy some kind of need. Maybe sexual, maybe something else, but his victims are usually either random or of a certain type. Petite blondes, for instance. These murders have a wide range of victims— male and female, young and old, well older. At any rate, they have nothing in common in terms of physical appearance, where they work or where they live. What if our guy isn't really a serial killer, but more of a hit man? Like he's on a mission, crossing people off a list."

Miller considered this. "It's possible. That theory would explain some things, but it also creates the question of the day, which is, what kind of list would all of these people be on, and who would want them dead?"

The question hung in the air as they looked over their menus. Upton stared at his without really seeing it. He pretty much had it memorized anyway. But Frannie took his distraction as a signal they were ready to order and approached the table.

"What's your pleasure tonight, Tommy?"

"Just a patty melt, I think. I'm not very hungry."

She looked at Miller.

"The same," he said.

"You guys better be big tippers," she said and walked toward the kitchen.

They continued to talk while they waited for their food, but the crime scene was still fresh in their minds and Miller's feeling of helplessness seemed to be contagious.

Upton was staring out the window and Miller was focused on his notes when Frannie brought their food.

"Geez, you guys are a barrel of laughs. Who died?"

Without turning away from the window Upton said, "Sandra Gibson."

Frannie blanched, and put her hand on the edge of the table for support, then collapsed onto the booth bench next to Upton.

"Oh my God. I didn't mean . . . I was just joking. I didn't know."

"She was killed this afternoon. Just outside her classroom at the high school," said Upton.

"She was just here for lunch yesterday."

Miller looked up from his notes. "Did you know her?"

"Yeah. I mean, we weren't exactly buddies or anything, but she came in here fairly regularly, and we've had drinks a couple of times."

"Was she with anyone?"

"You mean, was she dating anyone?"

"No, I meant was she with anyone when she came in for lunch yesterday but, now that you mention it, *was* she dating anyone?"

"She was alone yesterday, she ate at the counter, and as far as I know, she's not dating anyone, at least not seriously. She's nice looking, I know she's been out a few times."

Miller and Upton were watching Frannie as realization fell across her face.

"Was. She was nice looking. Oh my God. I can't believe this."

"Did you know any of the guys?"

"You think it's someone from town?"

"We're looking at all the possibilities, Frannie. Until we have somebody in custody, we have to look at everyone. Did you notice anyone paying special attention to her yesterday?"

"No. I mean, she said hello to a few people, but nothing more than that."

Frannie pushed herself up from the booth and went back to the kitchen. Tommy couldn't help but notice her hips had a little less sway than the last time he had seen her.

"We're missing something, Dave. I can't believe we're dealing with some kind of criminal mastermind. Could it be a gang?"

Miller looked at Upton, stopping his fork midway on its arc to his mouth. He took the bite, then shook his head.

"No, I don't think so. Our little gangbangers aren't really at that level. When it comes right down to it, they can't walk the walk. They'll mess up a wall with graffiti, maybe deal a little meth or weed, but they aren't tough enough for something like this. They do their stuff in the dark, like little cockroaches. They also take credit for anything they do, that's how they establish their street cred. There hasn't been a whisper from the gang unit about any of this. Whoever is killing these people is working at a whole different level than our gangs are capable of."

"You sound like you've made up your mind that it's one person."

"I guess I have, Tommy, but I don't know why. It's just a gut feeling. Maybe it's just easier to think it's one person instead of four, but Los Robles is just too small to have a bunch of cold-blooded murderers running around without someone hearing something. A single killer has a much better chance to keep the lid on things."

"Well, then let's play a little game. Let's just go ahead and assume it's one person we're looking for. What do we know?"

Miller slowly mopped gravy from his plate with a piece of bread. Upton let him think. Miller pushed his plate over to the end of the table, put his notebook in its place and started flipping pages.

"Well, I think we can assume it's a male."

"Why?"

"Except for Jen, all of the murders indicate some form of dominance. Anyone could have swung a pipe or something hard enough to kill Jen, but the other murders were all more confrontational.

"Lisa Erickson was stabbed repeatedly and with great force. I don't think Paul Mendez would have allowed himself to be forced into a car, walked out into an orchard, ordered to his knees and shot by a woman. And Mary Ellen said it appeared that Sandra Gibson's attacker was taller and stronger than her."

"Makes sense so far. Young or old?"

"Hmm. Probably younger. And somehow not threatening. He was able to approach both Paul and Lisa, they might have been a little more cautious if approached by an older male, especially Lisa. In fact, it might be possible that Paul and Lisa knew their killer. But Jen and Sandra were both blind-sided. Although, Jen was in a quiet neighborhood, a strange man hanging around would probably have raised her defenses. Same thing at the school. A younger guy hanging around the high school might blend in if he was spotted, not an older guy."

"But Jen wouldn't have been showing that house to a kid, it would have taken a pretty solid income to make the mortgage payments."

"True, so maybe like Lisa and Paul, we're back to somebody she knew."

"It's a small town, Dave. Everyone knows everyone."

"We all like to say that, but it's not true. Could you have told me who Mike Zepeda was before we went out there? How about Sandra Gibson?

"I mean, you've got a point, Tommy. There's only one high school, one major grocery store, that kind of thing. But we have two major industries—oil and plums—and there's almost no cross-over there. At last count, we had seventeen churches in town and about nine service or fraternal clubs. People tend to hang around with people who have similar interests. Sure, they might bump shopping carts at the store, but they don't know each other."

"With what you just said, though, it sounds like we're talking about someone who lives in Los Robles."

"I guess so. The murder scenes all indicate some local knowledge, at least."

"So, we're looking for a young male who lives in Los Robles."

"I guess we are. It helps to brainstorm like this sometimes." He pushed up from the table and reached for his wallet. "I want to get back to the office and get this up on my white board while it's still fresh in my mind; see if it helps clear anything up."

Upton waved off Miller's wallet. "I've got this, Dave. Can I come by tomorrow and talk a little more about this after we've had a chance to sleep on it?"

"Sure. I'm not sure why, but I think we made some progress tonight."

Upton remained in the booth, sipping his coffee, reluctant to take the short walk back to the condo. Frannie, eyes red-rimmed, brought him the check.

"Tommy, should I be scared?"

"No, I don't think so, Frannie. Whoever this person is seems to have some kind of agenda. I can't believe you would be on anyone's hit list."

She managed a small smile. "See you tomorrow, Tommy."

Tommy turned the key and let himself into the condo. It was dark. He liked it that way. The light brought back too many memories. Pictures on the wall, Jen's favorite chair under the reading lamp. Her desk, still littered with real estate documents. He turned on just enough lamps to keep him from running into the furniture and navigated the condo by going from one pool of light to the next.

He went to the kitchen but did not turn on any lights. He let the light from the refrigerator illuminate the room while he poured a glass of orange juice. Not long ago, he would have poured a glass of something stronger. More than one glass. He didn't crave the alcohol any more. He didn't even miss it. The physical need had disappeared long ago, and now the psychological need was growing weaker every day.

He didn't know if he was an alcoholic. He thought he probably was, and if not, he had certainly been on the road to it. The shock of Jen's death had somehow removed his craving and he hadn't looked back. Even Eddie's entreaties to return to the social hour at Louie's weren't particularly tempting. He was just over it.

His doctor had sent him for some addiction counseling, but he only went twice. He wasn't interested in a twelve-step program or anti-depressants. His doctor told him that stopping cold-turkey could have killed him. He could have had a seizure. But he didn't. And he didn't want a drink. For some reason, he craved chocolate every now and then, but not small-batch bourbon. He decided a slight addiction to Hershey bars wasn't the worst thing in the world.

When he sobered up, he had poured every drop of alcohol in the house down the kitchen drain. All the bourbon, all of Jen's wine, even the Nyquil. Eddie had been apoplectic. Tommy didn't care.

Jen's family wouldn't even speak to him, like her murder was somehow his fault. He didn't really care, they had never really liked him anyway. They thought he was after Jen's money. It was family money, and there was a lot of it. She didn't have to sell real estate, and he didn't have to work if he didn't want to, but they both wanted to, so the money grew. Now Jen was gone and all that was left was the money and the memories.

He put his glass in the sink and climbed the stairs to the bedroom. He undressed in the dark and slipped into the right side of the bed, next to the nightstand with the lamp and radio alarm clock. He couldn't bring himself to roll over onto his right side and face Jen's side of the bed.

CHAPTER FIFTEEN

Brewster was aware of the looks he'd been getting as he walked through the packing house and took his place on the line. The color of his bruises had deepened overnight and the scratch marks on his hands, arms and face were angry and red. On top of all that, he was sore.

He hadn't expected Sandra Gibson to put up such a fight. His earlier victims had died easily. Gibson's struggle had been extremely physical. He didn't know a woman could be that strong. And she had actually hurt him. That wasn't part of his plan. At least she had known who he was and why she was dying. That part of the plan worked fine. Everything else was a mess.

In hindsight, the garroting had been a mistake. At least in his hands, the garrote was neither elegant nor effective. And shooting her had been an act of desperation. He couldn't shake the feeling that using the gun would cost him somehow. Still, no one had seen him as he got away. He kept running the whole incident through his mind and now, he realized he had made another critical error.

He felt a cold sweat suddenly bead his forehead. It was terrible.

He had left the garrote on the ground after it broke. Even though he had been careful, he was sure that something he had constructed would contain some sort of forensic evidence of value to the police. He would have to be very cautious from here on out. He had no criminal record, so the police would have nothing to compare any DNA or physical evidence to, but that didn't mean he was in the clear.

The realization made him very uncomfortable. He didn't like it when one of his plans went awry, but now he knew the Sheriff's Department would be increasing their efforts to find a suspect, they might even call in outside help, like the FBI.

He resisted the urge to look over his shoulder and instead concentrated on the plums streaming past him.

He jumped and almost fell onto the conveyor belt when he felt a hand grab his left shoulder.

"Dude. What happened to you?"

Rico Garcia was only three or four years older than Brewster, but he had already worked at Plumrite for more than ten years. His name was Richard, but he insisted on being called Rico, because that's what the guys on the high school football team had called him. He had been the school's star fullback. But star fullback for a small-school football team would be as high as his star ever rose. He was the floor supervisor for Brewster's end of the packing line and he still walked with a jock's swagger, slapping men's backs and winking at the women. He personified why Brewster had yearned to escape Los Robles.

"Seriously man, you look like you lost a fight."

"Yeah, I wish, Rico. That'd make a better story. I just took a header off my mountain bike."

Brewster didn't even own a bicycle, but nobody at the plant knew that. He knew Rico would go up and down the line re-telling the lie and calling him a dumbass. But then everyone's curiosity would be satisfied and things would get back to normal. It was worth a little humiliation.

"You need to be more careful, dude. We can't afford to lose a good worker like you." Garcia laughed, slapped him on the back and moved on down the line. Brewster considered adding Garcia's name to the book in his bedroom, but decided against it. Garcia hadn't stolen his dream, just reminded him of it.

Brewster's hands were sweating profusely inside his latex gloves. He peeled off the gloves and threw them into the trash. He wiped his hands vigorously on his smock, trying unsuccessfully to dry them off. Glancing around cautiously he could see the line was operating normally, nobody was watching him.

He pulled on a new pair of gloves, adjusted his hearing protectors and started sorting plums, filling the boxes mechanically while his mind raced. He couldn't get the shooting out of his mind. It had been different with Mendez. Shooting him had been the plan, and the plan had gone perfectly, right down to standing far enough back to avoid being hit by back-splash when the bullet penetrated his skull. Mendez hardly spoke. Even after he saw the gun, and he certainly didn't struggle. It was like he had accepted what was about to happen. But Gibson had been so different. So primal. So intense.

When he finally abandoned the garrote he had panicked. Panic was not normal for him. Gibson's struggles had not only hurt him, they had dirtied him. She was crying and her nose was running. As she strained to breathe, she blew saliva onto his face and clothes. Her face rubbed against his shirt sleeves repeatedly, smearing them with tears and mucous. And when he fired the first shot, the blood started.

The first shot had probably been enough to kill her, eventually. But he couldn't afford to let her scream. So when she fell, he stood over her, looking into those eyes. Those eyes that had once promised him a future. Those eyes where he had once seen affection. He saw none of those things now. Instead he saw fear and resolve. So he fired. And fired again, and the eyes showed nothing.

He wondered if he should get rid of the gun. He'd watched enough crime shows on TV to know the sheriff would eventually discover the bullets taken from Mendez would match the ones in Gibson, but without the gun itself, that really didn't mean anything.

He loved that pistol. Not because it had been his dad's, but because his dad had left it behind and nobody knew he had it. To him, it represented power, ultimate power, and he had proved it.

Bobby Brewster had been a mean and nasty drunk. A brute. He had beaten his mother and him regularly and with equal brutality.

Alex remembered his dad's hands most of all. They were large, strong, work-calloused hands, perpetually stained with oil and grime from his job as a roughneck in the oilfields south of town. Those hands would grip his upper arms like vices as his dad started to shake him. The beatings always started with shaking.

Bobby Brewster would grab Alex's arms up near the shoulder and start to shake him. He would bring his face to within inches and Alex would smell bourbon and see the beard stubble and bloodshot eyes as his father shouted. Soon the slap would come. Alex didn't usually remember anything after that. He would just slowly become aware that his mother was there trying to comfort him, but often looking worse than he did.

He eventually came to hate his mother as much as his dad. She could have protected him. She could have taken him away. Instead, she stayed, and the beatings continued right up to the day his dad left town. When he left, his mother cried and said she wanted him back. That made Alex hate her more.

It was obvious though, that Bobby Brewster had left for good. The cash they kept in a mayonnaise jar in the kitchen was gone. He left the jar. His work clothes were gone, too, and a few other things. The rest he just left behind. A few weeks later there were rumors he was looking for work in the oil fields in Ventura and Santa Barbara counties. And then, a year later, that he had been arrested after a bar fight in Signal Hill. That was the last news they ever heard about him.

His mother found solace in vodka. Working at Plumrite she made just enough to keep the apartment and buy some groceries. Vodka was always the first item on the shopping list. Food for her son was much farther down the list.

One day after school, while his mother was still at work, Alex started going through the things his father had left. His mother had literally thrown everything of his dad's into a closet and shut the door on it and him.

Sifting through the closet, at first Alex found only clothes. But as he dug down through the pile, he started to find the things his dad had stored in the closet, not what his mother had thrown in. In the back corner, under a stack of soft pornography and union magazines, Alex found a box. It was a treasure chest as far as he was concerned. Inside was the .38 revolver wrapped in a soft cloth, the box of shells and just over fifteen dollars—all ones and a few coins. It didn't seem like a box his dad would forget. He might have left the gun, but not the cash. He might have left in more of a hurry than Brewster remembered. Regardless, the box would change his life.

Brewster took the box back to his room and spent the next few years moving it from one hiding place to another. Eventually, he found the spot behind the heating vent. He never fired the pistol, but he often took it down to look at it. He liked its weight and the way it felt in his hand. But always, it was carefully returned to its hiding place.

Shortly after he started high school he came home to find the landlord had repainted the apartment. Brewster hadn't known anything about it, but his mother must have, because all of the furniture had been pushed to the center of the rooms.

He ran to his room, certain his secret had been discovered. He climbed his desk chair and removed the vent cover and found the box intact. It was incredible. The painters had removed the cover to paint the wall but hadn't noticed the box in the vent. But as he was replacing the cover he noticed that the screws and the vent around them had become scratched over the years. The screws had originally been painted over by a low-bidder contractor, but years of Brewster unscrewing them had chipped off the paint. They seemed very obvious against the freshly painted wall.

Brewster had checked his watch, done some quick mental calculations and dashed out the front door. He had about two hours until his mother got home. First he ran to the hardware store and bought four new screws for the vent cover. Back at the apartment, he found the painters packing up for the day but convinced them to paint the vent cover. By the time his mother inspected the apartment, the vent matched his newly painted walls. He talked the painters into a little leftover paint as well and used that to keep the screws looking painted. After that, he was meticulous whenever he removed the vent cover and it remained unscratched.

He thought about the gun now, still in the same box he had discovered it in, and realized that the gun and his desire to leave Los Robles and his mother were the only things he had ever had in common with his dad.

But his dad was an oil worker. He worked with his hands and his back, not his brains. Brewster's brain was his ticket out of Los Robles. Sandra Gibson and the others had stolen that dream.

He looked down at his hands, the scratches and bruises covered by latex gloves and the gloves stained with fruit juice. He felt the anger rise in him.

Gibson's hadn't been the last name on his list. But he knew he needed to lay low for a while and let things settle down. The sheriff couldn't find any evidence if he wasn't leaving any.

The people left on his list weren't going anywhere, they were stuck in Los Robles, too. He had the rest of his life to make them pay, and the rest of their lives wouldn't be very long.

CHAPTER
SIXTEEN

Tommy Upton sat on his bench in front of City Hall. His hat brim was pulled down low, partly covering his eyes. The day's Los Angeles *Times* sat on the bench next to him, neatly folded. He read out-of-town newspapers as often as he could. It didn't pay to become too parochial. He wanted to know what was going on outside of Los Robles and maybe use some of that knowledge to give his local stories more depth. On top of the paper was his yellow pad of lined writing paper. He took it everywhere he went now, and the top page was stained with circles from coffee cups and greasy fingerprints, probably from too much time spent on the table at the café. The first ten or fifteen pages of the pad were filled with hurried-looking, almost illegible handwriting. Illegible to anyone but Tommy. These pages were curled and dog-eared from being carried around and frequently flipped through. The remaining pages in the pad were empty and neat, waiting to be filled by his thoughts.

He was staring at the oil derrick monument in the traffic circle, remembering how one of the local churches had come up with the idea to hang lights from it and decorate it like a Christmas tree for the holidays. He didn't know why he was thinking about Christmas. He was supposed to be thinking about Sandra Gibson. Her obit was due soon and he hadn't written a word.

It turned out she had no family in Los Robles. Dave Miller had tracked down her parents in a small town outside of San Diego. They were supposed to arrive in the next day or so to claim their daughter's body. Upton didn't want to imagine what that long car ride would be like. He hoped they'd talk to him, but if they didn't, Miller had promised him a few details to help fill out the obit. He had interviewed several teachers at the school and a couple of students, but it turned out nobody really knew her. They all liked her, and complimented her work ethic, but her personal life was something of a mystery. Apparently, she kept mostly to herself. Even Frannie couldn't give him any useful ideas.

Upton saw Miller turn the corner in his patrol car and head for the parking lot behind City Hall. Gathering his newspaper and pad, he decided to pay Miller a visit.

The Sheriff's Department had its own entrance behind and below City Hall. The department occupied the entire basement with its offices, lab, locker rooms and a few holding cells. Upton took the three steps down and pushed through glass door emblazoned with the Sheriff's star. His path further was blocked by a counter that stretched half the width of the room, backed by the formidable, if pleasurable, form of Carol Burnside. A low fence of blond wood with a swinging gate formed the remainder of the barrier. The small waiting area in front of the counter was empty except for two well-used oak chairs. Carol's desk was immediately behind the counter. There were several other desks, all unoccupied, behind hers. Behind them was a window that allowed Miller to look out from his office towards the counter. Upton suspected the glass was bullet-proof. Tommy could see Miller, head down at his desk, already absorbed in something. Just then, Miller looked up and waved Upton in. Carol saw the gesture and graced Upton with a smile as he passed her desk.

Miller immediately noticed the yellow pad in Upton's hand.

"Still working the case?"

"Can't let it go. But right now, I'm kind of working it back-handed, I guess. I'm trying to write Sandra Gibson's obituary."

"Trying?"

"Yeah, it's not going very well." He plopped himself down into one of the chairs facing Miller's desk and then fixed an unseeing stare at the corner of the ceiling over Miller's head. "Since Jen died . . . since Vic gave me a second start . . . I just can't phone these things in any more. They feel like a debt I owe. What I write in an obituary is the last the word the world will ever hear about that person. I can't bring myself to just write who, what, when and where, then close the book. Her family hated me for it, but I insisted on writing Jen's obit. It was the last thing I could do for her. I remember every single word of it. And you know what?" He looked down from the ceiling and into Miller's eyes. "I remember every single word of every other obit I've written since. Every obit. Every word. Verbatim."

Miller didn't say anything. Carol Burnside had been leaning against the doorjamb, listening. Her eyes were glassy with tears. She walked the few steps to Upton and gently laid her hand on his shoulder.

"I don't know what it is, Dave. I feel like I can't stay away from this thing. Like I'm not allowed to. It's not just justice for Jen, and it's not just my job at the paper. I don't know what to call it, it's like I've been given a *purpose*."

No one spoke. Only the muted sound of the police band radio scanner in the next room broke the silence. It was Upton who finally spoke.

"Did you find anything at Gibson's apartment?"

"Just the nice life of a nice lady. The place was neat as a pin, but not obsessively so. Everything was in its place, but the apartment felt comfortable, lived in. The bed was made, but there was a mug in the sink with the teabag still in it. She had a small desk where it looks like she kept her work for school and paid her bills. Like everything else, it was arranged and neat—as if she could walk in the front door, sit down and go to work. Her refrigerator was well-stocked—lots of salad stuff—and a couple bottles of white wine. The furniture was nice, but not expensive, Penney's, not Macy's. Same with the clothes. And no sign of a boyfriend."

"What about family or friends?"

"Well, I told you about her parents, and I guess there's a sister somewhere. Her parents hadn't heard anything about a boyfriend, but that doesn't really mean anything. There's lots of things a little girl won't tell her daddy. We found a few framed photos, one on her desk, one on an end table and two in the bedroom that looked like family photos, but we don't have a way to match names and faces. We're hoping her parents can help us out there. We found some family names in an address book on her desk, that's how we were able to make the notifications. The tech guys are going through her computer to check e-mails and all that stuff. It's an older HP model, they said it wouldn't take long to find the files."

"It's so sad," said Burnside.

"It always is, Carol," said Miller. "We always meet people on the worst day of their life. When people call us, something has gone bad in their life. They've been robbed, had an accident, seen a family member OD or . . . die. It's our job. It's their tragedy."

He stood up and walked over to the white board.

"I started adding some of the things we talked about, Tommy. I feel like maybe the fog is starting to clear a little. I have a feeling like it's coming into focus and I think, once it does, things will move fast."

A bang from the outer office caused all three of them to look out Miller's window towards the front counter. Ana Espinoza had barreled past the front counter through the swinging gate and was storming toward Miller's office.

"I want you to call the FBI," she said.

"They have no jurisdiction at this point and, besides, that's my call, not yours," said Miller.

"I'm the mayor."

"And I'm the sheriff. That means I got a gun and a badge, and you got a gavel."

"I can have you fired."

"No, you can't. That takes a majority of the council and you don't have it. Now, why don't you settle down a little and tell me what's bothering you."

"What's bothering me? People are *dying*, that's what's bothering me."

"That bothers me, too, Ana. I'm working on it." He gestured at the white board. "I've got deputies in the field running down leads and I'm trying to establish some kind of profile on this guy."

She looked around the room, taking in the white board and, finally, Burnside and Upton.

"What's *he* doing here?"

"Helping, which you're not. This might be a good time to let me get back to work."

"I'm not kidding, Dave. I want the FBI. I'd better see some progress fast or I'm going to start pushing. Hard."

She stared at Upton for a few long seconds and Upton stared right back. "I hate your hat," she said.

She left the office without looking back.

When the front door closed behind her, Upton said, "What's wrong with my hat?"

Miller and Burnside were laughing. "I happen to think your hat is quite stylish," said Burnside.

"It's not your hat, Tommy," said Miller, "it's not even you. It's an election year and she's already picking out targets. Looks like your hat made the list. Maybe it'll end up on a campaign poster."

"She's got a point, though," said Burnside. "If we don't make some progress on this soon, people are going to start asking tough questions."

Miller rocked back in his chair, ran his hand across his head, and then sighed.

"You're right, Carol. The thing is, Tommy and I have been 'round and 'round on this thing and it's like we can both feel something there, we just can't get our hands on it."

"Maybe the FBI could."

"Maybe. But once we call them, we're out, and I don't want to be out."

The room was quiet for a moment, and then Miller leaned forward in his chair and picked up a white board marker.

"Maybe we've been thinking too much. Carol, ask Bert if he could come in here for a minute and give me a forensics update. Maybe a little science will move us along."

———————

"I've got all kinds of science, Dave, I'm just not sure it's going to help much."

Bert Vega was holding four case files. Miller noted they were all about as thick as murder files usually were at this point in the investigation, but he also knew a lot of it was just required forms and that those forms had a lot of blank boxes on them for these victims.

Vega walked over and inspected the whiteboard.

"Been doing a little profiling?"

"Trying to, but that's mostly best guesses, that's why I asked you to come in. I decided to try adding a few facts to see if they might bring something into focus."

"Well, facts I got. Whether they'll give us any answers, I don't know. Most of what we've gathered will help us when we identify a suspect, but won't be of much help in determining who the suspect, or suspects, are."

"I think it's the singular. Tommy and I have really been brainstorming this and we think the circumstances point to a single assailant. A male."

Vega looked at Upton and couldn't quite disguise his look of doubt and disapproval. The look was not lost upon Upton.

"I'm a new man, Bert. And I want to help find this guy."

"A new man. I've never heard that before from a drunk trying to stay on the wagon."

An uncomfortable tension filled the room.

"I probably deserved that, Bert. I've burned a lot of bridges. But Jen didn't deserve what happened to her, and neither did Lisa Erickson, Paul Mendez or Sandra Gibson. I'm invested in this. I haven't had a drink since the day Jen died and my head is clearer than it's been in a long time. My heart is in the right place, Bert, and at least for now, so is my head. Give me the benefit of the doubt here."

Vega stared into Upton's eyes the way only a cop could. Then his features softened.

"Okay, Tommy. Benefit of the doubt."

With the tension lessened, Vega began laying out his files on a corner of Miller's desk.

"We've found all kinds of evidence, none of it very useful at this point," he said. "We're running everything through NCIC and CODIS, but so far, no hits."

"I've heard of the National Crime Information Center," said Tommy, "but what's CODIS?"

"CODIS is the FBI's program for criminal justice DNA databases. It stands for Combined DNA Index System. NCIC helps us to see if our crimes are similar to crimes elsewhere. We can compare crimes and criminals to see if we get a match, or at least something similar that might indicate a pattern. CODIS compares the DNA we collect with known samples collected by other agencies. A match gives us a suspect."

"And you've been finding DNA?"

"Some, mostly from the Gibson case. Let me go through it case by case and I'll show you what I've got. We'll take them in order."

Upton felt a small knot form in his stomach as Vega picked up the first file. That would be Jen's. Vega made the realization at the same time.

"Are you sure you want to hear this?"

"No, I don't want to hear it, and I don't want to see it in my dreams any more, either. But I really want to catch this guy. Go ahead."

"Jennifer Upton was a clean crime scene. There was almost no physical evidence found there. Cause of death was blunt force trauma. We can't identify the weapon. It appears to have been long and roughly cylindrical. We searched for several blocks around the crime scene, but couldn't turn up any possible weapons, probably because it was something very common. It could have been anything—a baseball bat, pipe, axe handle—no shortage of possibilities. We weren't able to recover any trace evidence from near the wound, so we really have no idea.

"She was struck from behind with a vicious blow. It was like the killer just walked up behind her and hit her. No indication of any other interaction. No defensive wounds.

"There was no sign of sexual assault or robbery and no DNA, hair or fibers that might have been the suspect's."

Upton was sitting quietly, hands in his lap. His face had gone pale and light sheen of perspiration covered his forehead.

"Unfortunately, there is next to nothing that gives us a hint about the perpetrator, his motive, or that even ties her murder to the others."

Vega shuffled the folders, and opened the next one.

"Lisa Erickson," he said. "Big change in MO here. She was attacked from in front. She had to have seen her killer and, while I don't have any forensics to support it, I think she must have known him, too. She would have been suspicious of a stranger approaching close enough to stab her.

"Stabbing is a very intimate form of violence. You have to be close and it has to be personal, especially when there are multiple stab wounds. Some criminal profilers have said there is a sexual component to the act. I don't know about that in this case. There was no evidence of any kind of a sexual assault, or robbery for that matter. Just another vicious murder.

"According to Mary Ellen, Lisa was stabbed four times in the abdomen. He must have delivered them very quickly because she said any one of the wounds would have been fatal. Together, they resulted in so much blood loss Lisa must have died very quickly.

"There was some indication Lisa may have tried to fight off her attacker, but not effectively, the wounds were just too devastating. We did recover some biological material from under her fingernails, but we're not sure what it is at this point or whether it will give us any DNA to work with. If there is DNA, we can at least compare it with what we got at the Gibson scene, because we found plenty there.

"With Lisa, we didn't recover any trace evidence we think is significant, but maybe it could be used for comparison and confirmation once we identify a suspect.

"The one thing we know about Lisa's killer is that he would have left the scene covered in her blood. No way to escape it. Again, that might be helpful when we have our suspect. Traces may still be on his shoes or other clothes. We didn't recover a weapon in this case, either. Mary Ellen said it was some kind of a large knife. It's hard to imagine a guy with a big knife, covered in blood, running down the street and nobody seeing him, but that seems to be what we've got."

Miller rocked back in his chair and ran his hand across the top of his head.

"Two murders, two MOs. Anything besides our guts that tie them together?"

Vega sighed. "No. Although the next two give us a little hope."

Vega walked to the whiteboard and pointed at the photo of Paul Mendez.

"Again, there was a change of MO with Paul. You can make the argument that our killer is escalating. Blunt object, knife, now a gun. In addition, this victim was abducted. There's an indication that Paul, too, knew his attacker. Paul was in good shape, his work is physical by nature, yet he appears to have gone with this guy with no struggle. Now, the threat of violence would certainly account for some of that. But it was a long ride from where he was abducted to where he was killed, and there is no sign that he was tied up or struggled.

"Cause of death was a single .38 round to the back of his head. Mary Ellen said the entry wound was high on the back of the head, with no exit wound. She recovered the slug from behind Paul's mouth. The trajectory suggests that the shot was fired from above and behind him. That supports our theory that he was in a kneeling position when he was killed."

"Execution-style," said Upton.

"Well, yes, but we really don't like that term much. He was executed no matter how he was standing. The other evidence—body position, grass stains on his knees—all supports the kneeling theory and that the killer wanted him in a subordinate, if not humiliating position.

"Again, there was no evidence of robbery and we found a small bag of meth next to the body. Our working theory on this one is that the meth was a clumsy attempt to mislead us. Leaving both the wallet and the meth makes it just plain murder. I don't know what the suspect gained by leaving the drugs. He was probably trying to get us to focus on the meth crowd, but he actually took a bigger risk by just obtaining the drugs in the first place. A dealer somewhere might remember him. In fact, the deputies have been working their informants to see if anyone remembers selling to someone new. Also, the baggie was wiped clean. No prints at all. That suggests a plant as well."

"Is there any indication Paul was a user?" asked Miller.

"None. No meth—or anything else—in his system, none on his clothes, hands or in his nostrils. The only trace evidence we recovered that might be of some use are some automotive fibers. We can't use them to trace the vehicle, but again, they can confirm it when we find it. We're hoping to be able to at least confirm a make or model."

The four fell silent at they stared at the whiteboard that was covered with information but, to this point, no help.

"Go ahead, Bert," said Miller. "Let's do Sandra Gibson, too, so we have all the information."

"The news there might be a little more positive," said Vega. "When things go wrong for the bad guy, they tend to go right for us. Obviously, his attack on Sandra Gibson didn't go as planned. As a result, he improvised and, by doing that, he left a lot of evidence behind.

"Let's start with the bullets. We've recovered two .38 slugs and we're looking for the third. They're the same caliber as the Mendez murder and I suspect we'll be able to match them with ballistics if they're not too damaged. That may not give us our guy but it will tie two of the murders together. On top of that, he left his garrote. We have confirmed that it was used in the attack, by the way. There's a lot of blood on it, but it all seems to be Sandra's. We're sampling for other DNA that might have been left on it and we're looking at the device itself.

"It was pretty simple. A couple pieces of broom handle, or something similar, a length of baling wire and some tape. They're all pretty common materials, but hopefully, they'll give us something.

"And, once again, there was no robbery or sexual assault, but clearly, Sandra was fighting for her life. We found significant amounts of biological material under her fingernails. That'll do two things. One, it will give us a very solid DNA profile of our suspect and, two, it means that whoever attacked her has war wounds. In addition to scratching the guy, it looks like she connected with a few right hooks. Her knuckles were bruised."

The room again fell silent. Upton flipped through a couple of pages on his yellow pad, then looked up at Vega.

"You said there were no hits in NCIC or CODIS?" Vega nodded his affirmation. "So, does that mean our guy is a new criminal, or a first-timer?"

"Not necessarily. It could mean that he's just never been caught, or that he never left any DNA trace before. Or, he might not have any felony busts since California started requiring DNA samples from convicts. We're also running the sample through some secondary databases hoping something will pop for us."

"For the sake of argument, if he is new, could that mean he's a kid? Two of his victims were barely out of high school and one worked there."

"Again, not necessarily. Criminal activities start at all ages for all kinds of reasons. Marital or financial problems, drug or alcohol abuse, a mental condition—all of these can be triggers to send some-one off down the wrong path. Even if it is a kid, something had to have triggered him."

Carol Burnside hadn't spoken since Vega entered the room. The details of the crimes had turned her face pale and in a voice barely above a whisper she asked, "Is there a serial killer in Los Robles?"

"Not in the classic sense, but yes, Carol," said Miller. "I think there is and so does Ana Espinoza, that's why she's pushing me to bring in the FBI.

"What do you mean by 'not in the classic sense,'" she asked.

"I don't mean to make it all about semantics, but here's what I mean: Yes, this person is killing people one after the other, so in that sense, he's a serial killer. But he doesn't seem to exhibit some of the typical behaviors of serial killers. For example, he keeps changing his MO. Most serial killers do the same thing every time. Exactly the same thing. This guy is all over the map, like he's playing a murder game. Or maybe he's just messing with us. Maybe he thinks we're too dumb to catch him.

"He's also not taking any kind of a souvenir, at least not that we know of. Many serial killers collect something from each of the vic-tims—a lock of hair, a piece of jewelry, or even a body part, like a finger or ear.

"And finally, there's the murders themselves. Most serial killers have some kind of obsession. There's a sexual assault, and then the victim is killed. Or the victims are all similar in appearance, or some-thing like that. Our guy is different. I don't think he has an obsession. I think he has an agenda."

"Could it be that his agenda has turned into the obsession?" asked Upton.

"Yeah, maybe," said Miller. "But even if that's true, it's his agenda that will lead us to him, not his obsession with it. It's his mindset that's the big difference here. Serial killers are driven to kill, they can't help themselves. That's why they're so ritualistic. This guy is more like an assassin, a hit man. He's killing these people for a reason and it's all planned."

"So you don't think our guy is crazy?" asked Upton.

"Oh, no. I think he's bat-shit crazy, but I also think he's smart. I'll even admit that I'm splitting hairs about the whole serial killer thing. My gut is saying that our guy is local and something set him off and," Miller paused and looked at each of them, "I don't think he's done."

CHAPTER SEVENTEEN

U pton walked around the traffic circle back to the office. He took, for him, the road less traveled, going around the circle opposite Louie's and the café.

Back in his office he pulled up the Word document whose few sentences represented the sum total of his work on Sandra Gibson's obituary. While he was at the sheriff's office, Miller had given him the few additional details on Gibson's life he had managed to glean. Upton took out those notes and his previous ones and scooted his chair closer to the keyboard and started to type.

> *"A light in the community was snuffed out when Sandra Gibson was murdered outside her office. A light that led the way to a brighter future for the high school students of Los Robles . . . "*

The page filled as Upton's fingertips danced across the keyboard. Sandra Gibson's brief life was outlined, a mere sketch of what was probably a much richer life than anyone in Los Robles would ever know. This was the town's thank-you. The town's goodbye. It didn't seem like enough.

Upton proof-read the obit one more time and pressed a key to send it to Vic Yanuzzi's computer.

He looked at the small digital clock on the corner of his desk. Five o'clock already. It had been one of those days when the time passed without him realizing it. It was an exquisite form of torture to Upton. The faster the day sped by, the sooner he had to return to the condo. He wasn't up to another meal at the café. Frannie's reaction to the news about Sandra Gibson's murder had reminded him how personal these crimes were. Out the window he saw Eddie push through the door to Louie's. You could set your watch by him, he thought. He felt the old familiar temptation to join Eddie and the other regulars, but resisted. He had come too far to fall back into his old habits. He knew those habits would kill him if he relented to them. But he was still thinking about it when Yanuzzi stepped up to his desk.

"Thanks for Gibson obit, Tommy."

"Yeah, well, I'm not feeling very good about it, Vic. I feel like I phoned it in."

"You're being too hard on yourself. It was good work. It sounds like she was a very nice lady."

"A 'nice lady,' that's great journalism."

"Look, Tommy, you know how talented you are, but you can't turn water into wine. You didn't have much to work with, but you did right by her."

Upton stared down at his shoes for a beat and then slowly nodded his head.

"Thanks, Vic."

As Yanuzzi walked away, Upton stared out the window across the traffic circle. It was quitting time in town and Louie had just turned on the neon light over the bar's door. The tubing spelled out "Louie's" in bright red cursive script. The red light beckoned him and he longed to succumb to its siren's song. To pour liquid comfort from a square bottle, hold the glass of amber painkiller up to catch the light, and then feel its warmth coursing down his throat on its way to calm his soul.

He blinked his eyes slowly and refocused his gaze on his desk, turned off his desk lamp and shut down his computer. As he stood he pushed his chair in and picked up the thin leather portfolio that held his yellow pad and the day's paper, the latter still unread.

Outside, he hesitated on the sidewalk. He felt an almost gravitational pull from Louie's. He decided to eat at home and skip the café. It was too close to Louie's and he just couldn't bring himself to face Frannie. The fear and pain in her eyes the day before had unnerved him. He still had his own pain, he wasn't ready to take on someone else's.

He tucked the portfolio up under his left arm and shoved both hands into his pants pockets as he trudged home.

The condo was quiet when he stepped inside. As quiet as death. Before Jen died, the condo had always hummed with activity and light. Her phone warbled almost constantly and the printer on her desk spit out page after page of real estate or loan documents. She always had the blinds open so sunlight streamed into the room. The coffee maker in the kitchen was usually on, its bubbling and hissing trying to drown out the upbeat music coming from Jen's iPod. Now there was only silence.

Upton walked to the kitchen, carefully avoiding even a glance into Jen's office just off the dining room. The day would come when he'd have to go in there, but today was not that day. He opened up the refrigerator and took out a bottle of decaffeinated iced tea. There was not a drop of liquor in the house, but the bar glasses still gleamed behind the glass doors of the kitchen cabinets.

His freezer and refrigerator weren't empty, but nothing in them seemed very appealing. He reluctantly slid out a frozen meal box—pasta, meatballs, broccoli and carrots—and set the oven to preheat to 350 degrees. While the oven warmed up he pulled out his yellow pad and scooted a tall chair up to the kitchen's breakfast bar. He sipped his tea and stared at the pages, but no inspiration came from them. Snippets of the obituaries he had written started running through his mind in an endless loop.

Somewhere deep inside himself he realized he was missing something. A clue. An avenue of investigation. An unanswered question. Something was there but he couldn't see it. In his head it felt like a slot machine. The reels were spinning, stopping one by one, but he couldn't see how they lined up.

There had to be a common denominator, something that linked Jen, Lisa, Paul, and now, Sandra Gibson. It wasn't gender, Paul broke that link. And it wasn't age—two kids and two adults. They weren't related by birth or marriage. They didn't live in the same neighborhoods and they went to different churches, if they went at all. So where was the link?

A chime rang on the oven indicating it had warmed up to 350 degrees, so Upton slid in his dinner and then returned to his spot at the breakfast bar. He and Miller had spoken many times about the number of things people in a small town share, things like one major grocery store, one high school and a small hospital that reflected the life—and death—of the town. The kids all grew up together. Even if they didn't attend the same elementary schools, they knew each other through Little League, scouts, church groups or other organizations. And, by extension, their parents knew each other as well. And that was the problem. How do you find a common denominator in a town full of them?

The oven timer chimed again and Upton took out his dinner. He picked at the pasta as he flipped back and forth through the pages of his yellow pad. One by one he started eliminating possibilities.

Churches were out. None of the victims attended the same church and he and Jen didn't go to church at all. He eliminated stores based on nothing more than it seemed too random. Ultimately he was left with the high school. Right back where he started.

Because all of Los Robles' elementary schools fed into the one high school, all the kids attended there, and that involved many of the parents as well. Many generations of families grew up in Los Robles and followed the same path. So Jen always made sure to market to the high school audience. She bought an ad in the yearbook, she put up banner ads at the football and baseball fields and, though the Petrolia Club, she mentored students and participated in the scholarship program.

Because of this, she had contact with hundreds of students or their parents. Upton shook his head. Even if he thought of all those people as suspects, what could Jen have done that would make one of them want to murder her?

Sandra Gibson's contacts at the high school were obvious. Students, parents, teachers, coaches, even the janitors would have to appear on the suspect list if he could establish a link to the school.

He forked a bite of pasta into his mouth and discovered it had grown cold. He pushed the plastic tray and the remains of his dinner away. Night had fallen and the condo was now dark and quiet. He sat in a pool of light from the lamp over the breakfast bar. He couldn't even see into the living room.

He rubbed his face with both hands. There was too much darkness in his life, he decided. Jen had been his light, and he thought that illumination had been extinguished with her life. Now he realized it hadn't. He had been covering her light, not allowing it to shine. Sitting in the kitchen, pen and yellow pad in hand, she had been inspiring him, driving him, just like always. She had always been his inspiration, his motivation. She still was. This whole investigation hadn't been about revenge or redemption, it was because that's what Jen would have wanted. All this time he had been shutting her out instead of letting her shine in his memory and his work.

He walked into the living room and turned on the floor lamp next to the antique Steinway that Jen had loved so much. She had never taken piano lessons, she played by ear, teasing songs from her imagination as her fingers played lightly over the keys. The light of the lamp fell on the portrait of Jen that sat atop the piano. The height of the piano put Jen's eyes nearly level with his own. Her eyes sparkled at him, just as they had in life. The portrait was the one she had taken for her real estate business, but they both loved it. Upton thought it captured her perfectly. Her lips were slightly parted in a small smile, allowing a glimpse of the brilliant white teeth just beyond them. He could see small, fine lines at the corners of her mouth and eyes. Jen had never worried about wrinkles. She called them the road map of her life. But the truth was she had very few, her life was smooth. He could almost smell the perfume in her hair. And then there were those eyes. He saw joy in them. And he saw love. And forgiveness.

He realized his face was wet with tears, but he also knew that something had changed. He felt lighter. Not happy, he missed her desperately, but as if he had been held back and was now moving suddenly forward. For too long he had suppressed all that he loved about her and their life together, concentrating instead on her death, on his drinking and the loss of his career. Somehow tonight, she had broken through and set him free.

He walked around the condo turning on lights, smiling as his tears flowed freely. He looked at photos he had kept hidden in the dark and remembered their trips together. Their love and love-making. Her loss was every bit as real, but her love was stronger.

He wiped his eyes with the back of his hand and took two long, deep breaths. He couldn't stop smiling. He went back into the kitchen and turned on the rest of the lights.

He was suddenly ravenously hungry so he made himself a sandwich using every kind of deli meat and cheese he could find in the refrigerator. Then he grabbed a can of Diet Coke and sat back down at the breakfast bar.

He flipped the pages on his yellow pad, scanning his notes on Lisa Erickson and Paul Mendez. They were both recent graduates of the high school but he couldn't see any connection to either Jen or Sandra Gibson. It stood to reason they probably at least knew who Gibson was, but it seemed to him like there would have be a deeper connection than passing in the hallway to involve them in the murders.

He could feel the instincts of an investigative reporter reawakening in himself. Thinking in clichés he would never write, he knew that a weight had been lifted off him and he was seeing things in a new light. He chuckled to himself; an editor would blue-line those phrases faster than he could type them but he knew, at least this one time, they were true.

Now, seeing things more clearly, it was obvious there was only so much he could accomplish as a disgraced reporter trying to regain his credibility. The common link was the high school. He was sure of it, but somebody with more authority than him was going to have to do the digging. It was cop work. The kind they never showed on TV. Hours of knocking on doors and poring through records.

He decided to pay Dave Miller a visit right after breakfast.

He put his dishes in the sink and turned off the kitchen lights. But for the first time in weeks, he flipped the switch for the light on the stairs and he looked at every photograph on the wall on his way up to the bedroom.

CHAPTER EIGHTEEN

A lex Brewster thought the shift would never end. Working on the packing line was boring, repetitive work on the best of days, and today wasn't a very good day. Generally, people knew him as a loner and left him alone with his thoughts so could pass the day mechanically, his mind somewhere far from Los Robles. But today, he had been the center of attention.

He didn't need or want attention, especially now. But the small, petty, ignorant people working around him bothered him all day asking about his appearance. Some asked with a smile, amused by the mountain bike story. Others seemed to be concerned about his health. He supposed they were just trying to be friendly. He didn't know anything about that, but he knew he didn't want their attention.

He was behind on the line all day because of the questions and that had brought further unwanted attention. When the shift finally ended, he was the first one out the door. Now, safely back behind the locked door of his bedroom, he was slowly starting to relax.

His mother had arrived home shortly after he did, but he claimed—honestly—that he was sore and not feeling well and stayed in his room. He was afraid she was going to push the issue but, soon after he closed his door on her he heard the TV go on and the door to the cabinet where his mother kept her vodka bang shut. She wouldn't bother him.

He needed to think about his next steps. Things had gone very wrong with Sandra Gibson. He had left a lot of evidence behind. Fortunately, he knew the evidence was no good until they had someone to test it against. As long as he was never a suspect, the garrote, blood and whatever else they found would just sit in a box somewhere.

He leaned back in his chair, closed his eyes and decided to take an analytical approach. He was very good at analysis. In fact, he had written at length about his analytical skills in his application to Harvard. They had accepted him so they must have been impressed.

Now he had to dissect his problem and put those skills to work. He had murdered four people, the last one very poorly. The big question was, he thought, should I stop?

On the one hand, every murder increased his chances of being caught. He wasn't impressed with the Sheriff. He had been a football player at UCLA. A state school. How smart could he be? But if he gathered enough evidence, he might get lucky. He wouldn't need to be smart. Brewster didn't think somebody like Dave Miller could figure out his plan, but a witness or some other piece of evidence might get Miller looking in his direction, and that could bring the DNA evidence into play. That would be bad.

It made sense to stop. The cops had no idea who was committing the murders or why. All four would go unsolved and slowly fade from memory. If he stopped at four, he could do so knowing he had extracted at least some measure of revenge. He should stop. But he couldn't. He didn't want a measure of revenge. He wanted full, complete, total revenge. Besides, he found that he was rather enjoying himself.

That didn't mean that he wouldn't have to be careful. He had been perfect on the first three, but the mistakes he made with Sandra Gibson could be enough to get him caught.

He wondered if he had left any evidence at the earlier murders the Sheriff could use. He didn't think so. Jennifer Upton had been so easy he almost laughed. She never saw him coming. He had called the number on her sign in front of the house and asked if he could take a walk-through. They agreed on a time. He knew she would arrive early to be sure the house was presentable, so he arrived even earlier. She smiled when she saw him, and as she turned toward the front porch, he raised the tire iron he had kept hidden behind his leg.

He took a tremendous swing at the back of her head. The tire iron made a slight pinging sound as it struck her skull, but she didn't make any sound at all. She just fell down onto her back, eyes staring but no longer seeing. After that, he just walked away. He dropped the tire iron into a recycling dumpster on his way home.

The only mistake he had made with Lisa Erickson was underestimating the amount of blood she would lose. God, who knew that much blood could come out of a few stab wounds? Fortunately, he had planned for some blood loss and that planning turned out to have been enough for too much blood as well.

He had stolen a white Tyvek jumpsuit from the processing side of the Plumrite plant. Because the people on that side were turning the fruit into other food products, they had different sanitary requirements. Everyone had to wear a jumpsuit, hairnet, latex gloves and booties. There were stacks and stacks of the jumpsuits. All he had to do was pick out his size. No one would even miss it. When he had walked up to Lisa wearing the suit, she had looked at him funny. But, then again, she had been looking at him funny since second grade. He smiled and she relaxed and she never saw the knife until he had buried it to the hilt in her abdomen. He didn't think she felt anything after that, but he had to be sure, so he kept stabbing.

The large kitchen knife he had used was untraceable. He bought it at the 99¢ Store, ironic since he'd paid almost five dollars for it. Nobody had questioned him at the time and the knife was about as generic as they come. The dumpster behind the Burger King was emptied every afternoon at about three o'clock after everything from the lunch rush had been cleaned up. He simply put the jumpsuit and knife into a trash bag and tossed it all in the dumpster. It was long gone before anyone might have thought to look there. It hadn't been a perfect plan, but it had worked perfectly, and now the knife was under tons of dirt at the landfill.

Paul Mendez was a little more problematic. In retrospect, the bag of meth he had left next to his body was probably an unnecessary risk, if not an outright mistake. Mendez wasn't a user and he didn't know if the deputies would try to follow the drug trail or not. It had seemed like a good idea at the time.

He was surprised by how easy it had been to get the meth. At first, he thought he'd have to buy it from some lowlife, and he was pretty sure that was a bad idea. But then he'd heard Rico Garcia and one of his old football buddies talking in the locker room at Plumrite. His friend had just "scored" a "dime bag," whatever that was. He waited until they went into the showers and searched the friend's locker. He found a small plastic sandwich bag filled with white powder. He stuffed it into his pocket and left the locker room as casually as he could. He didn't think they knew he was in there, but he couldn't be too careful. He didn't know how Rico's friend would react to the theft, probably badly, but what was he going to do, call the cops?

That brought him back to Sandra Gibson. There was nothing he could do about the mess he had left there, but he felt like he had covered his tracks on the other ones just fine.

He took the box down from behind the grate and centered it on his desk. He raised the lid and carefully lifted out the .38. He unwrapped the small gun and then laid it down in the center of the soft cloth. He pulled a small rod, releasing the cylinder. He swung the cylinder out and pushed the mechanism at the front to eject the shells. They fell into his palm and he stood them up in a perfect line on the desk. Three pieces of brass topped by ugly little lumps of gray lead. And three empty shells, with small black stains showing where exploding gunpowder had sent lead sailing into Sandra Gibson's body.

He picked up one of the shells and sniffed it. Closing his eyes he let the smell take him back to the high school parking lot.

He would always remember her eyes. She had looked into his when he told her she had stolen his dream. She *understood*. She knew why she was dying. The others hadn't. Going forward, he would make sure they knew. He had decided, he realized. He was going forward, he wasn't done. He had more work to do.

He took the book out of the box and opened it to the list of names. He drew a line through Sandra Gibson's name and then began looking over the remaining names.

Who should be next? He finally focused on one name, Darrell Bingham. Brewster pictured him in his mind. Fat-assed and jowly. Bingham was an insurance agent, a successful one, and it seemed he celebrated his success with food. He was shaped like an upright football. He always wore a suit, but not one of his coats could button across his expansive belly. His neck fat rolled over his shirt collars nearly covering the knots on his ties.

Brewster wanted to do something special with Bingham. He had been president of the Petrolia Club during the scholarship competition. All he would have had to do was say the word and the scholarship would have gone where it belonged. Brewster had sat next to Bingham at lunch several times. Bingham had an annoying habit of clasping Brewster's shoulder and calling him "young man." And he ate like the pig he resembled. Brewster could hear the big man as he ate—slurping and burping was how he thought of it. The man was disgusting, but Brewster had always smiled and listened to the unsolicited advice the man spewed. He even had a pen from the man's insurance agency in his desk drawer. "A successful man is never without a pen," he had said when handing it to him.

Well, it was time to cancel his policy, so to speak.

The question was, how? Garroting was out, that was for sure. And he didn't think stabbing would be very effective on a man that large. The knife might never reach anything critical. That left him with two practical choices—the .38 or a blow to the head.

A blow to the head it was. It worked before and, besides, he liked the feel of it. The swing, the solid connection, the look of surprise. Only this time, he would swing from the front. He wanted Bingham to know who killed him.

A sharp rapping at his door startled him so much he knocked over the line of .38 shells standing on his desk. They rolled in little circles on the wooden surface.

"Have you had anything to eat?" He hadn't heard his mother approach his door. That wasn't good.

"I ate earlier, Mom."

"Are you feeling okay? You still look pretty bruised up."

"I'm fine, Mom. Just a little tired."

"You're sure?"

"Mom, I'm fine."

He heard her walk away without another word. He hated these little interactions. He called them Motherhood Moments. Every now and then, through the cigarette haze and vodka fog, a maternal instinct flared in his mother and she would express love, concern or even admiration. He didn't care. Too little, too late. When he lost the scholarship, her only words to him had been, "I told you not to get your hopes up."

He needed to go to the bathroom, but he decided to hold it until his mother stumbled off to bed. He didn't want to talk to her. He didn't even want to see her.

He looked down at his book and made a check mark next to Bingham's name. This one would be special. He would start planning in the morning.

After replacing the box behind the vent, he listened at his door. The TV was off and he couldn't hear his mother stirring. He slowly turned the door knob, his thumb lightly covering the lock button so that when it popped up it wouldn't make a sound.

Opening the door, he found the apartment dark. His mother was in bed, asleep or passed out. It didn't matter which to him, and he made it to and from the bathroom without encountering her.

Back in his room he slipped into bed and fell asleep quickly. Tomorrow would be another big day and he wanted to be rested.

The next morning he was still sore, but he felt better. Some of his bruises were turning from purple to yellow, and his right shoulder no longer ached. Best of all, the cuts and scratches were healing. They were scabbed over and they no longer looked so red and angry.

Still, they looked bad enough that, probably, nobody would complain if he took a sick day or two. He was pretty sure his mother would never know he wasn't at work, unless somebody told her. But that didn't seem likely since they worked in different parts of the plant and neither one of them was particularly friendly with their co-workers.

He needed a day or two to follow Bingham. He couldn't afford any mistakes this time. It had to go perfectly with Bingham so he could keep working through his list. He wanted every last one of them to die.

He was out of the apartment before his mother came out for breakfast. He hesitated only long enough to call the Human Resources department at Plumrite and leave a message saying he would be out sick for at least a day. Then he made his way to his pickup. He drove to McDonald's and bought a cup of coffee and two hash browns to go. Bingham's home address had been easy enough to find, it was listed in the old telephone book his mother kept in a kitchen drawer. He wasn't sure if having your number listed was a small-town thing or an insurance agent thing. Either way, he probably wanted everyone to know how to reach him. Well, thank you very much.

His truck was now edged up parallel to the curb about a half-block from Bingham's house, parked inconspicuously between a Dodge van and a Chevy Tahoe. Brewster could see both Bingham's front door and his driveway from his observation point.

Before he finished his second hash brown, Brewster saw Bingham walk out of his front door and around the corner of the house to the garage. Soon a shiny black four-door Mercedes backed down the driveway. Brewster waited until the Mercedes reached the end of the block and then pulled out from the curb and followed it.

He assumed Bingham would drive somewhere for breakfast. He didn't look like a guy who missed any meals, but Brewster was wrong. Bingham drove straight to his office. The Bingham Insurance Agency occupied a small, single story, stand-alone building a block south of the traffic circle on Petro Avenue, not far from Brewster's apartment. The front of the building had two large plate glass windows with a glass door between them. There was a drycleaner on one side of the agency building and a small-appliance repair shop on the other.

Brewster expected Bingham to pull to the curb right in front of the agency, but he didn't. Instead, he drove past the front of the building and turned into a small driveway between the agency and the dry-cleaner. There had to be a parking lot in the back.

Brewster started the engine on his truck. He was smiling. He would come back after business hours and checkout the parking lot. In the meantime, he had other things to do.

He could feel it inside him. He had found the place. Now, it was just a matter of time. He would be back to meet Bingham, and one of them wouldn't leave the meeting alive.

CHAPTER NINETEEN

It felt like the first day of the rest of his life. Upton couldn't get the tired cliché out of his head because that's the way he felt. He felt new, refreshed. Jen's loss was still there, visceral in its intensity, but now he was remembering good things and good times. He hadn't had a drink for weeks, but this was the first time he really felt clear-headed.

Coming downstairs he opened all of the window blinds, letting sunshine stream into the condo. He could see a thin layer of dust on most of the surfaces. Dusting. Another thing Jen had done without him ever noticing. There was a can of Pledge under the sink in the kitchen. He'd take care of the dust later.

He started the coffee pot and opened the refrigerator. There wasn't much to choose from, especially breakfast fixings. There was a half-carton of eggs in the door, but he wasn't sure how old they were. He couldn't remember buying them. It was an easy choice to decide to treat himself to breakfast at the café.

His notes were still on the kitchen counter. They seemed to hold new promise for him. He gathered up his yellow pad and slid a few loose sheets between the pad of paper and the cardboard backing.

He decided to take the Jeep into town. Normally he just walked the few blocks unless he had appointments or something, but he couldn't escape the feeling that events were beginning to move, and he wanted to be mobile enough to follow along.

At the carport he noticed the condition of the Jeep. It hadn't been washed in months. It was covered in dirt, clean only where the wipers swiped across the windshield. Inside, there were candy wrappers, soda cans and all kinds of other trash everywhere. It looked like he'd been living in the car, and in some ways, he had. He didn't have time to wash the car, but he unwadded a McDonald's bag he found on the floor behind the front seat and began stuffing it with trash. It wasn't big enough. By the time he made his second trip to the dumpster, the Jeep looked much more presentable, at least on the inside. He jumped in and drove downtown.

He parked along the curb in front of Louie's. The bar's siren call was quiet. He didn't know if it was the early morning hour or if he had crossed some kind of threshold, but he knew he was done with Louie's. Turning away he walked next door to the café. Pushing through the swinging glass door he saw Eddie Mercer already in the booth Upton usually occupied. Upton slid in across from him.

"I was hoping you might come in for breakfast."

"I usually don't, Eddie. You got lucky."

"I needed to talk to you."

"You don't look so good, Eddie. Did you eat?"

"Not hungry. I'm in trouble at work."

"What kind of trouble?"

"They think I have a drinking problem."

Upton looked across the table at his friend, trying to look into his eyes, but Mercer wouldn't look up. His head was hung and his gaze seemed focused on the Formica tabletop.

"Eddie. You *do* have a drinking problem."

"I don't Uptown. I have no problem at all drinking."

"It's not funny, Eddie. You're talking about your health and your career. Did they fire you?"

A small sob came from Mercer and he wiped the back of his hand across his nose.

"No. They want me to get help. Counseling or something. But they can't make me go. I've been thinking I'll just stop drinking for a few days and I'll be as good as new."

Upton watched Mercer's face. His expression was begging for understanding, for agreement, for support, but his appearance cried for help. His eyes were sunken and he had black circles under them. There was a sheen of sweat on his forehead and his combed-back hair looked greasy. He had both hands on the table and they were shaking slightly. His two index fingers were drumming softly on the tabletop.

"It's more than that Eddie, and you know it. You can't just take a vacation from drinking and make it all go away. Did they drug-test you?"

"No, but they warned me I was subject to random testing from now on."

"Well, I don't know how Plumrite works, but most companies offer you a chance to get help. If you don't get it, they cut you loose and never look back."

There was silence between them for a few moments.

"I don't know what to do."

"Get help, Eddie."

"It's not that easy. I'm not as strong as you."

"That's bullshit. It's not about strength. It's about wanting to change and then committing to it. I'll be there to help you every step of the way, just like you were for me, but you've got to take the first step."

Mercer just stared at the tabletop. Upton signaled the waitress over. He didn't know her, Frannie apparently didn't work the breakfast shift.

"Let's start with something to eat."

"Then what?"

"Then one day at a time, or one hour or one minute. Whatever it takes."

Mercer clearly wasn't interested in the food. He mostly pushed scrambled eggs around his plate and looked miserable. He asked Upton about the murders, mostly just to take his mind off his churning stomach.

"There's not much to tell. Sheriff Miller can't, or won't, tell me everything, but we're working together and comparing notes. So far though, it doesn't seem like either one of us is making much progress."

"People are talking, Tommy. You ought to hear the talk in the lunch room. They think there's a serial killer loose in Los Robles. After that lady was killed over at the high school, I heard people saying they were going to keep their kids home from school."

"How about you? What do you think?"

"I'm not sure I'm capable of thinking right now. My head feels like it's on the wrong body. Look, I don't know anything about serial killers, or any other kind of murderer for that matter. But no matter what you call him, how could this killer be anything else but a local guy? The paper said the Mendez kid got in a car with the guy. Sandra Gibson was killed in a part of the school nobody who hadn't gone there would know about and, sorry Tommy, but the guy walked right up to Jen. Maybe she knew him. Even if she didn't, the guy obviously knows the town. He could be anyone. And that's starting to scare people."

Upton was silent, staring into his coffee cup. He looked up at Mercer who was clearly suffering. His face was now covered in sweat, his skin pallid and his hands were shaking worse.

"You're right, Eddie. Jen was trusting, but she wasn't stupid. And she would have fought like crazy against an attacker. She must have known him. Either that or she never saw him coming."

Mercer smiled but the effort cost him.

"Eddie, what are you going to do?"

"Plumrite made me an appointment down at the clinic for ten o'clock. After that, I don't know."

"Let me take you over there."

"Nah. I'm all right." His breath caught and a tear ran out of his left eye. "Tommy, I'm scared."

"I know, Eddie. But you're not alone. I'm here. Anytime, anywhere."

They sat in silence while Upton finished his breakfast. Wadding his napkin under his plate, he leaned back against the booth. A little bit of color had returned to Mercer's face. He clenched his jaw and met Upton's gaze.

"I can do this, Tommy."

"I know you can, Eddie, and I'll help."

"Maybe I'll take you up on that ride."

Upton dropped Mercer off at the clinic after making him promise to call as soon as he was through. He reached into the back seat to retrieve his yellow pad, put the Jeep in gear, made an illegal U-turn and drove back to Dave Miller's office.

Miller was leaning back in his office chair, back to the door, spinning a football in his hands when Upton walked in.

"You're going to rub off all the autographs if you keep spinning that ball."

Miller looked down at the ball and seemed almost surprised to see it in his hands. He stood up and placed it back on the shelf. Still facing the wall he looked up at the ceiling as if he could see something written there.

"I'm getting a lot of pressure, Tommy."

"I know. I think Vic has that worm Jerry Morris out putting a story together. And facts aren't always a big part of Morris' reporting."

"Great. I'm sure Ana Espinoza will give him plenty of material." With a sigh, he turned to face Upton.

"You look different."

"Wow, it's like you're channeling Sherlock Holmes. But yeah, and I feel different, too. I had an epiphany or something last night. I'm a new man."

"What happened?"

"I don't know exactly. It was sort of like the reels of a slot machine. They've been spinning and spinning inside me and, last night, they stopped and came up a jackpot. I made my peace with Jen and I made peace with myself. The weight is off. I can't undo anything I did in the past, but now I think I can go forward the way she would want me to. I can try to make her proud of me again."

"You know she never lost her faith in you, Tommy."

"I know that, but it's up to me to prove her right, to show that her faith wasn't misplaced."

A slightly uncomfortable silence fell between them, but it was brief.

"I have a theory."

Miller put his feet up on the desk and locked his hands behind his neck. "Let's hear it."

"It's the high school. It has to be. It's the only common denominator that makes sense. And it has to be someone local. A stranger to town might have pulled off one of these murders, maybe even two, but not all of them. Together they represent too much local knowledge for an outsider to have. These victims all had something in common at the high school, we just have to find it."

"And how do you propose to do that?"

"I don't propose to do it, I propose to benefit from it, because I think it's called good, old-fashioned police work, and that's your job.

"We need to go through every smart phone, calendar, date book, class schedule and note pad we can find and start listing people, activities, appointments—everything—and see where we find matches."

"We've looked at the high school and we didn't find anything there."

"You didn't look hard enough. I think we've been underestimating our killer. He's clever. Except for Sandra Gibson, he's left almost no evidence behind. All of the killings appear to have been carefully planned. He's got the whole town talking, including the mayor, and he's got us twisting in the wind. These aren't perfect crimes. We have to find the flaws, because that's how we'll find him."

Miller stared at Upton for a few beats, then slowly nodded. "If you're wrong, we'll have wasted a lot of time and manpower. But if you're right, we might be able to see a motive, maybe even a suspect."

"Do you want me to do the research on Jen, or should I bring you all of her paperwork?"

"Well, you're right, it *is* police work, so my people should be doing it. But we're stretched thin and nobody knew Jen better than you, so if you can do the research on her, it will free someone up here."

"I'll start today."

"So will we, but don't get too excited, Tommy. This feels a little like grasping at straws to me."

Upton left Miller's office, walked around to the front of City Hall and took his customary seat on the bench. This morning, not even Los Robles looked the same. He could see some of its charm, so much of what had appealed so much to Jen.

The U.S. flag atop the oil derrick monument in the center of the traffic circle rippled gently in the breeze. The breeze was from the north and Upton could smell the sweet aroma of plums being carried in from the Plumrite plant.

He pushed the brim of his fedora up off his forehead and titled his head back so he could see the sky. He couldn't believe the way he felt. The sky seemed bluer, the air smelled sweeter. At first he thought maybe he had just managed to somehow compartmentalize his grief and guilt, but he realized that wasn't right. Both were still with him, but less intense, and with some perspective. There was something—someone—else with him, too. Jen. He could feel her presence. He could feel her approval. He could feel her love. And it felt good.

"I was such an idiot," he said out loud. He felt a twinge of sadness, then laughed. Jen would have agreed with him and edited the statement to "complete" idiot.

He stood and took the shortcut straight across the circle to the newspaper leaving the Jeep in the City Hall parking lot. He was tempted to walk around the long way, stick his head into Louie's, and make sure Eddie wasn't there drowning his career, but he decided to follow up with him later.

At his desk, his in-box was half-full. He had two new obituaries to write and a short stack of faxed news releases. He wondered if newsrooms were the only place left on the planet that still received faxes.

He'd sort through the news releases later to see if there was anything worth a story. Mostly, they would probably just be material for briefs. He wasn't a big fan of writing club news or society blurbs, but it kept him busy and it kept him in the game. He finally decided he'd start with one of the obits.

Actually, it was an easy call because Los Robles had just lost a leading citizen. Elizabeth Hartley was the grand-daughter of Albert Hartley, one of the first people to settle in Los Robles. Albert had come west from Titusville, Pennsylvania. Titusville was the birthplace of the oil industry in the United States. The first oil well was drilled there in 1859. A few years later, crowded out of the oil fields by growing oil companies who were buying up leases at exorbitant prices, Hartley joined the steadily growing stream of independent operators heading west to stake their claims in the oil-rich soil of California. Stopping for the night in the small crossroads town that was called Oakville then, he studied the geology in the surrounding hills and decided to start buying leases right where he was, down at the south end of the small valley. He struck oil with his very first well. Soon other operators and speculators followed and Oakville was transformed into Los Robles with paved streets and stone buildings.

His fortune made, Hartley became a benefactor of the city. He donated the land for the high school, started the town's first service organization—the Petrolia Club—and when plums proved to be a new kind of boom discovery for the town, planted hundreds of acres of plum trees. The family ranch was still one of Plumrite's biggest growers and a member of the family had held a seat on the Board of Directors for decades.

Elizabeth grew up tall, beautiful and elegant. She became the guardian angel of Los Robles, contributing generously to charities large and small. She formed an art society and, once a year, hosted a grand ball at the family mansion with all proceeds going to charity. An invitation to the ball was the town's highest social achievement. Now, at eighty-four, she was gone and Los Robles was bereft.

Like most newspapers, the *Register* kept extensive biographical files on all of its prominent citizens. Upton had almost everything he needed for the obit already sitting on his desk. His hands flew across the keyboard and line after line of copy rolled across his computer screen.

The only time there was a benefit to being the obit writer was when someone important died. When that happened, the obit went to page one. At least it did for Upton. Because of his experience, he knew Vic wouldn't pull the story from him and that it would appear above the fold in the next edition.

By the end of the day he had filed the Hartley obit, started on the second, and written three briefs. He straightened his desk, shut down his computer and then started thinking about dinner. After Jen died he had never really stopped eating, but he had never felt hungry. Tonight, he was famished.

On the way home he stopped by a small market and picked up a rib-eye steak, a can of ranch beans, a bag of mixed lettuce salad, a six-pack of Diet Coke and some coffee and eggs for breakfast. Back at the condo he slid the patio door open to let in some fresh air.

Opening cabinet doors one after the other he finally located a skillet. He poured in a little cooking oil and started heating it. The beans he dumped into a small pot, adding a little Tabasco sauce, and he filled a bowl with part of the salad. The oil had warmed up so he laid the steak down across the pan, enjoying the sizzle. He added just a little salt and pepper to the steak.

The kitchen smelled great, like food and life. Popping the top on a can of the Diet Coke, he placed it on the breakfast bar and then opened the silverware drawer. He suffered a pang of guilt as he realized he was setting the table for only one. When the food was ready he filled his plate and sat down to eat. As he did, another wave of melancholy washed over him.

The steak was huge, much more than he could eat. Most of the beans were still in the pot and his salad had used only about a quarter of the bag. He was going to have to learn how to cook for just one person. How to live as just one. How to live without just one.

Jen's memory was his dinner companion and, ultimately, he decided it wasn't such bad company. He polished off more of the steak than he probably should have and decided he could have the leftover meat with a couple of eggs for breakfast.

He had cleaned up the kitchen and sorted through the mail when his phone rang.

"Uptown, it's me. Eddie."

"Eddie, I thought you were going to call me after your appointment. Where are you?"

"I never left my appointment. I went straight to rehab. They want to keep me for a while."

"Well, Eddie, that's probably a good thing."

"I know, I know, but it doesn't feel like it right now. They've got me on some drugs to help me detox. It's pretty rough."

"It'll get better, Eddie. They know what they're doing. Just do what they say."

"I will. Listen, Tommy, could you do me a favor? Could you go by my place and bring me some clothes? They wouldn't let me go home today."

"Of course I will. What do you want?"

"I can't have anything with any kind of a string on it. I guess they're afraid I'll hang myself or something. But, you know, some socks and underwear, a few shirts, a couple pair of pants. Toothbrush. That kind of stuff. There's a spare key hidden under the planter by the front door."

"I'll do it right now, Eddie. I'll see you in a little while."

"You're a good friend, Tommy."

"So are you, Eddie."

He found the planter, and the key, but there was no plant, just a box of dirt by the front door. The mailbox was full so he took the mail in with him. It had been months since he'd been to Eddie's apartment – maybe a year—and he didn't have a strong recollection of it.

He had last seen it through a haze of bourbon. As he pushed the front door open he was a little afraid of what he might find. Eddie had been spiraling down for some time and Upton suspected the apartment had been going down with him, but he was wrong.

There was a strong smell of stale cigarettes and a more subtle smell of alcohol. The apartment smelled a little like a bar that had been closed for a while, but it was very neat. It looked lived in, but orderly.

Upton put the mail on the kitchen counter. There was a fork, plate and coffee cup in the sink. Everything else was put away.

Upton wondered if he should look for booze and throw it out before Eddie came home, but decided he needed to let him find his own way. If Eddie wanted him to throw it out, he would. He crossed through the living room to the bedroom.

He wasn't sure what to take. He felt a little uncomfortable going through Eddie's dresser and closet, but there was no way around it, so he started opening drawers. Socks and underwear were in the top two drawers and Upton took a few pairs of each. He found some golf shirts one drawer down and took two of those. In the bottom drawer there were sweat shirts and sweat pants and he thought those might work to sleep in. Remembering what Eddie had told him, he took out the drawstrings. In the closet he pulled out two shirts and two pairs of casual pants. He stacked everything on the bed. In the bathroom he found a toothbrush, toothpaste, shampoo, deodorant and a hair brush.

Upton surveyed everything on the bed and figured it would be enough to hold Eddie for a few days. He noticed a half-read paperback on the nightstand, so he grabbed that, too. He would bring Eddie anything else he needed. There was a small duffel bag on the top shelf of the closet and Upton packed it with Eddie's things.

An orderly met him at the door of the clinic. He wouldn't let Upton in to see Eddie.

"He's pretty heavily medicated right now to help him detox," he said. "Patients can have visitors two times a day for one hour, at nine in the morning and six in the evening. If you come at six, you can buy dinner for three bucks and eat with him."

Upton thanked the orderly and got a phone number he could call for updates or to talk with Eddie.

When he got back to the condo, he turned on all the lights and then did his best to steel himself for what was to come next. He remembered some homily about the longest journey starting with a single step so, taking a deep breath, he walked into Jen's office.

A light layer of dust covered everything. Other than that, the office looked exactly as it did the last time she left it. He felt his breath catch in his throat but he continued across the room to her desk.

A Dell laptop sat in the middle of the desk. It was closed and a small leather case stuffed with Jen's business cards sat on top of it. An empty wire basket was in the upper left hand corner of the desk. Upton had forgotten about that. The basket was where Jen had kept the files for her current listings. Another agent Jen had a loose partnership with had come by to pick up the files a few days after the funeral. He had never liked the guy and suspected the feeling was mutual. Upton had a fleeting thought about the listings and figured none of Jen's commissions would ever be sent his way. He might have to think about that—some other time.

Jen's calendar and address book sat on the desk directly to the left of the laptop. Both books were leatherbound. The right side of the desk held a printer, a phone, the computer mouse, a stapler, a box of paper clips and a coffee cup from their insurance agent that was filled with pens and pencils.

Upton decided to start with the calendar. He pulled out the desk chair and as he sat he seemed to feel her with him. He could smell a hint of her perfume and she felt near to him as he occupied the space that was so much a part of her life.

Her calendar was in a leather binder small enough to fit into her purse. The pages behind the calendar were for notes and about twenty business cards she had collected were confined by a rubber band and tucked into a pocket in the cover of the binder.

He had decided, since he had to start somewhere, that he would start with the first day of January and go through the calendar chronologically. He had brought a fresh yellow pad to the desk with him. He pulled out a sliding work surface from the left side of the desk and put the pad and his pen on it. He spread Jen's calendar out on top of the closed laptop and began flipping through the pages.

As a successful Realtor, Jen had been very well-connected electronically. The chime for incoming e-mails had sounded regularly and she had a website and a smart phone. But now, looking at her calendar, there was no doubt it was the heart of her business.

Each month in the calendar consisted of two facing pages, so she could see her entire month at a glance. As he turned to January, Upton saw that every square on the pages, each square representing a day of the month, had at least one entry. There were also notes scribbled in the margins.

Most of the entries looked like appointments with potential buyers to show a house, but clearly Jen had committed her entire life to her calendar. She put everything on it. Upton wrote down names and dates as he scanned doctor's appointments, meetings, deadlines and even lists of errands.

When he finally got to the end of the calendar it was after midnight. He'd gotten everything written down, but hadn't been able to do any analysis. It was too late for that now. He'd start fresh in the morning.

He pushed the desk chair back under the desk and walked to the door. He looked back at the desk, and then turned out the light.

CHAPTER TWENTY

The sun woke Upton up the next morning. He'd gone to bed so late he'd forgotten to close the bedroom shades and now the morning light was streaming into the bedroom. Despite the short night, he felt rested. After showering he went downstairs and started the coffee-maker. The paper was on his front doormat and he brought it in and spread it on the breakfast bar. His obit for Elizabeth Hartley was on the front page, right where he thought it would be, above the fold. There was a file photo from last year's grand ball and, in the background, he could see Jen and himself seated at one of the tables near the stage.

He cracked two eggs into a small frying pan and put the leftover rib-eye on a plate in the microwave. He couldn't remember the last time he'd had steak and eggs for breakfast. He read the rest of the paper while he ate.

Checking his watch he saw he still had about an hour before he could visit Eddie at the clinic, so he went back to Jen's desk.

On the day she was murdered, there were two appointments on Jen's calendar. She had her nails done at nine in the morning, and she met her murderer at seven that night. There was no name, of course. Just the time and the address of the house.

He stared at the small square in the calendar as if some sort of answer would magically appear, but nothing did. Just a note written in Jen's neat handwriting for an appointment with the last person she would ever meet.

That appointment was where he had stopped his research the night before. It had seemed logical at the time, but he could see that Jen had other appointments and meetings scheduled past that date, so he added all of them to his list as well. By the time he was finished it was time to go see Eddie. He gathered up both of his yellow pads, put on his hat, and drove the Jeep to the clinic.

Eddie didn't look good. His face was haggard, he hadn't shaved and, though it appeared he had showered, he looked like he had just toweled his hair dry, then left it. He looked a bit like a wild man, but he was undeniably sober. He was wearing a set of the sweat shirt and pants he had dropped off.

"How're you feeling?"

"Worse than I look."

"That bad, huh?"

Eddie managed a smile. A small one.

"Tommy, we've gotta talk."

"Sure, Eddie."

"C'mon in here. There's coffee. There's always coffee."

They each filled a Styrofoam cup and Eddie led the way to a distant corner of the day room where they would have a little privacy.

"I've already been to two sobriety meetings since I got here. We have three a day. I'm learning some things. One of the twelve steps says that I should admit to God, and to myself and to someone else the things I've done wrong. I know I let booze take over my life and I know I've done some wrong things."

"Eddie, you don't have to do this for me."

"It's not for you, Tommy. It's for me. Look, I realize now I have a bad drinking problem. And I screwed up at work. Plenty. I made mistakes. I left early or came in late, sometimes both. I broke things. But there's something I didn't tell you yesterday."

Eddie was staring down into his coffee cup, unable to meet Upton's eyes. Upton said nothing, giving his friend time to organize his thoughts.

"The company told me to get help, but they also said they're opening an investigation on me. For stealing. Look, I'm in the finance department. In this economy, things are tight at Plumrite. They're literally watching every penny. They inventory pencils, for cryin' out loud. And lately things have started to turn up missing. Little things, all over the plant. Stupid stuff. A broom. A roll of baling wire. A Tyvek suit. They said I'd been seen in all of the areas where those things went missing. What would I want that stuff for? If I was going to steal from the company, why would I take a broom? I'm in finance, I could take *money*. But here's the thing, Tommy. I *was* in those places, but not to steal anything. I had bottles hidden there. I'd sneak off to a quiet part of the plant to get a drink, not to steal something. I didn't take a thing."

"Eddie, one thing I know about these meetings is they say 'one day at a time.' You've got to take one problem at a time, too. Get healthy first and then deal with the investigation. You have an explanation for what you were doing in those places. When you're healthy, I think they'll accept that explanation."

Mercer looked at Upton with tear-filled eyes. "I hope you're right, Tommy. My job is all I have."

Upton reached over and put his hand on his friend's shoulder. "You have more than that, Eddie. You'll be all right. You're on a good path now. I'll do everything I can to help you stay on it."

A soft bell rang signaling the end of the visiting hour. Patients exchanged hugs with supporters and a slow tide of visitors started towards the door.

"I'll see you tonight, Eddie. If you think of anything you need, let me know."

Mercer offered a small smile and a nod in gratitude.

Upton sat behind the wheel of the Jeep staring through the windshield. He knew that he could have been in the same place as Eddie. In some ways he was. He had lost his reputation and the respect of his family, friends and co-workers. And he had lost Jen. But for some reason, he had been able to overcome his dependence on alcohol while Eddie was overwhelmed by it. It seemed arbitrary and unfair somehow. Eddie had managed to save him from alcohol even while he was drowning himself with it. Upton wasn't part of a twelve-step program, but he felt an obligation to Eddie and he wouldn't let him down.

He started the Jeep and drove to the paper. Vic Yanuzzi met him at the front door.

"The Hartley family loved your obit on Elizabeth. Her grandson came in and bought a whole stack of papers so they could send it to the family who couldn't get here for the funeral. It's also the most popular page on our website right now. Most hits we've ever gotten on a story, more than the murders, even."

"It's the writer, Vic. Jerry Morris couldn't write a decent grocery list."

"Don't be that way, Tommy. He's trying, and now you've got him running scared."

"Good. I hope he runs the whole way out of town."

"Be the bigger man, Tommy. Be the bigger man."

At his desk he discovered his in-box was empty. He went back over to Yanuzzi.

"Vic, my desk's clean. You mind if I go spend some time with Dave Miller?"

"Have at it. Just be sure you end up giving me a story that will justify your time. And hey, if you can throw Jerry a bone, give him a break, will you?"

———————————

Dave Miller waved Upton to his customary seat on the opposite side of the desk.

"I made good progress with Jen's stuff last night."

"Yeah, well I got my ass handed to me last night. The city council spent about an hour grilling me. All that goddamn Ana Espinoza can talk about is the FBI. Seriously, what could the FBI do that we're not already doing?"

"Dave, you know it's all about the next election."

"Of course I do, but she's trying to make me seem incompetent and, worse, she's trying to make it look like I don't care, and that really pisses me off."

"Are your people having any luck with the other victims?"

"They working on them. They were all very busy, active people. But just ordinary folks. There's a lot of stuff to go through. Although Lisa Erickson seems to be the exception. She was just a nice, normal girl. It's not that we've established any kind of pattern or anything, but somehow she just doesn't seem to fit."

"Is it possible her murder isn't related?"

"It's possible, sure, but my gut says no. We just haven't figured out the connection yet."

Miller left to check on the progress his deputies were making, so Upton walked around to the front of City Hall and took his usual place on the bench.

The sky was cloudless and the sun was warm without being hot. He closed his eyes. The warmth felt good. He kept his eyes closed and listened as life in Los Robles went on around him. There was the traffic navigating the circle, a lawn was being mowed somewhere. The drone of a small plane reached him from above, and then another one of his senses kicked in. A breeze had carried over the aroma from the café—a combination of fried food and pie. Close enough to lunch time, he decided. So he walked around the circle to the café. His step never faltered as he passed Louie's.

As he pushed through the door, Frannie met him with a smile.

"Haven't seen you in a couple of days, Tommy."

"I've been trying home cooking."

"How was it?"

"I'm here, aren't I?"

His favorite booth was empty, so he slid in.

"You want a menu?"

"Nope. Diet Coke, grilled ham and cheese and fries."

"Comin' right up."

He pulled out the yellow pad he had used to write down Jen's appointments. First he scanned them all again to make sure none of the other victims showed up. Then, on a separate page, he began to list any of the appointments that had anything to do with high school. There were more than he expected, but most of them had only a minor connection to the school.

There were a number of appointments with three teachers at the school, two who were looking to buy a house, and one who was trying to sell. There was a career day where Jen was supposed to make a presentation. He wondered if Sandra Gibson was involved with that. He found a meeting with the yearbook committee about a sponsorship and one with the athletic boosters for some advertising at the football field. Jen had also marked the date for the homecoming football game and, later in the year, for a scholarship banquet.

Frannie set his plate and glass down at the end of the table and Upton looked up at her and saw tears in her eyes.

"I'm sorry about the other day, Tommy."

"Don't be sorry, Frannie. It's a terrible thing, it's all right to feel bad about it."

"I know, it's just, well, I'm embarrassed about how I reacted, like I was a little girl or something."

"Frannie, we all read the paper, watch TV, surf the Internet and see this stuff. We think we're desensitized to it, but we're not. We just don't realize it until violence strikes close to home. Then it becomes real. The horror is real. The blood is real. The loss is real. It hurts your heart because it's real. And none of us should be ashamed to mourn the loss of a friend."

She reached down and patted his hand.

"Thank you, Tommy." One tear escaped as she turned and walked to the kitchen.

Upton pushed his yellow pad out of the way and dug into his sandwich. The bread was a golden brown and the fries were so fresh they were almost too hot to eat. He pushed them into his mouth anyway, using the Diet Coke to reduce the heat. There was only a small piece of bread crust and half a pickle left on his plate when his cell phone buzzed in his shirt pocket. The caller ID read "Sheriff."

"Upton."

"Tommy, it's Dave. There's been another attack. Darrell Bingham. Tommy, he's alive. Meet me at his office."

Upton left a wad of bills on the table and was out the door before Frannie knew he was gone.

CHAPTER
TWENTY-ONE

A street light on the next block over provided enough light for Brewster to explore the parking lot behind Bingham's office. It was a postage stamp of a parking lot with four parking spaces and an enclosure for a dumpster. He bet the trash trucks hated trying to get in and out of the lot. But it couldn't be any more secluded. The back wall of Bingham's office was solid cinder block except for a small frosted window that was probably a restroom. The solid cinderblock walls of the cleaner and appliance shop on either side had no windows at all, and the back of a large brick building on the next street over made the final side of the parking lot. The only window was Bingham's bathroom.

The lot was a box, completely enclosed by the buildings except for the driveway between the insurance agency and the drycleaner's. Looking carefully, Brewster discovered a small gap between the dry-cleaning building and the brick building.

It was only about five feet long and the ground was covered with blown-in trash. He realized that, standing sideways, he could slip through the gap. It was perfect. He could enter and exit the parking lot without being seen from the street.

Smiling to himself, Brewster realized his timing was perfect. The Petrolia Club met every Thursday over lunch. Bingham never missed a meeting and always returned to his office immediately afterward to catch up on the calls and other business he missed while he was at the meeting.

The Orchard Hotel was less than two blocks away, but Bingham always drove. Brewster didn't know if it was because Bingham liked showing off his Mercedes or because he was just too fat to walk that far without arriving covered in sweat. Either way it worked for Brewster. Tomorrow, Bingham wouldn't return to an empty parking lot, Brewster would be there. Waiting.

In his room that night, Brewster spent some time thinking about the next day. He would take the .38, just in case, but that's not how he wanted Bingham to die. Like with the Upton woman, he would find a weapon of opportunity. Something that couldn't be traced.

He slept peacefully and was up early. He called in sick at Plumrite again but left the house so his mother would think he was at work.

He stopped at the grocery store and bought doughnuts and a cup of coffee. Then he drove south out of town. He didn't have any particular destination in mind, but he didn't want to be seen hanging around town during the morning.

The land to the south of Los Robles was where much of the oil production had been and where what still existed was operating. The area was crisscrossed by oil roads and there were a few scattered orchards. Mostly it was rolling hills covered with oak trees and brush. The only oasis of green was the country club and golf course. The far end of the valley was defined by Derrick Grade. It was named for the oil derricks that had dotted its sides during the boom times and the road that ran over it was the only paved road out of the south end of the valley. The road was steep and curvy, but it was the fastest way to the junction that led to Bakersfield, about forty miles away.

Brewster passed the country club and then turned off onto an oil road. When the pavement ran out and turned to dirt he parked under an oak tree and ate his breakfast.

The morning was quiet and calm. The day was warming up but Brewster felt comfortable parked in the shade. He had the windows in the truck down and he could hear birds above him in the tree and small animals—probably squirrels—rummaging through the carpet of dead leaves under the oak.

He didn't think much about Harvard any more, but he thought about it now. He wondered what class he would have been in, where he would be living, and he wondered if, at Harvard, he would be able to find an intellectual equal. He thought he might. Maybe even a girl. Wouldn't that be something?

He checked the time on his cell phone, 11:30, Bingham would be leaving for the Orchard Hotel, arriving early so that, in true insurance agent fashion, he could shake everybody's hand and ask about their wives and children.

Brewster wadded up the bag from the grocery store and threw it through the sliding window behind the seat into the bed of the pickup. He decided to take a leak before returning to town, so he stepped out of the truck and walked behind the tree. As he was relieving himself he looked past the tree and saw a small pile of old lumber. He wondered what it was from and as he walked toward it, a small shack came into view behind the brush. The shack was abandoned, and obviously had been for years. Faded letters painted on the door read "Drilling Foreman."

Anyone who had grown up in Los Robles knew old shacks like this could be found in any of the areas where there had been oil exploration activity. The shacks were cheaply constructed and not worth the time and effort to take them down when the oil ran out. Many of the shacks closer to town were well-known to the high school students who used them for parties and romantic encounters.

One of the oil companies must have tried to sink a well nearby sometime in the past. Since there were no wells anywhere around, Brewster figured this particular well must have come up dry. There was an orchard that ran right up to where the paved road ended, but he hadn't seen any wells on his drive up the road. And he didn't know how much further the dirt road went, but he hadn't noticed any sign of recent activity.

He refocused his attention on the lumber pile. He kicked at it a little to be sure it wasn't home to a snake or some other animal, and then picked a 2x4 off the top of the pile. It was about two feet long. Brewster hefted it and it felt good in his hand. He could swing it with one hand, but it was long enough he could use two hands if he really wanted to get his weight behind it. It would do.

He put the board in the pickup bed, right behind the driver's door. It was time to get ready.

Brewster drove down the street that ran behind Bingham's office. The building that backed up to his parking lot was a plumbing supply store. The gap between the buildings came out into the back corner of the store's parking lot. He pulled into the lot and with the engine running got out of his truck and left the board just inside the gap. He then drove down the street to the Los Robles Shopping Center. It was about a block south of Bingham's office, on the same side of Petro Avenue.

The shopping center was typical for a small town. There was a Safeway grocery store on one end and a CVS drug store on the other. Between them were a drycleaner, a hardware store, a hairdresser, a UPS store and a Chinese restaurant. Brewster parked his truck in the middle of the parking lot figuring nobody would pay any particular attention to it parked among the other cars. He walked to the back of the shopping center and then back up to the plumbing supply store. After making sure the parking lot was clear, he walked to the back, picked up his board and slipped into the gap to wait for Bingham.

He pulled out his cell phone again to check the time. He really didn't know why he even owned a cell phone. He had bought it in anticipation of leaving for Harvard. Everyone in college had cell phones and he wanted to belong. Now, he just carried it around. No one had the number, not even his mother, and he never called anyone. He didn't play games on it and he didn't take photos. He used the calculator and checked the time.

He looked up when he heard the sound of tires crushing sand and gravel. He peeked into Bingham's parking lot and saw the Mercedes making the turn from the driveway into the parking space with Bingham's name on it. It was his lot and his business and he still had to paint his name on a parking space, it wasn't like there was any competition for it.

Brewster watched to make certain Bingham was alone. He was. He waited until the big man opened the driver's door and then started across the parking lot.

Brewster and Bingham met at the back of the Mercedes. Recognition flashed in Bingham's eyes as he saw Brewster but, before he could say anything, Brewster yelled at him.

"You stole my dream!" he shouted and then he swung the 2x4 with both hands. Bingham reflexively flung up his left arm to block the blow. The board glanced off his forearm and struck him on the forehead just above his left eyebrow. He screamed in pain and threw a blind punch at Brewster with his right arm. He felt more than heard the crunch of cartilage in Brewster's nose as his fist connected.

Brewster looked down, surprised to see blood on his clothes. His left hand went to his face and came away bloody. Bingham's forehead was streaming blood and Brewster didn't know whose blood was on his clothes.

"You stole my dream," he shouted again and swung the board one more time. This time Bingham turned and took the blow across his broad back. The blow staggered him, but didn't knock him down. As Brewster followed through on his swing, Bingham gave him a shove and ran for the driveway and the street, screaming the whole way.

Brewster ran, too. But he ran for the gap between the buildings. As he crossed the plumbing supply parking lot he could still hear Bingham screaming.

He paused in the parking lot and turned his shirt inside out, hoping it would help hide some of the blood. He held his hand across his face and pinched his nose, trying to stop the bleeding. He could feel his heart pounding against his rib cage. He forced himself to walk, not run. His best chance was that he would be seen, but he wouldn't be noticed. He almost smiled at his clever semantics. It's hard to be clever with blood leaking between your fingers, he thought.

Back at the shopping center parking lot he made his way to the truck zigzagging through the lines of parked cars, avoiding as many people as possible.

As he climbed behind the steering wheel he grabbed a discarded McDonald's napkin off the seat and wiped his face. Inspecting his nose in the rear-view mirror he didn't think it looked broken, but it had bled copiously.

He could hear sirens. Lots of them. Leaning over and looking through the passenger-side window, he looked up the block and saw emergency vehicles beginning to converge in front of Bingham's office.

He was in trouble. Bingham had recognized him, and Bingham didn't die.

Unless he was hurt worse than he thought, he knew Bingham could and would identify him. He had to get away. But first, he had to go to the apartment, change, and get rid of the bloody clothes.

He didn't have much time.

CHAPTER
TWENTY-TWO

From the café, it almost didn't matter which way around the traffic circle Upton took to get to Bingham's office, although he could cut straight across if he was willing to brave the traffic on both sides. He wasn't. Instead he took the slightly longer route that would take him past the *Register*. He stuck his head in the door and yelled to the back.

"Vic! Darrell Bingham has been attacked at his office. Send Morris."

Yanuzzi looked up but Upton didn't wait for a reply. He continued around the circle and the short distance down Petro Avenue to Bingham's office.

Yellow crime scene tape was already stretched across the sidewalk, but the deputy standing guard held it up for him to pass under.

"When Jerry Morris gets here, let him in, will you?"

"Really?"

Upton smiled. "Yeah, really." The deputy just shrugged.

The back doors of the ambulance were closing as Upton approached the driveway. The hospital was only about two blocks further south on Petro, but it wasn't like Bingham could walk. Dave Miller squatted on his haunches next to a pool of blood.

"He's alive, Tommy. This might be our break."

"Can he I.D. his attacker?"

"I don't know yet. Apparently he was talking like crazy after he ran out of the driveway to the sidewalk, but he wasn't making much sense by the time I got here. He was hit in the head and there was a lot of blood. A lot of blood. By the time they had him loaded into the ambulance he wasn't looking very good and he was unconscious."

"He was attacked right here?"

"No, behind the building in the parking lot. I've got guys back there going over the scene. We can go back as soon as they're done." He tilted his head down the street. "Right now I want to talk to Margaret Chu. She was the one who called 911."

Chu owned the drycleaning business. Like the Hartleys, the Chus had lived in Los Robles since the town was formed, although at different ends of the social spectrum. Margaret Chu's grandfather had brought his family from China, selling everything they owned and a little they could steal, to make his fortune in America.

At first, all he found was back-breaking work in the oil fields. Some of the big companies, and most of the wildcatters, used Chinese labor like slave labor. They paid very little, often late, and sometimes not at all. But Wang Chu managed to find honest operators and he saved money as hard as he worked. He learned English and dressed like the other roughnecks, not like his fellow countrymen. Eventually, he saved enough to open a store and supply the oil workers instead of laboring beside them.

The business prospered and so did the family and now, two generations later, the Chus owned several businesses in addition to the store—now a menswear and tuxedo rental store—and some acreage north of town full of plum trees, not oil wells.

Margaret Chu was small in stature, but her voice was loud enough to knock plums off a tree. Upton supposed it came from shouting over her drycleaning equipment every day. Plain wouldn't describe her, she was better looking than that, but her features were toughened by hard work. Her black hair was short, cut above her shoulders, but standing next to her Upton could see streaks of gray. Miller didn't even have to ask her a question to start her talking.

"He was acting crazy, Dave. I heard this commotion out on the sidewalk and there's Darrell, covered in blood, screaming like a little girl."

Miller and Upton had to smile a little at the description even though both of them knew it wasn't really funny.

"Did he say anything?"

"He kept screaming at me that he had been attacked and to call 911. I went back inside and made the call and brought out a towel. After he calmed down a little he told me again that he had been attacked, but he punched the guy in the nose and got away."

Miller held up a finger to stop Chu's story and called one of his deputies over.

"Call the ER at the hospital. Tell them there may be blood evidence on Bingham's hands. We need them to collect samples." He turned back to Chu. "Did you see anyone?"

"No, but I didn't go looking, either. He was hurt pretty bad."

"Did Darrell say anything else?"

"Yeah, one thing, but I didn't understand it. He said, 'I don't understand why he would attack me.' He said it a couple of times."

Miller entered the information in his notebook and Upton added it to his yellow pad. Before Miller could ask another question there were voices raised behind them. Jerry Morris was pushing his way through the crime scene personnel like he was a running back trying to break into the secondary.

"Where's the body?"

"There is no body. Darrell Bingham survived, Jerry. He's on his way to the hospital," said Upton.

"Jesus, Tommy. The guy lives so you throw the story to me? Not important enough for you?"

Dave Miller's mouth was actually hanging open, too stunned to speak. Upton was considering punching Morris in the nose. He was trying to hold up his end of the bargain with Vic Yanuzzi, but Morris was making it hard.

"Jerry. He lived. If he was attacked by the same guy, we have a witness. It might be a big break in the case."

Morris stood still for a couple of beats while Upton's words registered. Finally comprehending, he spun on his heels and began jogging back toward the crime scene tape. "I'm heading for the hospital," he said over his shoulder.

Miller looked at Upton. "What's he going to do at the hospital? Bingham's probably in surgery or something and, if he isn't, the first guy he talks to isn't going to be a reporter."

"Morris is an idiot. Vic told me to give the guy a break, so I told him about Bingham as soon as I heard. Vic sent Morris, but he can't hold the guy's hand and I'm certainly not going to do his job for him." Upton shook his head. "I handed the guy a scoop on a platter."

As they watched Morris jogging down the street toward the hospital, a deputy came down the driveway between the buildings and approached them.

"Sheriff, it's clear to go back now."

Bert Vega had taken charge of the crime scene and he met them where the driveway opened into the small parking lot. Once again Upton experienced a sense of the surreal as he saw the perfectly ordinary parking lot now dotted with numbered tent cards identifying evidence and yellow crime scene tape festooning the cars and buildings. He could smell the copper-like odor of fresh blood and an even less pleasant smell as blood pools in the sun slowly coagulated.

"There's so much blood. It's hard to believe Darrell survived."

"Remember, it may not all be his blood," said Miller. "But yeah, it's a lot of blood."

Vega started walking them through the crime scene.

"It looks like the attack began at the back of the car. My guess is the suspect waited until Darrell got out of the car and met him as he came around the left-rear quarter panel. Most of the blood evidence is there. There's spatter on the trunk of the car, probably from the impact, and then there's a spray pattern consistent with blood coming off an object that's being swung. So Darrell might have been hit more than once."

Vega pointed to the ground. "It doesn't look like they moved around much at first. There's a large pool of blood, probably Bingham's, but then things look like they started to get crazy.

"There's another pool of blood, a smaller one, just a few feet away. There are a couple of bloody footprints through what we think is Bingham's blood pool that lead me to believe he advanced on his attacker."

"Margaret Chu said Bingham told her that he punched the guy in the nose," said Miller.

"That fits. And it looks like he connected. We can't tell until it's tested, but I'm guessing the second pool isn't Bingham's. And Bingham stepped in that puddle too as he ran toward the street. Our suspect left a blood trail on the way out as well, but not footprints, just drops. He must be quite a bleeder."

Vega led them along the trail of blood droplets, staying carefully to the side. He pointed to a gap between the buildings. A technician wearing white Tyvek booties was in the narrow space tagging evidence.

"It looks like our suspect went out through there. My guess is he also waited there for Bingham to arrive. He would have been almost invisible unless you were specifically looking down there. We also found our weapon at the other end. An old two-by-four."

Upton walked to the corner of the building and peered down the opening. "Does this seem right to you?" he asked. "This was a major screw up. If it's the same guy, his previous attacks were much more efficient and well-planned."

Dave Miller didn't say anything. He just dropped into his customary squat and appeared lost in thought as his eyes followed the blood trail running between the buildings.

"Don't forget Sandra Gibson," said Vega. "That attack was very well-planned. The only thing that messed it up was his choice of weapons. That may be the case here too.

"Our suspect had obviously done some research on this. He found an isolated, nearly invisible location. Then he found an alternate route in and out that would keep him from being seen. And finally, he must have known something about Bingham's schedule. Personally, I think we'd have another body if the suspect had used a different weapon."

Miller and Upton nodded. Upton began flipping through pages on his yellow pad. Several pages in he found what he had been looking for.

"Margaret Chu said Bingham told her 'I don't understand why he would attack me.' That statement could be interpreted in a couple of different ways. For someone who had just suffered a senseless, random act of violence, the statement would be: Why me? Out of all the people, why me? But you can look at it from another perspective too. Isn't that something a victim might say if he knew his attacker? It can be kind of a contraction of the statement like: I know him. I don't understand why he would attack me."

"That may be how the suspect was able to approach him from the front," said Miller. "The same could be said for Lisa Erickson and Paul Mendez. If they knew their attacker, it would allow him to get much closer before he struck. If they knew the guy, it would be too late by the time they sensed trouble."

"I've got two deputies following the blood trail on the other side," said Vega. "I'll let you know where it leads."

Miller started walking toward the street. "Let's head for the hospital, Tommy. If Bingham can talk, we might be right on this guy's tail."

"You don't think Jerry Morris will have pumped him dry by this time?"

Miller just smiled and kept walking.

Mary Ellen Driscoll met them at the door to the hospital room. Her presence alarmed both Miller and Upton and she could see it on their faces. She offered them a small smile.

"Relax, boys. He's not dead. I'm on rotation today. For now at least, I'm his attending."

"That's a relief," said Miller. "Has he said anything?"

"No. He suffered a serious blow to the head and he was unconscious when he arrived. He still is. He also has a fractured left ulna and severe contusions on his back."

"His arm is broken?" asked Miller.

"Yes. I'm thinking it saved his life. The location of the fracture is consistent with a defensive action." She raised her left arm as if shielding her face from a blow. "I think he deflected the blow by the attacker, reducing the impact on his skull."

"When can we talk to him?"

"Not for a while. Even when he regains consciousness, he's heavily medicated, and he's also not out of the woods yet. It may not be when he regains consciousness, it may be if he regains consciousness. The impact on his skull produced a serious subdural hematoma and that's putting a lot of pressure on his brain. We're trying to relieve that pressure right now but, if we can't, we'll have to airlift him out of here. We've already got the Kern Medical Center in Bakersfield on standby."

"When do you think you'll know something?"

"Soon. We can't wait. If we don't start seeing some improvement, we'll have to transport him."

"He was talking at the crime scene. Did he come around in the ambulance and maybe say something to the paramedics?" said Upton.

"No, not that I heard about anyway. But that's not unusual, Tommy. After the attack, he was pumping a lot of adrenaline. That kept him going for a while, but then shock set in from the blood loss. And you guys may run into another problem; he may not remember anything when he does come around. It's very common for someone who suffers a serious head injury to not remember what happened."

Miller nodded. "Will you keep me posted?"

"Of course, Dave. As soon as I know anything." She shifted her attention to Upton. "Tommy, it's good to see you. You look better."

"I am better. Thanks, Mary Ellen."

As they waited for the elevator, Upton turned to Miller. "Coffee?"

"Sure."

They settled in to Upton's customary booth at the café and decided on slice of Key Lime pie to go along with the coffee. Neither spoke much, their thoughts were too heavy on their minds.

Thick white ceramic coffee mugs full of steaming coffee sat in front of them. The mugs had a drawing of the traffic circle oil derrick on them and the insides were stained from thousands of earlier cups of coffee. Miller wasn't drinking his coffee. He kept turning the mug around with his hands, leaving rings of spilled coffee on the table. Upton could see Miller was gathering his thoughts, so he just sipped from his mug and waited.

"This should do it," Miller finally said. "If Darrell can identify his attacker, I think we'll have our murderer as well."

"What makes you so sure?"

"Well, at this point we're pretty sure Darrell recognized his attacker. At least that's our working assumption. If that's true, it means the suspect is a local. A local suspect answers a lot of our questions about how he was able to get close to his victims. A name would also give us something to work back from. We've collected evidence from every scene, but we haven't had anything to compare it against. With an identified suspect, all that evidence either helps us make our case or becomes exculpatory."

"You said 'he or she.'"

"I know, but I don't mean it. I think the level of violence and the strength required for some of the attacks is too high to be a woman. I just don't want to lock myself into one theory. If you think about it, a woman, even a stranger, is a lot less threatening than a man, and that might also explain how the attacker was able to approach the victims. Like I said, I really don't believe it, I just can't allow myself to lose sight of the bigger picture."

"So, assuming Darrell remembers his attack and can identify the guy, what's the next step?"

"Depends. We're putting a lot of stock in the word 'identify.' It may be someone that Darrell just recognized. Someone he's seen around town or something but doesn't really know. On the other hand, if Darrell can give us a name, we'll go full speed ahead. We'll have to establish motives for all of the attacks, but if Darrell can give us a name we can at least pick him up for questioning. But even that might not be so easy. The guy got punched in the nose today and he knows that Darrell wasn't dead when he left the scene. He's got to know we're after him and that could mean he's on the run."

"So what do we do now?"

"We can't do much with Darrell until his condition improves so, for now, it's all about forensics and how good a job my guys did following that blood trail. I'm going to head back to the office and touch base with Bert. Want to tag along?"

"I don't think so. I need to stop by the paper and then go check in on Eddie."

"How's he doing?"

"So-so. He's got a couple of things going. The booze, of course, but there's also some kind of issue at the plant. They haven't exactly accused him of stealing, but they're close."

"They think he was embezzling?"

"No, that's just it. There have been a lot of petty thefts and they suspect Eddie because he's been seen in some places he shouldn't be. He says he wasn't in those places stealing, he was visiting his booze hideouts."

"I don't remember seeing any theft reports from Plumrite."

"You probably wouldn't. From what Eddie said it was all small stuff, like a broom. They only made it an issue because Eddie was seen in all of the areas where the thefts occurred. Well, that and the drinking."

"Hmm. I guess he has a bigger problem to deal with first."

"That's what I told him."

Miller scooped up the bill as he stood. "I'll be in touch."

"Me too."

Upton walked over to the newspaper office and as he pushed through the door he saw Vic Yanuzzi perched on a corner of Jerry Morris' desk. Yanuzzi saw him come in and waved him over.

"Jerry here says the murderer is as good as caught."

"Jerry should go back to J-school and learn the meaning of corroboration."

"Hey, I'm sittin' right here. Besides, it's a slam dunk. There are deputies following a trail of blood and Darrell Bingham saw his attacker."

"Couple of problems there, Jerry. First, the deputies are following a blood trail, but there's no telling what they'll find at the end of it. It stands to reason the suspect probably had a car parked nearby. The blood trail probably ends at a parking spot somewhere. And second, Darrell Bingham is still in trouble. He has a subdural hematoma that's producing severe swelling. They're talking about airlifting him to Bakersfield. And Mary Ellen Driscoll says that, even if everything turns out all right, he may have no memory of what happened. Even if he does remember, there's no guarantee he can identify his attacker, even if he saw him."

"So how's this a big break in the case then?"

"It's a big *potential* break. The guy started out like a ghost. Now he's making mistakes. One of those mistakes will give us the clue we need to catch him."

"So what am I supposed to write about?"

"You write about how Darrell Bingham fought back and may have saved his own life, and then you talk about the blood trail and ask people to call the sheriff's office if they see someone who looks like they've been in a fight. Go over to the sheriff's office, request a copy of the crime report to help you fill in any blanks."

Morris looked over at Yanuzzi. Yanuzzi just nodded. Upton walked back to his desk with Yanuzzi following.

"Thanks for trying, Tommy."

"Jeez, Vic. What a putz. How could you hire that guy?"

Yanuzzi's face reddened and Upton saw his fists clench.

"I needed a writer, Tommy. The one I had let me down."

Now Upton's face reddened, but it was from a different emotion.

"I'm sorry, Vic. I let you and a lot of other people down, especially Jen. I appreciate that you didn't abandon me, it would have been easy for you to cut me loose. I'm back on track now, and I'm going to stay that way."

Neither man said anything. The only sound in the room was the clicking of the keys on Jerry Morris' keyboard.

"I'll keep working with him, Vic. I know I owe you for a second chance, and I'll pay you back with interest."

The tension left Yanuzzi's body and his features relaxed.

"You've turned a corner, Tommy. Just keep heading in the right direction."

As Yanuzzi walked back to his office Upton looked over his own desk. His in-box was empty. No obits to write, no social announcements. The bloody image of Darrell Bingham flashed through his mind and hoped the in-box would stay empty.

Glancing at his watch he saw it was only a few minutes until visiting time at the rehab clinic. He grabbed the keys to the Jeep and drove over to check on Eddie.

The evening visiting hour coincided with meal time. Upton saw Eddie sitting by himself in the corner of the large common room, staring morosely at a tray of food on the table in front of him.

"Aren't you going to eat, Eddie?"

"Tommy." He looked up and smiled. "I'm glad you're here." He looked back down at the tray. "I can't seem to decide about the dinner."

An orderly noticed Upton and wheeled a cart across the carpet towards him.

"Visitors are invited to eat with our patients, sir. The dinner is only three dollars."

"Sure, I'll join my friend." Upton peeled three singles from his wallet and the orderly placed a tray in front of him. Upton unrolled his napkin to get the utensils inside. There was no knife.

"What've we got here, Eddie?"

"Not sure. That's one of the reasons I haven't tried it. I think it may be a breaded chicken breast."

Upton forked a bite into his mouth. "Nope. It's fish."

"Great. Institutional fish. Sounds delicious."

"Yeah, not so much. But you've got to eat. Your body needs fuel."

"I know," said Mercer as he tried a small bite of fish. "I just don't have much appetite. I think it's the drugs they're giving me."

"Your color looks a little better."

"Yeah, I guess I feel a little better, too. I'm just really tired. And now that I'm sober, I keep thinking about my job."

"I talked to Dave Miller about that. Plumrite hasn't filed any kind of a report, so right now, it's a private matter. Let's get you healthy and then we can deal with Plumrite."

They spent the rest of the visiting hour talking, mostly about the therapy Eddie was receiving and his initiation into a twelve-step program. When he left, Upton couldn't decide which one of them was more depressed.

He drove back to the condo and realized that for the first time in a very long time, he was glad to be home.

CHAPTER
TWENTY-THREE

He was covered in blood. It seemed impossible that all of the blood had come from his nose.

He leaned back in the driver's seat of his truck and closed his eyes. His pulse and breathing had just about returned to normal. He had to move. The cops would be looking in the neighborhood. He had no idea how many people might have seen him on his way to the truck. But, if anyone did, they'd be sure to remember. That much blood would be noticed by anyone.

He started the truck and slowly rolled it out of the parking lot. He turned onto Petro Avenue but he really didn't know where to go. He had seen recognition in Bingham's eyes. If Bingham lived, he would certainly tell the sheriff who attacked him. Brewster drummed his fingers on the steering wheel. He'd have to lay low until he could find out if Bingham lived.

Making up his mind quickly, he cut over a block and pulled into a parking space behind his apartment. He needed some clean clothes.

He checked the parking lot before getting out of the truck. All clear. He took the steps two at a time and let himself into the apartment. He grabbed a backpack from his closet and began to carefully pack it. He knew he needed to hurry, but he couldn't help himself.

It had to be neat. He packed two shirts, two pairs of boxer shorts, two pairs of socks and a hoody sweatshirt. He opened an envelope in his desk and found the cash he had stashed there. Just under sixty dollars.

The .38 was in the truck. He had taken it with him to Bingham's but when Bingham hit him, he was too surprised to pull the gun. Bingham started screaming so he had started running.

It was fully loaded. He looked up at the heater vent and decided he didn't have enough time to retrieve his box. He thought it might look like the paint on the screws had been scratched, but he didn't think so. His room looked just like he had left it.

He peeled off the bloody shirt and wadded it into a trash bag. He would have to find a place to dump it. In the bathroom, he looked at his face in the mirror. There was caked-on blood under his nose and around his mouth. His nose was swollen and one of his eyes was turning black. He didn't have enough time to clean up thoroughly so he splashed water on his face and managed to wash off the worst of the blood. Then he swallowed four aspirin from the bottle in the medicine cabinet. He thought it might help with the swelling.

He went to the kitchen and put two bottles of water, a box of crackers and a stick of hard salami in the backpack. At the front door, he cracked it slightly and peered outside. He couldn't see anyone in the parking lot or looking out their window. He dashed down the stairs and into the truck.

As he backed out of the parking space he remembered Plumrite was harvesting south of town, near the golf course and the old oil fields. The harvest usually started in the southern end of the valley and worked north. If he went south, all of the activity would be moving away from him. And, if things got really bad, he could just keep going and head over Derrick Grade toward Bakersfield and the Interstate.

Brewster checked the time on his phone. The harvesting operations should be about ready to shut down for the day. The workers would be leaving, but the portable toilets would still be there for when they returned in the morning. The toilets all had hand-washing stations attached to them with four sinks, soap and paper towels. Brewster could use one of them to finish cleaning himself up. He passed the golf course and as he reached the orchards he saw several areas where the picking had moved far enough off the road that he thought he could clean up undetected. He drove until the road began sloping gently up toward Derrick Grade and turned off on an old oil company road.

A short way down the road he came to a fair-weather crossing on a dry creek. He drove into the creek bed and under the shade of a cottonwood tree. He couldn't be seen from the main road. He'd stay there until dusk and then go clean up while there was still a little light to see by. That way he could be sure everyone would be gone and he wouldn't have to turn on his headlights and give away his position.

He rolled down the windows and sat listening to the engine tick as it cooled. The shirt in the trash bag was stiff with dried blood and it had started to give off an unpleasant odor. His nose hurt and now his lip felt swollen. The drying blood in his nose made him want to sneeze but he refused to let that happen. He was afraid a sneeze would start the blood flowing again.

He slapped the steering wheel and was surprised to feel tears welling up in his eyes. Things were unravelling. He had planned so carefully. The first three had gone perfectly. And then the disaster with Sandra Gibson and now the even bigger disaster with Darrell Bingham.

He checked the time again on his cell phone. It was almost six. Right now, everything depended on whether Darrell Bingham lived or died. He thought about Radio 670—KPLM—it called itself the Voice of the Valley. It was Los Robles' only local radio station, except it wasn't really local. It broadcast local commercials between music and talk shows that were fed in from its owner's corporate headquarters somewhere in Ohio. Besides the commercials, the only local programming was a newscast at six in the morning and six in the evening. That's when all the locals tuned in to get the Los Robles weather forecast, the farm report and about two minutes of local news.

Brewster started the truck and tuned into the station. The attack on Bingham led the broadcast. Not surprising. It was certainly more interesting than the planning commission report that followed it. But the report did nothing to improve Brewster's situation.

Someone from the Sheriff's Office had called in the report. He described what had happened based on interviews with witnesses and evidence collected at the scene. He even talked about deputies following a trail of blood away from the scene—blood thought to belong to the attacker. Brewster realized if he had sat in his truck any longer at the shopping center the deputies would have walked right up to him. He wiped sweat off his forehead. Everything was starting to fall apart. He blinked back tears and fought for control over his emotions.

Finally he heard what he had been listening for: "Mr. Bingham remains in very guarded condition. The attack was brutal and his injuries are severe."

It wasn't the news he had hoped for. Bingham wasn't dead. If he lived, Brewster would have to leave. Bingham would almost certainly identify him. If Bingham died, Brewster was still in trouble, but not as much. He could lay low for a while. Let things settle down.

As the sun started to set he drove out of the creek bed and back down to the orchards where they had been harvesting. As he expected, it was deserted. He pulled the pickup into a row between the trees so it couldn't be seen from the road.

The bloody shirt was smelling worse and worse and he was glad to get rid of it. There was no sense in trying to wash it, so he stuffed it down into one of the portable toilets. He knew it would eventually plug the toilet and be found, but he also knew it would be worthless as evidence.

He pulled a stack of paper towels out of the hand-washing station and wet them with water from the reservoir. After a day's use he knew it might be low on water so he tried to conserve. He soaped up his face, arms and torso and started to scrub. The pile of paper towels turned pink by blood grew next to the sink. Finally, he felt reasonably clean.

He gathered up the paper towels and stuffed them down a gopher hole a little ways from the wash station, then he kicked dirt over the hole to cover it up. He didn't want the Plumrite supervisors showing up in the morning and finding a trash bin full of bloody paper towels.

He walked back to the truck and put on a clean shirt from his backpack. He felt much better.

He figured his mother would be well into her bottle by this time, but he wasn't sure if it was safe to go home. If Bingham had talked, the sheriff could be waiting for him.

He decided to wait for the morning newscast. He drove back to the spot in the creek bed and sliced some salami. He ate the salami with crackers and washed them down with a bottle of water. Feeling clean and fed, he settled down to wait.

CHAPTER TWENTY-FOUR

"He's stable, Dave. But he's still unconscious. We decided not to transfer him to Bakersfield, although that's still a possibility if we don't see improvement soon," said Mary Ellen Driscoll.

Dave Miller was standing next to Darrell Bingham's hospital bed looking at all the wires and tubes attached to him. A monitor on a stand next to the bed blinked Bingham's pulse rate, respiration and blood pressure.

"If you had sent him out last night, do you think it would have made a difference?"

She shrugged. "Maybe. I had to weigh the risks against the benefits. They might have been able to do more for him in Bakersfield, but the increased air pressure he would experience during the flight could have killed him."

"You willing to take a guess on whether he'll be able to tell us anything?"

"There's still no guarantee he's going to make it, Dave. If he does, I'd say it's about a fifty-fifty chance he'll remember anything. Physically, I think he can overcome the damage, but his memory of the trauma may be gone. We won't know until we know. Any luck on your end of things?"

"I don't know. I came by here first. I'm heading to the office next."

"Hey, Dave. What was with Tommy yesterday? He seemed different. Better."

"I think he managed to flip some kind of internal switch or something. He's been able to let some things go. Maybe forgive himself for what happened to Jen."

"It may take a while, but that sounds like a good step towards recovery."

Miller looked at the doctor through slightly narrowed eyes. He had heard the same sound in her voice that he had noticed in Frannie's at the café. It hadn't really registered when Frannie spoke, but hearing it again now from Mary Ellen Driscoll, he realized there was a subtext in what the women were asking. Los Robles was a small town and Tommy, admittedly through tragic circumstances, was now available. Neither woman wanted to dishonor Jen but, as they say, life goes on. He wondered how he would fit in that equation. His marital status was well known. Maybe he needed to start paying more attention.

"I think you're right, Mary Ellen. He seems reenergized and refocused."

Miler nodded towards Bingham, festooned with wires, tubes and leads. "Let me know if anything changes."

As he walked into the Sheriff's Office he caught a look of warning from Carol Burnside. Looking through the window into his office he could see Ana Espinoza sitting in one of his visitor's chairs, waiting.

"I expect my sheriff to work full days."

"What's that supposed to mean, Ana?"

"I've been waiting for more than an hour."

Miller looked into her small, black eyes that glistened like a snake's. Her mouth was pursed, a blot of bright red lipstick on a pasty face framed by shoulder-length black hair. The hair was chemically black. It had lost its natural Hispanic luster years ago.

"First of all, I'm not your sheriff. I serve the people of this community and I'm elected by them just like you are. And secondly,

I don't owe you any explanations, it's not like you had an appointment to see me. That being said, I wasn't here when you arrived because I thought it might be a good idea to stop by the hospital to see if Darrell Bingham is still alive."

Espinoza said nothing, continuing to glare at Miller.

"He is, by the way. Alive. Thanks for asking."

"I want the FBI."

"I don't really care what you want, and neither does the FBI."

"What?"

"I'm good at my job and if you don't like it, why don't you see if you can get enough votes to have me recalled. Or try to. And part of doing my job well is making sure I've covered all the bases. There is a murderer in my town and I have no intention of letting him get away. Last night I called the Special Agent in Charge at the Bakersfield FBI field office. We talked for about an hour. He agreed with the course of our investigation and was unable to see any avenue where he could assume Federal jurisdiction. And, of course, he offered to help in any way he could."

Espinoza remained silent.

"I have work to do. You'll be leaving now. If you have anything else to discuss with me, make an appointment with Carol on your way out."

Miller walked to his office door and held it open somewhat cere-moniously for Espinoza. As she left, she did not look back. As soon as the front door closed behind Espinoza, Carol Burnside stuck her head through Miller's office door.

"That was awesome."

Miller allowed himself a small smile.

"Was it all true?"

"Mostly." The smile appeared again. "The jurisdiction is an issue but with the number of bodies we have, the FBI could make a case for stepping in if they wanted to."

"But they won't."

"For now. I explained Darrell's condition. If he is able to talk, we may be able to wrap things up. We've got all kinds of evidence. We just need to match it to a suspect."

"I may be able to help with that," said Bert Vega as he entered the office, a thick manila folder under his arm. "Thanks to your conversation with the FBI they gave our DNA search a little priority and we got a hit right away. We've got a familial match on the DNA. It's not our suspect, but it's his father."

"First things first. You said 'his.' Our suspect is a male?"

"Yes, and you're right to use the singular. All the suspect DNA we've recovered from the crime scenes belongs to the same individual."

"Who's our match?"

"Comes back to a guy named Robert L. Brewster. Goes by Bobby. It comes out of Texas. Seems Bobby was a bit of a brawler. He has a record in Texas for a number of assaults, mostly bar fights. During his last one he took a pool cue to a guy's head and the guy died. Now Bobby's in Huntsville for good. Okay, here's the part you've been waiting for, his record shows he was married to a woman named Alice. Alice Brewster lives here."

"Does Alice have a son?"

"Don't know, we're checking. Turns out Bobby had a rap sheet here, too. Again, mostly barroom stuff. Apparently he left years ago because his name pops up in Bakersfield, Long Beach, New Mexico and Oklahoma. He was an oil field roughneck in every sense of the word."

"A prince."

"Yeah, he left a trail of bloody noses and cracked ribs halfway across the country."

Vega's cell phone chirped with a text message. "We've got an address for Alice Brewster."

Five minutes later they were knocking on the door. There was no answer.

"She may be at work," said Vega.

Miller nodded and then suddenly dropped into his customary squat.

"This looks like a blood drop."

Vega peered over Miller's shoulder and then started looking around the apartment landing.

"There's another one over here by the stairs."

Miller rose halfway up and looked closely at the door. "It looks like there's a smear next to the door knob. Let's get the crime lab over here and call for a warrant. Under the circumstances, I think the judge will agree we have probable cause. I want to get inside the apartment and I'm not waiting for Mrs. Brewster to get off work."

It turned out he didn't need the warrant. Alice Brewster arrived home right behind the crime lab van.

"What do you want here? They told me at work you were looking for me and told me to go home."

"Mrs. Brewster? I'm Sheriff Dave Miller. Do you have a son?"

"Is he all right?"

It seemed to Miller that she really didn't care. She was just asking the expected question. But her response gave him the answer he was looking for; now they had a suspect.

"We don't know, ma'am. We're looking for him. We want to talk to him. What's his name?"

"Alexander. He goes by Alex."

Miller heard a noise on the stairs and saw Tommy Upton picking his way around the evidence technicians as he made his way to the landing.

"Ma'am, this is Tommy Upton. He's with the newspaper but he's been helping us with our case. You don't have to talk to him."

She shrugged. "I got nothin' to hide."

"About your son. Do you know where we might find him?"

"We usually get off work about the same time. He works at Plumrite, like me. I left early so I expect he's still there."

"So you saw him there today?"

"Not exactly. I don't always see him. We work at opposite ends of the plant. I know he was gone when I got up this morning. I figured he went to work. Why are you looking for him?"

Miller ignored her question. "Does he do that a lot? Leave before you do?"

Another shrug. "He's a strange kid. Spends a lot of time by himself. He's real smart. He could have gone to college, but he stayed here. Now he just mopes around."

"And he goes by the name Alex Brewster?"

"Alexander Robert Brewster."

"Bobby Brewster is his dad?"

"The son of a bitch. Got me pregnant, beat me and left me a few years after Alex was born."

"I'd like to look at Alex's room. I've got a warrant coming, but all I need is your permission."

She unlocked the door, pushed it open and waved them in. "It's the one on the left. You shouldn't have any trouble, it's the cleanest room in town."

Miller and Upton surveyed the room and came to the same conclusion as Brewster's mother.

"A teenager lives in this room?" said Upton. There's not one thing out of place."

At first glance, neither man could see anything in the room that didn't look like it was exactly where Brewster intended it to be. Upton looked at Miller.

"Can I open the drawers in his desk?"

"Go ahead. His mother gave us permission to search, but put these on." Miller reached into a leather pouch on his duty belt and tossed Upton a pair of latex gloves. "There could be evidence and, since we really don't know what we're looking for yet, let's treat everything like it might be important."

Upton pulled out the center drawer of the desk and whistled softly.

"Honest to God, I've never seen anything like this. Jen was neat and organized, but this is like, psychotic. There's everything you would expect in a drawer like this—pens, pencils, paperclips—all that stuff, but it's all laid out precisely. He's got paperclips laid out flat on the bottom of the drawer, each one in a row, the same distance from the next one. I'll bet he knows exactly how many paperclips there are."

Miller shook his head and snapped a photo using his iPhone. "I'm starting to think we'd better get the crime lab guys in here. I want to make sure Bert has the warrant on the way, too, just in case Mrs. Brewster changes her mind."

Since Alice Brewster hadn't yet come to stop them, they continued to open drawers, more carefully now so they wouldn't disturb any contents. They teamed up and opened each drawer cautiously. Upton would slowly pull out a drawer and then Miller would photograph it. The photos weren't so much for evidence as they were for documentation. Every drawer in the desk, and every drawer in the dresser was the same. Neat. Precise. Clean.

"I'm no psychologist," said Upton, "but I don't see how anything could be hidden in here. It would break the pattern."

"Maybe," said Miller. "There really isn't a pattern, it's more of an obsession. He's making sure everything is in its proper place. If he had something to hide, it would have its own place."

"Like taped under a drawer or something?"

"Again, maybe. I'm no psychologist either, but under a drawer isn't really a place. I think it would have to have its own place. Its own drawer. Maybe a box, or a coffee can buried somewhere. It's hard to say because we really don't know what we're looking for."

Miller continued to search slowly and methodically. Despite his earlier comments, they looked under and behind drawers. He checked under all of the furniture and he inspected the baseboards and along the edge of the carpet to see if anything might be hidden there. He checked every pocket in every piece of clothing in the closet.

Finally, the two men stood in the center of the room, hands on hips.

"Nothing," said Upton. "Other than the neat freak weirdness, I didn't see one thing that looked unusual or suspicious."

"Me either, although I'm not sure how effective a search can be when you don't know what you're looking for."

Miller slowly scanned the room again.

"Did you check the electric outlets and switches to see if any of the plates looked like they might have been removed recently?"

Upton shook his head. There were two outlets, one each on opposite walls, and a light switch near the door.

"I can't see anything that looks to me like the screws have been removed recently," said Miller, "but when the crime scene guys get in here I'll have them remove the plates just to make sure."

Miller heard conversation in the hall outside and Bert Vega walked in.

"I've got the warrant, but it's only good for the boy's room and his vehicle. The judge wouldn't give us the whole apartment, not without some supporting evidence."

"Mrs. Brewster gave us permission for his room, but we haven't turned anything up so far."

"Hey, we didn't check that heating vent," said Upton, pointing up near the ceiling.

Miller walked over and looked up.

"There's paint covering the slots on the screw heads. I don't think it's been tampered with."

"Wait," said Upton. He went over to the desk and opened the center drawer once again and removed a small glass bottle. "Look, it's paint. The same color as the walls. I saw it earlier, but I didn't attach any importance to it."

Miller dropped into a squat and peered at the carpet. He took a flashlight off his belt and held it an inch or two off the carpet so its beam played across the surface at a very low angle.

"Bring that desk chair over here, Tommy. Look at these impressions under the vent."

The flashlight beam revealed four impressions in the carpet. Miller carefully settled each leg of the chair into one of the small indentations. It was a perfect fit.

"Bert, get the techs in here right now. We need to check that vent. Tommy, this could be the place we were talking about."

They watched as a technician placed a six-foot stepladder under the vent and climbed up onto the second rung so he could inspect the vent.

"You're right Sheriff. There's paint covering the screw heads, but it's fresh. I can smell it."

He took out a flashlight and shined it through the slots in the vent plate.

"There's something back there."

After the area around the vent was photographed and thoroughly dusted for fingerprints, Miller borrowed a screwdriver and removed the vent cover himself.

"It's a box. Just to cover our bases, let's get some photos before we take it out."

Miller exchanged places with the technician. When he stepped back down, Miller climbed back up and removed the box using both hands. He walked the box over to the desk before opening it. Using just two fingers he carefully lifted the lid.

"I think we've found our guy," he said, "there's no gun, but there's a box of .38 shells."

"How many are missing?" asked Vega.

"Enough."

Miller slowly removed items from the box as the crime lab documented and photographed them. A small notebook was laid flat across the bottom of the box. He set it on the desk and slowly started turning pages.

"Bert, we need an arrest warrant for Alex Brewster. He will be charged with the murders of Jennifer Upton, Lisa Erickson, Paul Mendez, Sandra Gibson and the assault and attempted murder of Darrell Bingham. He is to be considered armed and dangerous."

Vega left the room without another word. Upton hadn't heard anything after Miller had said Jen's name. His knees buckled and his stomach churned. He reached out to a corner of the desk with his left hand to steady himself.

"What does it say? It's him?"

"It's him all right. No doubt. He has a list of targets and detailed descriptions of each murder. You wanna take a look?"

"Yes. But I can't. Not now. Maybe not ever."

"Maybe you should sit down. You're looking a little green."

Upton managed a small smile. "Green's a good color on me. It all just kind of took me by surprise. We've been looking for this, but hearing it out loud made me feel like I got gut-punched."

"Yeah, well, it's not over yet. Now we know who it is, but we don't know where to find him."

Bert Vega came back in writing notes in his report book while he held his cell phone between his ear and his shoulder. He grabbed the phone and punched the "end" button before he spoke.

"The warrant's in the works. He didn't show up at Plumrite today, or yesterday for that matter. I put out a statewide BOLO on his truck. If he took off right after he left Bingham he could be anywhere by now, so we'll have every cop in the state looking for him."

"He hasn't left town," said Upton.

"What? Why do you say that?" asked Vega.

"He's not done." Upton had finally gathered the will to look at the notebook and was now staring at the list of targets. "He's on a mission. He's got a list. He's not leaving until he's done. Look at this room. Like they say, there's a method to his madness. Leaving now would mess up his perfect order. And there's something else. I've just skimmed the murder descriptions." He paused for a moment, cleared his throat and wiped the corner of his right eye. "He thinks he's smarter than us. He thinks he's smarter than everybody. He doesn't think he can be caught."

Miller stuffed his hands into his front pants pockets and stared up at the ceiling as he thought.

"I saw a cell phone bill in one of his desk drawers. Bert, see if you can get a GPS hit off the phone. Talk to Mrs. Brewster and get a list of friends and associates. Put some manpower on that list and maybe we can find where he hangs out. As soon as the lab is done with it, Tommy and I will go through Brewster's little murder book and see what else it can tell us. Seal off this room, but give the rest of the apartment back to Mrs. Brewster."

Upton and Miller waited while the crime lab bagged all of the evidence and collected Miller's signature and initials to establish a chain of custody.

When they were finished they left the bedroom and walked to the living room where Vega was taking notes as he talked to Alice Brewster. Vega shrugged his shoulders. He wasn't getting much information. Miller stood in front of Alice Brewster and stared down at her. She smelled of booze and cigarettes and Miller was losing his patience.

"Missus Brewster. Where would your son go if he was trying to get away?"

She shrugged. "Men leave me, they don't tell me where they're going."

"What's he drive?"

"An old Ford pickup."

"What color?"

"Used to be white. It's mostly rust now."

Miller looked over at Vega who confirmed the white truck was the vehicle they had issued the lookout for. He turned his attention back to Alice Brewster.

"Have you ever heard of obstruction of justice?"

"Have you ever heard of I don't give a damn?"

Trying to cut the tension and make some progress, Upton stepped up beside Miller.

"He's in trouble, you know."

"Figured."

"Have you noticed anything different about him lately?"

"Don't hardly see him."

"Did you use to see him much?"

"Not much, but hardly at all after he graduated high school. He was so smart I figured he'd go to college. But he stayed. He acted mad. Like it was my fault."

"Like what was your fault?"

"I don't know. Whatever was making him so mad."

"We're going to find him, Missus Brewster," said Miller. "We have a BOLO out on him right now."

"What's a BOLO?"

"Be on the lookout. Every cop in the state is going to be looking for him. Missus Brewster, we think he's murdered four people."

She looked up at Miller. Her face seemed to sag and her eyes filled with tears. Then just as suddenly, her face set itself into a grim and determined mask.

"What are you going to do when you catch him?"

"That's up to him. He has a gun."

Alice Brewster looked down at the glass of clear liquid she held and swirled it slowly. She looked like she was about to say something when Bert Vega came back through the front door in a rush.

"Dave, Darrell Bingham is awake."

CHAPTER TWENTY-FIVE

B rewster was growing increasingly more nervous. The creek bed hid him from view, but that also meant that he couldn't see someone else coming. They had to be looking for him. He couldn't afford to have the police simply drive right up on him.

It was starting to get dark. He decided to move while he could still see. Besides, if he moved during the daylight hours he wouldn't have to use headlights. Headlights up the hills can be seen from a long ways down in the valley.

He started the truck and then sat for a moment, thinking about where he should go. Ultimately, he decided he didn't want to be seen out on Petro Avenue, so he simply continued further up the dirt road he was already on.

The road climbed slowly into the hills, becoming narrower the further he got from the highway. There were more turns as the road grade followed the topography. As he gained elevation from the valley floor he began to pass abandoned oil works. His senses suddenly became prickly, like something was coming into focus. And then he realized what he was feeling. He knew this place.

His father had brought him up this road when he was a boy, maybe three or four years old. It was just before he left town. His dad had to pick up a paycheck or something and his mom had made his dad take him along for the ride.

Brewster stopped the truck in the middle of the road. His heart was beating faster and his eyes had filled with tears. He didn't have many memories of his dad, and the ones he had were bad. Had this been a fun time for him? He didn't know and he couldn't explain the emotion to himself. He tried to turn the memory to the problem at hand. He seemed to remember some kind of an office. Even as a boy, it had seemed small, not much more than a shack, like the one where he had found the board he used to hit Bingham. He had waited in his dad's truck while he went in. But he remembered it being in a heavy stand of trees—oaks—cool, even on the summer day that he had been there. From where he was, he could see mostly scrub brush and knee-high grass. He rolled forward a few feet and caught a glimpse of some treetops visible just over the rise in front of him. He drove up on the rise and saw the trees and short side road off to the right. In the middle of the trees stood the shack, even smaller than he had remembered.

He coasted down the rise and onto the short track leading up to the shack. Brush scraped the undercarriage of his truck and there was a fine fuzz of green grass growing in the twin tire tracks. He pulled the truck behind the shack and got out. It was quiet and night was beginning to set in. Looking around he realized the tree canopy would make it very difficult for his truck to be seen from the air. He walked carefully through the tall grass up to the shack, wondering about rattlesnakes.

The shack was a simple wooden affair, mostly solid. Just four walls and a roof. The four-pane back window was intact, but almost opaque with fly specks and cobwebs. One of the side walls had no window at all. The other had one small window with the lower left-hand corner of the window pane broken out. The front of the shack had a single board step leading up to a door set into the left end of the wall. Another four-pane window was to its right, with all of the glass gone.

Brewster stood on the step and examined the door. It was secured with a hasp and a padlock. He tugged on the lock and it remained firmly latched, but the hasp didn't. At some point, someone must have kicked in the door, popping the screws loose from the door. Brewster pushed and the door swung open.

He stepped into the one-room office and wrinkled his nose in disgust. It was filthy and in disarray, things he didn't usually tolerate. Whoever vandalized the shack must have done it a long time ago. There was a heavy layer of undisturbed dust covering everything. In one end of the room there was a round wooden table and two chairs. Only one of the chairs had all four legs. A desk sat against the back wall. It had three drawers, all open, all empty. Above the desk there was an old calendar from an oil equipment dealer and next to it the centerfold from a Playboy magazine. The centerfold looked almost innocent compared to what could now be downloaded in seconds from the Internet. The rest of the room was empty except for a little trash and some rodent droppings.

The shack would work for temporary shelter until morning. Not ideal, but acceptable under the circumstances. He would reassess the situation when the sun came up.

He went back to the truck and took inventory of his supplies. The water, crackers and salami he had taken from the apartment were plenty to get him through the night and, if necessary, maybe one more day. But it would be small rations. He had one clean shirt left.

Analysis had always been one of his strengths and he didn't like his analysis of his own situation. The more he thought about it, the more convinced he became that he couldn't stay in Los Robles. But he also knew he couldn't leave town without retrieving the box from behind the heating vent in his bedroom. It held all his secrets. He would decide in the morning. Things always seemed clearer in daylight.

Brewster took a flashlight from the truck's glove box, gathered his supplies and walked back to the shack. He set everything down out-side and then walked over to some nearby brush. He broke off a leafy branch and used it to sweep the worst of the dust and trash out of the shack.

Even after the sweeping the shack didn't look much better. He considered sleeping in the truck but he thought he might be better protected in the shack.

If someone were to approach, he'd hear them better from the shack and, if the shooting started, he wasn't quite as exposed. But he really didn't think there would be any shooting, at least not until morning.

He spread a couple of napkins out on the table and ate. Salami, crackers and a bottle of water, and for some reason, it tasted like the best meal he had ever eaten. He stared disinterestedly at the Playboy centerfold as he chewed. He wished he had his book. He wanted to re-read what he wrote about Jennifer Upton, Lisa Erickson and Paul Mendez. Everything had gone so well with those three. Then came the mess with Sandra Gibson and the disaster with Darrell Bingham. What had gone wrong with those two? He had planned just as carefully. It was a mystery to him.

He briefly considered that, perhaps, murder just couldn't be reduced to a purely intellectual exercise. He quickly dismissed that notion. He was much smarter than any of them. He proved it with the first three. The problems started with Sandra Gibson. And even that one worked out, eventually. She died, so she couldn't identify him. Darrell Bingham was a different story all together.

Brewster replayed the scene in the parking lot in his mind. The spot was perfect and Darrell Bingham had played right into his plans. Right up until the point he raised his arm. That changed everything. Even as the board struck Bingham's arm Brewster somehow knew the blow would no longer be fatal, or even disabling.

That fat, greasy bastard had fought him. How could anyone have seen that coming? And now he had a problem.

He tried to review his options. His hope was that his first option was "business as usual." But that didn't seem likely. Everything hinged on whether Darrell Bingham lived or died.

If Bingham died, option one still might be feasible. If he lived but was in a coma or something, Brewster might still be safe and might—might—be able to finish the job at some point. But if Bingham talked, Brewster was in trouble.

To Brewster's way of thinking, it wasn't much of a puzzle. If Bingham lived, he needed to get out of town, at least for a while. He had no doubt he could evade the cops. The best of them couldn't even approach his intellectual level. But he needed to get out of town first, and he couldn't leave without the box.

He pulled the two chairs together and prepared to settle down for the night. He was sitting in the good chair and he propped his feet up on the chair that was missing a leg. He didn't really think he'd sleep. The shack was dirty, the chairs were uncomfortable, his mind was racing and he was starting to hear the sounds of the night.

As the light grew dimmer in the shack Brewster resisted the temptation to turn on his flashlight. He thought the light would be comforting, but he also knew that out in the country, light could be seen from far away. He didn't want to make anyone curious.

His eyes slowly adjusted to the darkness and soon he discovered he could vaguely make out the objects inside the shack and he could clearly see each window. He stood up and stretched. He didn't want to check the time on his phone. For one thing, he suspected time was passing slowly. For another, the bright screen would ruin his night vision, at least for a while. He made his way to the window next to the door. Moonlight, starlight, he wasn't quite sure what it was, but he was able to see the small clearing in front of the shack. He could see the grassy area near the front, the oak trees with their giant limbs that seemed to grow back towards the ground, and he could see the twin tire tracks, ghostly in the night, slowing fading into the darkness until they disappeared.

The thin walls and the cheap glass remaining in the windows offered little insulation against the sounds from outside. There were crickets. He could hear a few night birds and there were soft rustlings out in the grass.

A single tear appeared at the corner of his left eye and slowly traced its way down his cheek. He quickly wiped it away with the back of his hand. He wouldn't allow himself the luxury of crying. His life wasn't what he had planned for himself, but now it was the life he had made for himself and he would not back down.

He went back to the chairs and took out his cell phone. He needed to set an alarm so he wouldn't miss the morning newscast. He had to know about Bingham. Bingham was now the key to his future.

He set the alarm, night vision ruined, closed his eyes and hoped to sleep.

He did.

CHAPTER TWENTY-SIX

Darrell Bingham was sitting up in his hospital bed. There was a bandage on his face that only partially covered a mass of ugly black and blue bruises, some tinged with red and yellow. His left eye was shot with blood. His left arm was in a cast and supported by a sling. When Miller and Upton entered his room he started talking like he was sitting behind the desk at his office.

"Did you catch him?"

Miller and Upton exchanged glances. Clearly Bingham was in possession of all of his faculties. Just to be sure, Miller asked, "Who are we looking for, Darrell?"

"A kid named Alex Brewster. The little shit. After everything I did for him. I was coming around the back of my car and all of a sudden he was there. He yelled something about me stealing his dream and then swung a board at me. I partially blocked it and then he swung again. I punched him in the face and then we both ran."

Miller gave Bingham a small smile.

"You look like hell, but obviously you haven't lost your memory. We tossed his room at the apartment he shares with his mother. We found plenty of evidence. It's not just you. We want him for murdering Jennifer Upton, Lisa Erickson, Paul Mendez and Sandra Gibson."

Bingham paled under his bruises. "Alex Brewster is a, a . . . serial killer? And I was supposed to be next?"

"It looks that way."

Upton stepped towards the bed. "Are you all right Darrell? Do you want me to get the nurse?"

"No, no. I'll be fine. It's a shock."

Mary Ellen Driscoll charged through the door with a nurse following close behind her.

"Darrell, I was at the nurse's station when all the alarms went off. Your blood pressure spiked severely."

"We just told him he was almost victim number five," said Miller.

"Way to sugarcoat it, Dave."

"I'm okay," said Bingham. "It was just a shock. I know that kid."

"Darrell, are you up to answering a few more questions?" asked Miller.

Driscoll stepped forward and took Bingham's pulse at the wrist, checking it against the readout on the monitor behind the bed.

She looked him in the eyes and said, "You sustained some serious injuries. You have a major concussion, your vision may be blurred for a while and, obviously, you have a broken arm, contusions and bruises. You're not totally out of the woods yet. I'll let you talk to Dave and Tommy, but I'm going to stay right here and I'm going to stop all of this if your blood pressure goes up again." She looked over at Miller.

He shrugged. "Fair enough."

All three of them watched for a moment as Bingham tried to regain his composure. When a little color returned to his face, Miller resumed his questioning.

"What can you tell us about Alex Brewster?"

"I thought I knew him pretty well. He was a finalist in the Petrolia Club's annual scholarship contest. The kids who were finalists attended a number of club meetings so the members could get to know them a little better. He sat right next to me three times. He was a tremendously gifted student—nothing but straight-A report cards as far back as you want to look—but he had the personality of a bowl of plain yogurt."

"Did he get the scholarship?"

"No, and at the time, I felt a little guilty about it. He had been accepted to Harvard but there was no way he could ever go without a lot of scholarship help. But the thing about the Petrolia Club is that we've always looked beyond just good grades when we award our scholarships. We're looking for leaders, for kids who will give something back to the community someday. Josh Slater got the scholarship. His marks were actually slightly lower than Alex's, but Josh was the class president, a wide-receiver on the football team and just a really engaged kid. He went off to Stanford."

Upton was furiously flipping through the pages of his yellow pad. When he found what he was searching for everyone was already looking at him.

"Lisa Erickson was Josh Slater's girlfriend. Remember her mom talking about a long-distance relationship? Josh left town, Lisa stayed. Brewster couldn't get to Josh, so he killed Lisa."

"You think the scholarship is the connection?" asked Miller.

"I think it's possible. Can we tie in all of the victims?"

"We can tie in Darrell, obviously," said Miller.

"Tommy, Jen was one of the committee members," said Bingham. Mary Ellen Driscoll's hand flew to her mouth. "Oh my God."

"Sandra Gibson counseled all of the college-bound kids," said Bingham, "and she was our contact at the school for accepting the scholarship applications."

"What about Paul Mendez? He wasn't college-bound," said Upton.

"He was like your wife, he was on the committee. He was our student representative. We chose him because he was an outstanding student but wasn't competing for the scholarship."

The small group was stunned. The only sounds in the room came from the machines monitoring Bingham's vital signs.

"There's not much we can do tonight. The BOLO is already out," said Miller. "I'll have the deputies start grid searches and maybe I can get the Highway Patrol to fly a night mission for me. They can use their FLIR to search outside of town."

"What's FLIR?" asked Upton.

"It stands for Forward Looking Infrared Radar. It picks up heat signatures. Maybe we'll get lucky and spot something where it shouldn't be. But tomorrow, it's a full-blown manhunt. We'll cover this valley from one end to the other, and we won't stop until we have him."

CHAPTER
TWENTY-SEVEN

Upton managed to get to the Rehabilitation Center with twenty minutes left in the visiting hour. He found Eddie in the common room sitting upright in a straight-backed chair, his hands resting on his knees. He looked tense, but there was good color in his face.

"Tommy! You came!"

"Hi, Eddie. I'm so sorry I haven't been by. Things are breaking in Jen's case."

"Tell me what's happening."

"I'll tell you what I can. It's a kid. He just graduated from the high school. It looks like he's responsible for four murders and the attack on Darrell Bingham."

"Who's the kid? Do you know him?"

"No, I don't, but you might. He works out at Plumrite on the packing line. His name is Alex Brewster. Right now, officially, he's just wanted for questioning."

"I don't know an Alex, but I know an Alice. Is that his mother?"

"It is, and she's a tough old bird."

"That's putting it mildly. She's tougher than a two-dollar steak. But she makes up for it by being mean as a badger."

Upton smiled. "Yeah, that describes her pretty well." Upton's smile vanished as a new thought entered his head.

"Eddie, what was it that Plumrite accused you of stealing?"

Eddie shook his head. "Stupid stuff. A broom. Some wire. A Tyvek suit. What the hell would I do with a Tyvek suit? There might have been some other stuff, too. Why do you ask?"

"Just a theory. I'll let you know if I come up with anything."

Orderlies were starting to herd visitors toward the door so Upton said his goodbyes and climbed into his Jeep. He decided to have dinner at the café.

"Tommy! It's been a while."

Upton grinned up at Frannie as he settled into his favorite booth. He put his hat down on the seat next to him.

"Seems like it to me, too. I guess I can stand my own cooking for only so long. Besides, I'm certainly not going to make a meatloaf better than here."

"I'll bring you a big slice. You want your usual mashed potatoes and gravy?"

"You bet. And a cup of coffee."

Upton was flipping through the pages of his yellow pad before Frannie even got to the kitchen. He realized it was an idle exercise. Brewster was their guy. It seemed incredible. Brewster was just a kid. A kid who carefully planned a series of murders. And why? Because he didn't get a scholarship? It didn't make sense, although he wondered if murder ever did.

Upton kept rolling it over in his mind. There was something Darrell Bingham had said; Brewster yelled something at him when he attacked. He found his note. Brewster had yelled that Bingham had stolen his dream. Stolen his dream? His dream was winning the scholarship? Then he saw it. Of course it wasn't the scholarship. It was what the scholarship represented, the opportunity to go to college. Harvard, Bingham had said. Brewster must have seen the scholarship and his acceptance to Harvard as his ticket out of Los Robles.

The dream was a common one for kids from small towns, Upton realized. Growing up in a small town meant growing up with the same kids, grade after grade. Social positions were established early and didn't change much over the years. Generations of the same families attended the same churches, worked in the same businesses and participated in the same activities.

Brewster worked at Plumrite with his mother. Darrell Bingham took over his father's insurance business. And Jen had worked with many parents helping their children buy their first home.

Jen. She had died. Been murdered. All because this kid hadn't received a scholarship. Upton felt his face growing hot as anger welled up inside him.

"Tommy? Are you all right? You look a little flushed." Frannie slid his plate in front of him, the mashed potatoes steaming and the slab of meatloaf slathered with a thick coat of ketchup.

"I'm fine, Frannie. Just a little worked up. With a little luck, this whole thing will be over soon."

"The murders? Tommy, that's great news."

"We've got a suspect, but now we have to find him." The bell rang at the kitchen counter and Frannie spun away to pick up her next order. Upton ate his meal in silence, his thoughts on Jen and injustice. On the way out he gave Frannie a little smile and she patted his shoulder.

Out on the sidewalk he looked over and saw the lights still on at the newspaper office. He pushed through the front door just as Vic Yanuzzi was reaching to turn out the lights.

"I was just closing up, Tommy."

"I know. I won't keep you, but I wanted you to know. We know who it is. It's my story, Vic. I'm not giving it to Jerry Morris."

"I wouldn't ask you to. Run with it and don't look back. What can you tell me?"

"Not much, officially. Dave has given me incredible access, I don't want to blow it. But it's a kid, from here in town."

"A kid?"

"About nineteen. Right out of the high school. Works at Plumrite now."

Yanuzzi shook his head in disbelief. "All of them? A kid killed four people and almost killed Darrell Bingham?"

"We've got him cold, right down to his DNA at the crime scenes."

"What's next?"

"Well, we know who he is, but we don't know where he is. Dave Miller has already notified all the nearby law enforcement agencies and of course his guys are out looking, but tomorrow, it turns into a full-fledged manhunt."

"Sounds like you'd better get some sleep."

They walked out together and Upton made the short drive home. The condo was dark, but the dark no longer intimidated him. He turned on the lights and walked over to his favorite photo of Jen. As he stared into her face it seemed like her smile grew brighter. He felt like she was proud of him. With that thought in his head he climbed the stairs to the bedroom.

CHAPTER TWENTY-EIGHT

A t first it was just a pulse to Brewster, a vibration barely penetrating his consciousness. Then the reality of the sound jolted him awake. It was closer now and the sound was unmistakable. A helicopter. Moving fast.

He stood up, stiff and cold from sleeping on the chairs. It was not quite dawn and the small shack was still dark. He could just make out the windows, small squares just slightly lighter than the darkness around them. He stumbled to the window near the door. Peering through it he couldn't make out the details outside, but the helicopter sounded very close. As he looked he saw it appear over the nearby oak trees, its navigation lights blinking. It roared past, its sound peaking and then receding. He knew it was moving too fast to have spotted his truck in the dark, but he suspected the helicopter would be out searching for him after first light.

He checked the time on his cell phone and saw he had enough time to warm up the heater in his truck before the news broadcast came on. The helicopter had been his wake up call, so he turned off the phone's alarm and left the shack. He took what was left of the salami and crackers with him and opened a fresh bottle of water in the cab of the truck.

The Darrell Bingham story was the lead item on the newscast. He was alive and talking to the police. Brewster could feel the search closing in.

He formed a plan in his mind. Instead of heading south across Derrick Grade towards Bakersfield and the Interstate, he'd go north. Back through town. His mother should be leaving for work soon. He'd dash into the apartment, pick up the box and a few other things for the road, and then head north out of town. His guess was that the sheriff would figure he would make a break for the Interstate and concentrate the search to the south. So he'd move to the north keeping to the back roads until he could hook up with Highway 99 up near Fresno somewhere. But he'd have to be careful, they would almost certainly have a few people to the north of town just in case.

Fortunately, Los Robles was full of white Ford 150 pickup trucks. Like many towns with large agricultural interests, a white pickup was one of the most common vehicles around. They would all be camouflage for his. Caution. That was the key.

There was about an inch of water left in his bottle. He poured it into the dirt behind the truck and used the mud to smear his license plate. It didn't obscure the numbers, but it made them much harder to read.

Brewster turned off the radio and sat listening to the engine idling. He hadn't thought about his future much lately, and right now, he couldn't see much of a future at all.

Soon, Los Robles would be in his rear view mirror, but in his mind, he couldn't see what was in front of the windshield. He didn't know where he would go. North. But that's a direction, not a destination.

When he followed Petro Avenue out of town he would be leaving Los Robles behind, but that was the only thing he was sure of.

He was surprised again when a tear rolled down his cheek. He hated Los Robles. He hated the people. He hated his job. And he hated his mother. He had done well in school despite her and, instead of escaping to higher education and even higher aspirations, he found himself figuratively working shoulder-to-shoulder with her. Stuck on a packing line with plum-stained hands and no discernible future that held anything but a never-ending stream of plums.

She was the last name on his list. He had planned it that way. Her death would complete his revenge. But now it seemed unlikely he'd ever get to the names above hers. Maybe killing her would be the last thing he did in Los Robles. She would be different. No big plan. No carefully thought out escape after she was dead. He would just look her in the eyes and shoot her. He'd leave her where she fell, close the door behind him and disappear from Los Robles forever.

Brewster didn't know when the helicopter would start its search, or if the sheriff would set up roadblocks, so he decided he would start working his way back into town just as soon as the sun was clearing the ridge on the east side of the valley.

Brewster had no idea how the police conducted a large-scale search, but he assumed it would be organized and regimented to make certain the search area didn't have any holes. Logically, they would start at the apartment and work their way out. So, if he could some-how reach the apartment, he should be relatively safe for a while—like being in the eye of a hurricane. If the logic followed, when he got ready to leave town, he would be behind the search lines. They'd all be look-ing in the wrong direction. He'd carefully work his way north behind them and then—with a little luck—slip through the lines after dark and be gone for good.

He made his way back into town slowly, taking back streets and checking for black-and-whites at every intersection. He kept the .38 tucked between his right thigh and the seat cushion. By the time he got near the apartment he had seen only one sheriff's patrol car and it had been heading away from him on a cross street.

He parked the truck in the parking lot of an apartment complex that was adjacent to his. He found a spot that was partially obscured by an over-full dumpster and a tree badly in need of pruning.

With the .38 tucked into the small of his back behind his belt, Brewster slowly worked his way towards his apartment, crouching in the narrow spaces between the parked cars and the cinder block wall.

He came to a gate in the wall that would allow him to pass into his own parking lot. He opened the gate just wide enough to slip through. He closed the gate behind him and melted into the shrubs along the wall to watch his apartment.

He spotted the patrol car immediately. It was parked with the deputy behind the wheel looking directly at the apartment. Brewster glanced over at the carport and saw his mother's battered Toyota parked in their assigned spot. She was home. He hadn't really expected that. He had hoped he could just pick up his box and a few other things and then escape. But since she was home, he could take care of that little piece of business before he left. The deputy, however, was a problem.

He wondered if he could risk sneaking up behind the deputy and shooting him through the window of the car. He would get at least one more gun that way; and more powerful than the .38. But shooting a cop would probably take the search to a level he couldn't escape.

As he was running options over in his mind he saw the deputy pick up the microphone for his radio, say something, and then put the patrol car into gear.

The deputy slowly rolled out of the parking lot and turned north toward the center of town. There was no way the cops weren't going to keep an eye on the apartment. Fearful it was just a bluff to draw him out, Brewster settled down among the shrubs to watch his own apartment.

CHAPTER TWENTY-NINE

Upton awoke early but the morning *Register* was already on his front porch. Jerry Morris' story about the attack on Darrell Bingham was on the front page—below the fold. It was as dull and dry as the police report he had plagiarized it from. He had been given one of the biggest stories of the year and his telling of it had less drama than a report on a school district meeting.

Upton's obituary on Sandra Gibson had been elevated to a feature story and ran on page three. He saw where Vic had placed it and was pleased, but he couldn't concentrate on it. He was too keyed up. He was amazed he had been able to sleep. The knowledge that Alex Brewster might be captured at any time had his pulse rate up and his mind racing. Yet he had slept soundly and was surprised by his alarm clock.

He reheated a cup of coffee and spread some cream cheese across the top of what turned out to be a stale bagel. It didn't matter. He washed it down with the coffee and put the cup in the sink. He switched off the kitchen light, grabbed his hat, yellow pad and an extra pen and headed out to his Jeep.

When he pulled into the parking lot behind City Hall there were no spaces left. Every spot had been filled by some kind of a police vehicle.

He found a spot on the street and walked into a briefing that was too large for Dave Miller's office. Instead, law enforcement officers from all across the region were perched on desktops and chairs in the main office behind the reception counter. Miller was standing in front of the white board that had been wheeled out of his office.

"We put the copter down on the high school football field and it's being refueled right now," he was saying as Upton found a desk corner to sit on. "He'll lift off at first light and start working the areas outside of town. Our plan is to work the copter to the south on the assumption Brewster is going to head for the Interstate.

"We've had a car on Brewster's apartment all night. There was no activity there overnight, so I'm pulling him off the apartment and I'll assign the car to the search group. We'll be doing drive-bys at the apartment all day. It seems unlikely he'd go back there, but who knows? I'm going to stop by there personally when we're done here and talk to his mother again about what to do if he contacts her. She was under the influence when we talked to her yesterday and we want to make sure she understands what's at stake.

"Bert Vega will be in charge of the search group. I'll let him explain the plan."

"Good morning," said Vega. "We really don't know where Brewster might be at this point. He's hurt, but we don't know how badly. It's possible he left town right after the attack on Darrell Bingham and he's long gone. On the other hand, we've seen his list and he may be laying low hoping to put a few more notches on his gun.

"Overnight, as the Sheriff said, we put a car on his apartment and then started a grid search out from there. Mostly, we're looking for his truck, an older model white Ford F150. In some areas, the search is already approaching the city limits. In other areas it's been a little slower because of apartment complexes and other high-density occupancies.

"If we hit the city limits without finding him or his truck, it's going to be a lot more complicated. If we have to move out into the orchards and oil fields we're going to be turning over a lot of rocks. There are a million places out there to hide a truck. That's why we've requested all of this manpower. You all have your assignments, so grab a last cup of coffee and let's go find this guy."

Miller and Upton sat in Miller's idling patrol car watching the front door of Brewster's apartment. The apartment and the complex itself were quiet. Most of the occupants had already left for work. Here and there a young mother could be seen hustling her kids into a car for a short drive to school. Brewster's truck was nowhere to be seen, although Alice Brewster's car was parked in its assigned spot.

"Looks like Mrs. Brewster decided to take a day off," said Miller.

"Finding out your son is a serial killer is probably enough to make anyone take a sick day."

"I suppose so. Let's go see if she knows anything new."

Alice Brewster wasn't sick, but she was in no condition to go to work, or anywhere else. They knocked twice before the door opened and, when it did, a stale odor of cigarette smoke and alcohol wafted out. The apartment was dark—every curtain had been closed. The ashtray on the coffee table in the living room was piled high with cigarette butts. Next to it, an empty juice glass sat beside a 750 ml. bottle of off-brand vodka. About an inch of liquid remained in the bottle.

"I think you'd better sit down, Missus Brewster," said Miller.

"I'm fine. Your people were here for hours yesterday, what do you want now?"

"The same thing we wanted yesterday. We want to find your son. Did you hear from him last night?"

"No."

"He didn't try to contact you in any way?"

"I said no and I meant it. I've had a little bit to drink but I'm not stupid. My son is a genius and he didn't get that from his daddy."

"Well, Missus Brewster, then why don't you enlighten us? What do you think your son is going to do next?"

She stared at Miller, her eyes locked on his. She was swaying as she stood and finally broke eye contact.

"I'm going to sit down."

Miller followed her to the sofa but remained silent. She started to reach for the juice glass but stopped herself. She put her hands in her lap and stared at them. When she looked up her eyes were wet.

"I think he's going to keep killing people. You showed me his book. He has a plan. That's what he does, he makes a plan and he follows it. No matter what. If he made a plan to kill people, he intends to follow the plan. I don't think he really has any friends. He was always studying in school. He didn't hang out much. Nobody ever came over. Even at work he keeps to himself. I guess he's what you'd call a loner."

"Do you think he'll try to come home, or try to contact you?"

"I really don't know, but I doubt it. Like I said, he's smart. It's a small town, he has to know you're looking for him."

"How about if he left town? Where do you think he might go? Do you have any relations he might visit?"

"Nobody I've talked to in years and most of them he's never met."

She started to reach for the glass and stopped herself once again.

"The families. Do they know it was Alex?"

"They know he's our suspect."

"Are they mad?"

"No. Not really. Mad comes later. They're mostly confused. They don't understand why."

"Neither do I."

"So you don't think it's the college thing? Him not getting the scholarship?"

"That would be hard for me to accept. The Petrolia Club scholarship is a thousand bucks. A thousand bucks. I've never been to college but I don't think a thousand bucks goes very far at Harvard. He's smarter than that."

As they left her, Alice Brewster reached for the glass again and this time she didn't stop. Miller drove back to the Sheriff's office and they each poured themselves a cup of strong black coffee from the 40-cup urn that had been brewing coffee non-stop for more than twenty-four hours.

"So, do you think he's smarter than that?" asked Upton.

"Than what?"

"Are we wrong about the scholarship? Do we have his motive wrong?"

"No. I mean yes, he's smarter than that, but I don't think we have his motive wrong. All of the pieces fit in that puzzle. On the other hand, Alice Brewster is right, he's too smart to think that scholarship gets him to Harvard."

"Maybe he thought of it as a critical first, important step. If he got that, everything else would follow."

"Maybe. Or maybe it was just another disappointment in a crappy life and he just snapped, and not getting the scholarship was the catalyst for everything that followed."

They sipped their coffee while that thought hung in the air. They both looked up when the door to the dispatch office slammed and Carol Burnside came bustling toward them. Upton spilled a little coffee over the edge of his cup. To see Carol Burnside bustle was something of an experience. She stopped in front of Miller, her heaving chest straining her uniform buttons.

"The copter spotted something south of town."

"The truck?"

"No. They couldn't see a vehicle but they saw fresh tire tracks going to and from what looks like an abandoned shack up in the oil fields."

"How did they know the tracks were fresh?" asked Upton. Burnside gave him a glare.

"Flattened grass and tracks in an area otherwise undisturbed."

Miller stepped in to save Upton. "Get directions and radio them to me in my car. Have Bert start five patrol cars to meet me there. Ask the copter to orbit the site and watch for any activity."

As they pulled off Petro Avenue south of town Upton looked back out of the patrol car's rear window and saw a line of patrol cars speeding towards them, red and blue lights flashing. Miller keyed his radio and told the cars to park behind him on the shoulder of the road.

Miller walked a few yards to where a dirt road intersected with the pavement. He squatted down to inspect the tracks in the mixture of dirt and gravel. Upton stood behind him and was soon joined by five deputies.

"The tracks are fresh," said Miller, "but there are several sets. Coming and going a couple of times, maybe."

"Do you think it's him?" asked one of the deputies. Upton noticed the deputy's hand slide back to the butt of his gun unconsciously.

"I think it's possible. The tracks aren't conclusive. But the shack increases the possibility." Looking at one of the deputies he said, "Call off the copter and thank him. He's reported no movement around the shack and no sign of a vehicle. Tell him to continue his search pattern to see if he can spot the truck. We'll head up there and see what we can find."

They entered the dirt road single file, Miller in the lead, and drove slowly up the road. Miller's eyes scanned the road constantly.

They dropped down into a small dry stream bed and stopped as Miller saw tire tracks veer off a short way downstream. He stepped out of the car and again his deputies convened behind him.

"Looks like whoever it was pulled off here and parked for a while."

Staying well off to the side of the creek bed, one of the deputies worked his way up to where the tracks stopped.

"There's something here, Sheriff. I can see what looks like a bloody tissue or napkin down there. It's wadded up into a ball."

"We know he left his attack on Darrell Bingham with a bloody nose," said Upton.

"Call in the lab boys," said Miller. "Let's collect the evidence and document the scene. It doesn't look like anything happened here, but I want to be sure we've covered all of our bases if we end up in court."

Miller assigned two deputies to preserve the scene in the creek bed and everyone else got back into their cars and continued up the road.

Topping a small rise about a half-mile further up the road Miller spotted the shack the helicopter had reported. He reached over and keyed his radio microphone.

"The copter reported no movement around the shack, but let's be smart about this. We'll approach assuming the suspect is there and armed. Two of you head further up the road and get in a position to cover the back and the flanks. Let me know when you're in position. One unit come with me and we'll approach from the front."

The cars split up and Miller took the lead, bumping down the track that led to the shack. He glanced over at Upton who was staring intently out the front windshield.

"If he starts shooting, get down on the floorboards and don't get up until one of us tells you it's clear."

"If someone starts shooting I'll be running back down the road screaming like my ass is on fire."

Miller grinned, but he said, "Just get on the floorboards."

Miller and the second squad car pulled in front of the shack, stopping about thirty yards from the door. He and the deputy got out and stood behind the driver's door of their vehicles, weapons drawn.

Miller could see the other two deputies behind the shack and each gave him a thumbs-up signal. Miller checked to be sure a round was chambered in his 9 mm. He nodded to the deputy and he jacked a shell into his shotgun.

"Alex Brewster! Sheriff's Office. Show yourself."

There was no response from the shack. Upton had slid far down into his seat and was peeking over the top of the dashboard. The police radio beside him was chattering with sounds from the searches taking place elsewhere and the powerful engine was steadily idling.

Miller shouted several more times but there was no sound from the shack. He used hand signals to instruct the deputies behind the shack to advance and try to see inside.

They advanced cautiously and one deputy stood up on his toes and peered into one of the side windows.

Upton saw all of the deputies tighten their grips on their weapons as they closed in. Finally, the deputy at the window held up four fingers—Code Four—it was safe.

One deputy entered the shack—weapon drawn—to make sure the structure was unoccupied.

"It's clear, Sheriff. But it looks like he was here. Or somebody was."

Upton followed Miller through the door. He took in the entire room with just a glance.

"It was him."

"What makes you so sure?" asked Miller.

"He tried to clean up. Look. The table has been wiped off and you can see marks on the floor where he swept."

"Well, I'm not sure we could convict him on that evidence, but I agree with you."

"If it was him, where is he now?"

"That's the question, for sure," said Miller. "He's obviously gone, but is he gone for good, or just moving round, trying to stay ahead of us?"

"I don't think he's gone," said Upton. "If he was going to run he could have just kept going instead of holing up here. And his mother said he finishes what he starts and, according to his book, he's far from done. He was only about halfway through his list."

"True, but we have to factor in his intelligence. He knows the heat is on. The smart thing for him to do would be to leave Los Robles and never look back."

"Maybe. It might all depend on Darrell Bingham."

"How?"

"We all agree he's smart, so think about this. Until this morning, Darrell's condition was unknown. He could live, he could die. If he lives, he identifies Brewster. If he dies, Brewster can keep working his way through his list."

"Darrell's condition was released this morning."

"That's right, but that means Brewster couldn't make a decision until this morning. And, by the time he heard Darrell would live, he had probably also heard there was a massive search underway. He would have to devise some kind of an exit strategy."

"What do think that would be?"

"I don't know. He's the genius, not me, but he would probably try to put himself in your head."

"Yeah, I really don't want him there."

"I'm sure. But let's try to approach it like he might. He has to assume we're looking for him. We know who he is and what he's driving. If he's listened to the radio, he knows Bingham is alive and a search is going on. We're in a valley with, essentially, only two ways out—north and south. The kid's no outdoorsman, he's not climbing a ridge and living off the land to survive. South is the Interstate. That's the most likely escape route, so it's also the most likely to be sealed off. That leaves him only one way out—back through town."

"But you said we have to assume he knows we're looking for him. That would take him back right into the teeth of the search."

"Yeah, but he's a genius, remember? Think logically. If you have to cover a wide search area, what kind of pattern would you most likely use?"

"A grid."

"Correct. And I think that would be his guess too. So I think he'll slink back into town and try to hopscotch through the grids. He'll watch for patrol cars and try to stay behind them."

"Geez, that would be a pretty gutsy plan."

"Dave, the kid is bold and arrogant. He thinks he's smarter than all of us. I'm invested in this too, and I think he's heading back to town, and if he does that, he might try to scratch a few more names off his list."

Miller thought for a few moments, then nodded.

"So, what do we do?" asked Upton.

"I'll have the lab document the scene here and we'll head back to town. I'll contact the highway patrol and let them know Brewster's last-known location was south of town and have them watch the grade for us, just in case. I'll have my guys shift some additional resources to the south part of town and see if we can close the gaps a little."

When they got back to Miller's office they found Jerry Morris sitting in one of the hard wooden chairs next to the reception counter.

"I need a story," he said.

"Do you think you're going to find it sitting on your ass?" said Upton.

"Vic is pushing me for a story. I figured this was as good a place as any to start."

"What have you got so far?"

"Nothing. I was waiting for you guys to get back."

Miller glanced at Upton. "See me when you're done here," he said as he swung the counter door open and made his way back to his office.

Upton looked at Morris and wanted to slap him. A huge story was unfolding on the streets of Los Robles and Morris was sitting in an empty sheriff's office, with only Carol Burnside to ignore him. But, Upton still owed Vic Yanuzzi for his support, so he decided to counsel Morris instead of excoriating him.

"Jerry, you can't expect a story to come to you. Sometimes they will, but usually you have to go out and find them, and build them. Have you talked to Brewster's mother? How about his coworkers? Have you been to any of the crime scenes, talked to any of the victims' families?"

"No. I figured all that stuff was old news."

"It's not old news, Jerry. Talking to those people is how you paint a picture of Brewster. If all you do is write about his capture, Vic might as well just run a copy of the police report. Until Brewster is spotted, your job is to get out there and tell our readers how his actions are affecting our community. Are they nervous? Mad? Frightened? Take their pulse and find out what they're feeling."

"Sounds like a lot of work."

Upton shook his head. "Good luck, Jerry," he said and left Morris still sitting on the chair as he walked back to Miller's office. Carol Burnside rolled her eyes as he walked by.

Miller was staring at the white board.

"I just can't get inside his head, Tommy. He's supposed to be this brilliant kid, but he has a narrow escape and, instead of taking off, he spends the night in an old shack. And, to make matters worse, our best guess now is that he *still* hasn't left. I'm just having trouble getting my head around this, he knows everyone is hunting for him but he comes back to town?"

"He's brilliant, Dave, but clearly, he's also nuts. I think his mom nailed it, he isn't finished."

Miller ran both hands over the top of his head and looked up at the ceiling of the office.

"That's scary, Tommy. If what you say is true, and I happen to think you're right, it means he's more crazy than he is smart."

"He's killed four people, Dave, and tried to kill a fifth. I think the crazy ship has sailed."

Miller thought about that while he stared at the board. Coming to an internal decision he took his hands out of his pockets and walked to his office door.

"Carol, would you please get on the radio and have Bert come in?"

"No need, he just went 10-7 in the back parking lot."

"Good. Track him down and have him come see me."

Upton could see Miller was working on something in his head so he kept quiet while they waited for Bert Vega. Miller picked up the trophy football from the shelf behind his desk and spun it in his hands while he paced.

"What have you got, Dave?" asked Vega as he came in and perched on a corner of Miller's desk.

"We've got to be smarter than this kid. We can't just do a grid search, he could kill somebody else while we're looking. So here's what I'm thinking: If we accept that he hasn't left town, then we have to figure out where he's most likely to go."

Upton leaned back in his chair and pushed his fedora up onto his forehead. "I'll play, Dave. I'll tell you what I *don't* think. I don't think he's going to hole up somewhere. If we accept that he came back to town to finish the job, then I think we've got to think about the people left on the list."

"Who's next on the list?" asked Vega.

"I'm not sure we can go by the list sequentially," said Upton, "especially now. Jen was number three on the list, but the first victim. Lisa Erickson was number eight or nine. I think he'll prioritize somehow and try to take out his biggest targets before he has to run."

All three men went to the white board and stared at the photocopy of Brewster's list.

"Let's think about locations," said Miller. "Look at his life and his list and you can see there are three places that have meaning for him: his apartment, Plumrite and the high school. Those places are all known ground for him. They're where he would be most comfortable. There's too much heat on him to scout a new murder scene."

"Don't forget the hospital, Dave," said Vega. "Darrell Bingham is unfinished business."

"Good point. So is his apartment. He left some things there he thinks are important, and he doesn't know if we've found them or not."

"Oh no," said Upton. "There's something else about the apartment; his mother. She's on the list."

Miller nodded. "You might be right. There are a lot of things he can tidy up if he goes back there, Bert, get uniforms to the high school and Plumrite. I want you to check in on Darrell Bingham. Tommy and I will head for the apartment."

The three men stood silently, somehow knowing their next step was going to trigger a chain of events that would bring everything to an end.

"Tell everyone to be safe and protect themselves, Bert. He's desperate."

"This isn't going to end well, is it?"

"Probably not for him."

CHAPTER
THIRTY

He saw the Sheriff, and another guy in civilian clothes, leave the apartment and close the door behind them. It was a good thing he had waited in the bushes, watching. He had started to cramp up a little and had been just about ready to move toward the apartment as the Sheriff had driven into the lot.

Now, as the patrol car left the complex, Brewster sprinted across the parking lot and took the stairs to the apartment as he usually did, two at a time.

Practice makes perfect. He let himself into the apartment silently. He always kept his bedroom door shut and he knew how to get in and out of the front door without making a sound. Half the time his mother had no idea if he was home or not. His odds went even higher after the vodka bottle made its first appearance of the day.

She should have been at work, but he had seen her car in their parking space under the carport and saw the Sheriff come out of the apartment. His first thought was she had hit the bottle harder than usual. But it also occurred to him she was probably getting a lot of pressure from the Sheriff and others about him. The Sheriff might have had a warrant, but she was probably home.

As he pushed the door open and entered the living room he realized he was right on both counts. The vodka bottle was nearly empty and he could see business cards with large gold sheriff's stars laying on the coffee table. She was asleep, or more likely, passed out on the sofa.

He ignored her and went directly to his room. He knew at a glance it had been searched. The room was neat, and nothing seemed to be missing, but everything had been touched. Everything had been moved. He quickly folded some shirts and placed them in his backpack. He went through his desk drawers and added a few personal items. Then he took the screwdriver out of the center desk drawer and carried the desk chair to a spot under the heating vent. He took off the cover and stared into the duct work.

"The cops took it."

His mother was leaning against the door jamb, arms crossed, looking up at him.

"Took what?"

"The box you had hidden in there."

"You let them in my room?"

She shrugged. "They had a warrant."

"So they're looking for me?"

"Of course they are." She looked down and hesitated before she said, "Did you do it? Did you kill those people?"

He stepped down off the chair and stood facing her. "Yes. They deserved it after what they did to me."

"What did they do to you?"

Brewster thought his mother looked like she might throw up. He hoped she wouldn't do it in his room.

"They stole my dream. They ruined my life."

"I don't understand, Alex. What dream?"

"Harvard. A new life. A new town. Never eating, smelling, seeing or touching another plum again. I was going to overcome Los Robles and be someone."

"How did they steal this dream? That's nothing any of them wanted for themselves."

"The Petrolia Club scholarship. They all played a role in giving it to Josh Slater, not me. That scholarship was my ticket out of here."

"How can you be so smart and not realize how wrong you were? That scholarship was a drop in the bucket. It wouldn't have bought the books for one semester at Harvard."

Brewster's face turned red and spittle formed at the corners of his mouth. He reached under his shirt and pulled the revolver out of his waistband. Alice Brewster began backing down the hallway toward the living room.

"You stupid bitch! You don't understand anything. What do you know about college? You've lived in this crappy town and worked at your crappy job your whole life. I wanted something better. Something bigger. You're as bad as they were."

He stepped toward his mother but was halted by pounding on the front door.

CHAPTER THIRTY-ONE

"We're not going to drive right up to the apartment," said Dave Miller. "I'm going to start a couple of blocks out and we'll kind of circle our way in. I figure if he's coming back to the apartment he won't rush right up. He'll watch for a while to see if we're waiting for him."

"So what are we looking for?"

"Movement. As we circle in, be watching for his truck, he'll have to leave it somewhere. He'll be working his way to the apartment very carefully, but as fast as he can. Pay attention to what you see out of the corners of your eyes. That's where your brain will recognize movement. He's watching for us, so what you might see is just a blur as he ducks behind a car, or lets go of a branch in a bush he's peeking through. Keep your head moving back and forth, always scanning."

The men remained quiet as Miller circled the neighborhood. People were out, but nobody was acting suspicious and Upton didn't see any motion out of the corner of his eyes.

"Wait. Back up to that driveway. Does that look like the bed of a Ford?"

Miller looked down the driveway of an apartment complex and saw the vehicle Upton had pointed out. It was partially hidden behind a dumpster.

"That could be it, Tommy. Get out and wait for me here."

"That's not going to happen."

Miller looked into his eyes and knew he'd have a fight on his hands if he tried to force Upton out.

"Fine. I'm going to drive down there. Take your seatbelt off. If he starts shooting I don't want you stuck in your seat."

Miller called for backup and then rolled slowly through the parking lot. He turned his red and blue lights on, but not the siren. They were close enough to read the license plate.

"That's it," he said. He immediately got on the radio. "Dispatch, Sheriff Miller."

"Go ahead, Sheriff."

"Dispatch, advise all responding units this is a silent approach. I don't want to alert the suspect. I've confirmed the plate, I'm going to clear the vehicle now."

"Copy, Sheriff."

Miller turned to Upton. "Stay in the car. No argument. If he starts shooting, get on the radio and say, 'shots fired.' Don't get out until backup gets here."

"I'm not moving from here," said Upton.

Miller got out of the car but did not close the door. He unsnapped the flap on his holster and drew his 9 mm Glock. He went to the tailgate of the truck and started working his way down the driver's side, his gun leading the way.

When he reached the cab of the truck he risked a look through the back window of the cab. He slowly moved forward to the driver's door. The window was up. He took one step away from the truck, quickly pivoted to his right to face the driver's door and raised the Glock to chest level in a two-handed grip.

He heard other patrol cars coming to a stop behind him. Looking back to where Upton and the deputies were waiting Miller raised four fingers.

"Code Four," said the deputy crouched next to Upton. "Brewster's not in the truck."

Miller walked back to his car. "The hood's still warm, but it's cooling down fast. He's been here long enough to make it to the apartment. I'm going to head straight there. The rest of you tape off this scene and then spread out and work your way to the apartment. He may still be hiding somewhere between here and there. If he's at the apartment we may have a barricade situation or he might even be holding his mother hostage. Mobilize the tactical response team and get them headed to the apartment, too."

As they pulled into the parking lot at the Brewster's apartment complex, Miller gestured with his chin toward the carport.

"That's not good. Mrs. Brewster's car is still in their spot."

"So now we have a hostage situation?"

"Not necessarily. We've never seen them together. She may be in on the thing. It didn't seem that way, though. And, he may not be in there. We have to consider that as well."

They quietly climbed the stairs to the second floor landing. Upton stayed on the landing, his fedora pulled down tightly on his head and his yellow pad clutched in his hands. He watched as Miller approached the door. Looking back at Upton, Miller mouthed, "Can you hear them?"

Upton nodded. The sound of an argument could be heard coming from the apartment. Miller stepped to the right side of the door and then knocked loudly.

"Mrs. Brewster? It's Sheriff Miller. Mrs. Brewster, open the door."

The arguing stopped and it seemed to Upton that all of Los Robles had gone silent. Miller knocked again.

A bullet came through the door, narrowly missing Miller's hand. It was quickly followed by another.

Upton ran down the stairs without embarrassment. Three members of the tactical response team passed him on their way up, but he didn't slow down until he reached Miller's patrol car.

Miller, gun drawn, was at the side of the door, his back pressed against the wall. A member of the tactical squad handed him body armor. He removed his cowboy hat and set it down on its crown while he lifted the vest over his head and then tightened the straps around his chest. He settled his hat back onto his head and then started giving commands to the tactical squad.

Upton couldn't hear what Miller was saying, but he guessed by his hand gestures that he was giving deployment instructions.

One team member stepped to the stairway landing and started speaking into his handheld radio. The other two stayed with Miller. One crossed over and took up a position on the other side of the front door across from Miller. The other took up a position behind Miller.

Upton looked around and saw deputies moving to the rear of the apartment building and quietly escorting people out of the apartments on either side of the Brewster's. Behind him, he saw a sniper taking up a position on the roof across the parking lot. A fire engine and an ambulance silently rolled to a stop about a half a block away. Upton looked down and realized his yellow pad was still in his hands. He turned to a fresh page and started writing furiously, pausing only to make a few sketches.

At the door, Miller received the signal that everyone was in place. There had been no sound from inside the apartment. This time, Miller didn't knock.

"Alex. It's Sheriff Miller. We need you to come out of there." For a moment, there was nothing, and then there was a voice that sounded like it was coming from far back in the apartment.

"That's not going to happen, Sheriff."

"Alex, you're a smart kid. You have to understand the position you're in."

Miller left the two tactical officers on either side of the front door, ducked under the front window, and came back downstairs to his car. With the apartment's front door compromised with two bullet holes, they would have to be very careful. Brewster would be able to see light and shadows through the holes, making anyone who passed the doorway a possible target, so any personnel going to the far side of the front door would have to go the long way around using the staircase at the opposite end of the building.

When Miller reached his car he immediately picked up his radio microphone and announced to all units they were officially dealing with a hostage situation and barricaded subject, and the subject was armed and dangerous. His car was designated as the command post for the incident.

Miller ordered his command staff to the back of the car and they started to discuss their options.

"Bert, check with the tactical guys and find out of any of them have a clear line of sight into the apartment," Miller said. "I'd like to know where he is and if he has his mom restrained in any way."

"We're probably going to be here for a while, so call the County and get them to send a couple of units to cover the city for us. Cancel the BOLO and let the FBI know we have our guy cornered. I'll call Ana Espinoza and give her the news myself."

Vega was punching numbers into his cell phone before he even turned to walk away. Miller pressed a speed dial number into his own cell phone and waited while it rang.

"Mayor Espinoza, this is Dave Miller. We have Alex Brewster cornered in his apartment. Shots have been fired." He listened for a moment and then said, "I'll keep you posted," and hung up.

Tommy Upton moved up next to Miller. The Sheriff was staring up at the second-floor apartment.

"What's next?" Upton asked.

"It's up to Brewster. My gut is telling me this is going to end bad for Brewster, but all he has to do to prevent that is put his gun down and walk out the front door."

"That's probably not going to happen."

"Nope."

Bert Vega joined the two and announced, "Nobody has eyes inside. We're blind."

"When he yelled, it sounded like he was back a ways from the door," said Miller. "Like maybe in the kitchen."

"No guarantee he's still there, though."

"Nope."

"The FBI offered to send up a hostage negotiator," said Vega.

"Good. Let's get him or her on the road. I'm not sure how long this is going to last, I'd like to have that in my back pocket. My negotiating skills are kind of limited and a little rusty. If we can keep things calm until the negotiator gets here, we may get out of this with no one else getting hurt. But his mother is on his list so we're going to have to get the ball rolling and hope Brewster is willing to play."

Everyone at the command post had unconsciously imitated Miller's posture and now they were all staring up at the apartment like its front door had some kind of message for them.

"I wonder what's going on up there," said Upton.

Miller looked over at him and said, "Me too. I think I'll give him a call and see if we can find out. It might give us a chance to take his temperature."

Miller thumbed through his notebook, found what he was looking for, and started punching numbers into his cell phone.

CHAPTER THIRTY-TWO

The second shot startled Alice Brewster more than the first one had.

"Are you crazy? They're going to come in here shooting."

"Shut up. I'm trying to think."

"Yeah, well think about giving up. You know they're out there now, and there are probably more on the way. How do you expect to escape?"

He turned and pointed the ugly little pistol at her face.

"I said shut up. I don't plan to escape. Not anymore. I plan to kill as many of them as I can."

"With that?" She pointed at the pistol still aimed at her face. "What do you have left, three, four shots? Every cop out there has more bullets than you."

He swung the pistol backhanded, catching her on her right cheek. She fell backwards onto the living room sofa, a bright red line of blood tracing her cheekbone.

"I said shut up. Don't make me say it again."

This time, Alice Brewster remained silent. She watched her son as he paced back and forth the few short steps between the living room and the kitchen. He stopped mid-stride, turned and went to the living room window.

Standing off to the side, he moved the curtain just enough to get a view of the parking lot. It was filled with patrol cars and cops. Looking up, he saw a police sniper on the building across from his. The sniper was staring right at him over his rifle scope. He had seen the curtain move.

Brewster let the curtain drop and went to the kitchen. He took a cloudy glass out of the cupboard, filled it with water and drank it down.

"My mouth is dry," he said. Alice Brewster remained silent, watching him. He sighed, and the act seemed to deflate him. He sat down heavily in a chair at the kitchen table and stared down at the floor.

"Why are you doing this? Why did you have to kill all those people?"

"They stole my dream," he said, but he didn't sound convinced.

"That's not what I mean. You've said that and I told you it was crap. That's what you're using to justify your actions, but it isn't enough. You didn't have to kill them."

"What was I supposed to do?"

"I don't know. Grow up? Apply to a less expensive college? Start at the community college? You had options, Alex. And you decided murder was you're your best bet. Maybe you didn't deserve to go to Harvard."

He stared at her. There was no sound in the apartment, just the faint murmur of all the police radios out in the parking lot.

"I wanted to get away from here. Away from you. Leave Los Robles forever, just like dad."

"So your dream was to be like your father? No good, in and out of jail, a drunk, a wife beater?"

"No. My dream was to be better than him. Better than you. Better than everyone."

"And how did you expect to accomplish that? With more schooling?"

"Are you really that stupid? I was going to Harvard. I was going to be someone."

"I didn't believe it when the Sheriff told me, and now hearing it out of your own mouth, it sounds even more incredible. People died— people were *murdered* because of that tiny scholarship. Even if you had the scholarship, where were you planning on getting the rest of the money? The tuition, the housing, the meals, the travel? What I make in a year at Plumrite wouldn't pay for a semester at Harvard."

"The scholarship was a start. I was going to build on it."

She didn't respond. She just stared at him, her eyes slowly filling with tears.

"My God. You killed those people for nothing. They didn't do any-thing and you were in some kind of a fantasy world. I know I haven't been much of a mother, but I never thought I was raising a psycho-path. You're just like your father, a mean, selfish bastard."

She reached for the glass of vodka and took a long slow pull. Then she stood up carefully and slowly in front of the sofa, got her balance, and shambled toward her bedroom.

"You don't understand! They stole my dream. They deserved to die!"

She didn't slow or turn around as he screamed. She just closed her bedroom door quietly behind her.

Brewster glared at the closed door for a heartbeat and then went back to the front window. This time he approached it from the oppo-site side, wondering if the sniper had zeroed-in on where he peeked out the first time.

He knew the Sheriff would still be outside, but now it looked like every cop in the state was standing in the apartment parking lot. Red and blue lights were everywhere. Yellow crime scene tape had been spread across the driveway entrance and people were gathering behind it on the sidewalk.

This wasn't how his plan was supposed to end. He had been so careful. He had worked out all the details. Damn Sandra Gibson. That's where things had started to go bad.

"I should have killed her first," he said to himself. "She was the one who encouraged me. She was the one who said I was a lock for the scholarship. She was the one who gave me the Harvard catalog when I went in to ask about Fresno State. I hate her."

His fists were clenched and a tear leaked out of his right eye. He refocused and found himself once again staring into the eyes of the sniper on the roof. He quickly dropped the curtain and stepped back from the window.

He glared at his mother's closed bedroom door. He would finish that part of the plan no matter what else happened. Especially after the way she had just talked to him. Acting like she was the smart one.

He heard a helicopter pass low overhead. He walked backed to his bedroom and looked out the window there. There were more police. And another sniper. The helicopter was white with a multi-color peacock logo painted across the loading door. Not the police, NBC. Probably from the Bakersfield station, he thought. But they might send the feed to L.A. Maybe everyone would know his name after all.

He went back to the living room and started wandering around it. Looking at the kitchen he could see one magnet clinging to the door of the refrigerator. It was from a bail bonds company. He wondered how long that magnet had been there.

A few art prints from the dollar store hung on one wall of the living room. They had been bright and cheery when his mother brought them home. Now they were dull and faded by time and cigarette smoke.

Brewster stood staring at the art reproductions without really seeing them. A glint of sunlight caught his eye. A small ray of sunlight had found a crack in the curtains and was reflecting off the glass of a photo frame between two others on a shelf in the corner. It was an old Sears print of the family, taken when he was just a baby. His mother looked the same, just younger. Her eyes were sunken, her arms thin and sinewy. She looked tough. He guessed she probably always was. She had to be. He focused on his father's face. It had been a long time since he had looked at it. His father looked so young, but he could see no trace of the cruelty that lived behind the face.

The photo next to it was of his mother receiving some kind of an award at Plumrite. A man he didn't recognize was shaking her hand and presenting her with some kind of a certificate. She was smiling. She didn't smile very often, at least not that he could recall.

The third photo was of himself. His high school graduation photo. It wasn't a good photo. He wasn't smiling. It had been taken less than a week after he found out about the scholarship. He stared into his own eyes, but saw nothing. He compared his face to his father's, but saw nothing there, either. He wondered if his mother had framed the photo to mock him somehow, like graduating from high school was the crowning achievement of his life. He put the photo down and turned around to face the room.

He wasn't sure where to go in the apartment, there were police outside of every window. He thought they might be right outside the front door as well. Every now and then he heard small scuffling sounds from outside, like someone was shifting position.

He settled down onto the sofa not realizing he was occupying the same spot his mother had just vacated. He sat up straight, both feet on the floor, his hands on his knees, staring at the two beams of light streaming into the apartment through the bullet holes in the front door.

He jumped when the cell phone in his left front pants pocket buzzed.

CHAPTER THIRTY-THREE

"**I**t's time to get this party started," said Dave Miller. Bert Vega was standing next to him along with command officers from the county sheriff's office, the highway patrol and the Los Robles Fire Department. Tommy Upton stood behind the fire chief and tried to stay out of the way. "Let's see if he'll answer the phone."

He looked down at his notebook and ran his finger down the page until he found what he was looking for, and started punching numbers into his cell phone. "It's ringing."

The entire parking lot seemed to go silent, all eyes focused on Miller.

"Alex, it's Sheriff Miller. It's time to end this. No one else needs to get hurt."

Upton leaned closer as Miller listened to Brewster's response, but he couldn't make out anything that was being said, just a murmur. Miller's face hardened as he listened.

"You do not have a hostage," Miller said. "That's your mother. If she wants to leave, you're going to let her."

There was a brief pause before he spoke again. "Actually, I am the one in charge here and the sooner you recognize that, the better it will be for you. I can make your life easy, or I can make it hard. It's up to you."

Upton still couldn't make out anything Brewster was saying, but it was clear he was angry and shouting. Miller started to say something in return and then lowered the phone away from his face.

"He hung up."

"I don't know much about negotiating," said Upton, "but it kind of sounded like you pissed him off."

"That was my intent. He thinks he's smarter than us, I had to make him understand that he wasn't in control. Everything he's done so far he's tried to plan carefully, he can't plan for this. He's out of his comfort zone."

"Does that put his mom into further danger?"

"Maybe. That was a calculated risk. He's a coward. He's ambushed every one of his victims except for Paul Mendez, and he made him kneel so he couldn't fight back. I don't think Brewster is tough enough to shoot his own mother when he's surrounded by cops."

"So what's the next step?"

"We start applying pressure." He turned to Bert Vega and started issuing orders. "I want the tactical team to move their vehicle right to the bottom of the stairs. Have them put on a show prepping their forcible entry tools. Put spotters up on the roof with the snipers. I want him to think we're ramping up to breach the apartment."

As the deputies scattered to complete their assignments and the other command officers drifted off to update their agencies, Upton resumed his questioning of Miller.

"Did he make any demands?"

"He wants us to pull back and let him leave."

"Or what?"

"Or he shoots his mother."

Upton's face paled. "You said you didn't think he'd shoot her."

"I don't."

"Then how do you handle that kind of threat?"

"Well, not by letting him go. Here's my problem—Alice Brewster was on his list. He's been planning on killing her all along. In fact, she may already be dead. We haven't heard or seen her since we got here and heard them arguing. Both snipers report seeing him, but not her."

"But both bullets came through the front door."

Miller looked at his shoes before raising his head and meeting Upton's eyes. "Tommy, he doesn't always use a gun."

Upton caught his breath as a vision of Jen laying in a pool of blood filled his mind.

"He's mad, Tommy. There are two things that can happen now. He can open the front door and come out with guns blazing, or he can start bargaining.

"He's too smart to come out shooting. He's not Butch Cassidy. Like I said, he's a coward. He's a pissed off coward, but he's still a coward. I don't think he has the guts to take aggressive action against a show of overwhelming force. I think he'll try to play 'Let's Make A Deal' because he thinks he's smarter than us."

They watched as the armored tactical vehicle pulled into position at the base of the stairs. Upton couldn't be sure, but he thought he saw the curtains in Brewster's apartment move slightly.

Somehow the stairs leading up to Brewster's apartment reminded him of the stairs in his condo and the photos of Jen hanging on the wall. The photos he now studied every time he went up or down the stairs. The photos that, not too long ago, were too painful to look at, but now he couldn't wait to see. Jen's smiling face and shining eyes reaching out to him from every frame.

But the boy, the man, at the top of the ugly cement stairs in front of him had, for a while, replaced those beautiful images with a monstrous one. He wanted to hate Brewster, but Jen's memory wouldn't allow it. He felt a hand on his shoulder.

"Tommy, I'm going to call Brewster again."

Upton walked with Miller back to his patrol car. His command staff had reassembled.

"I'm going to see if I can get him negotiating. I'll start small and work my way up. He's had time to think now, maybe we can get him to make some concessions."

Miller pressed the redial button on his cell phone and waited while it connected. When it did, Brewster didn't even give him a chance to speak.

"Alex, calm down and let's talk," Miller said when there was a break. "Things may not have changed in there, but they've changed out here. I have deputies in place all around your building and the FBI is on the way. But hey, I'm not trying to be unreasonable. This has been pretty intense. Maybe we could take a little time-out. Are you hungry? How about your mom? Do you want me to order you a pizza or something?"

There was a pause as Brewster replied.

"No, I don't think you're stupid," said Miller. "I think you're hungry and it's starting to look like we might be here for a while. Think about what I'm saying."

Bert Vega caught Upton by the elbow and guided him a few feet away.

"He's trying to break the ice," whispered Vega. "Dave just wants to get him to agree to something, anything. Once he breaks that ice, Brewster has given us an opening and we can start chipping away at it. He might also give us a clue about his mother, like if she's still alive. Best case scenario is he surrenders. Second-best is he lets his mother go, assuming she's alive. But to get there, we need to get him making concessions; accepting food, letting us talk to his mother—anything that produces movement in the negotiations."

"Pizza. Does that work?"

"Sometimes. Not always. Sometimes none of it works and we end up with a big bloody mess. But he's had a stressful couple of days. He's hurt, he probably hasn't slept much and he probably hasn't eaten much. The mention of food might get his stomach rumbling and that might give us the opening we need."

Miller approached them from the back of the car. "Well, that went a little better than the first time."

"Did he agree to anything?"

"No, but he didn't hang up on me either. The problem is, I can't tell if I'm making progress or if he's simply become resolved to a plan of action."

"How do we find out?"

"Gentle pressure applied relentlessly. We have to stimulate movement. The status quo doesn't work for either one of us. Clearly, time is on our side, but we can't forget about his mother. We have to assume she's being held against her will if she's still alive."

The cell phone in Miller's shirt pocket rang, startling them all. Miller glanced at the Caller ID on the screen.

"It's him." He pushed a button to answer the call. "Sheriff Miller here."

Miller started pacing with the phone.

"Of course I'm willing to talk," he said into the receiver. Then he listened for, what seemed to Upton, a long time.

"That's not going to happen, Alex, and you're smart enough to know it."

Brewster was yelling. Upton could hear it faintly from both the phone and from behind the apartment door.

"It's pretty simple, Alex. Either you come out, or we're going to come in and get you. Send your mother out first and then come out behind her with your hands up in the air. If your hands are up, I guarantee your safety."

Miller looked down at his phone. "He hung up." But Brewster wasn't done talking. An ashtray sailed through one of the front windows of the apartment, crashing onto the parking lot below. The curtains remained closed with just a small gap where the ashtray had knocked them apart.

"Sheriff! Can you hear me?"

"I hear you, Alex. We can all hear you."

"This ends now."

"It doesn't have to end, Alex. We can keep talking. You have options."

"My options disappeared when that scholarship disappeared. My options disappeared when my dream disappeared."

"You can still dream, Alex. You're a young man. Call me on the phone. Let's talk about this."

"I'm done talking, Sheriff."

"Alex! Alex, are you there? Let me talk to your mother."

The parking lot was silent. Even the police radios were quiet. A light breeze rustled the curtain in the broken window.

A single shot sounded from inside the apartment. Every law enforcement officer ducked behind their car and drew their weapon. Bert Vega grabbed Upton's arm and pulled him down. Upton turned to look at Vega with a stunned look on his face.

"What just happened?"

"Nothing good."

Deputies took up positions behind their cars as Miller signaled the tactical team to prepare to enter the apartment. They approached the front door from both sides and then froze in place as the door opened a crack. Their weapons went to their shoulders.

"Hold your fire," Miller shouted. "Hold your fire." Then towards the apartment he yelled, "Open the door slowly and step out with your hands in the air."

The apartment door swung into the apartment and Alice Brewster stepped out onto the landing with her arms raised over her head. She was holding a pistol in her right hand.

She looked at the parking lot full of deputies and said, "I shot the little bastard. He was going to kill me. My name was in his book."

For a moment there was a stunned silence in the parking lot. Then a tactical squad member grabbed her right hand, pulling it down behind her as he disarmed her. Then stepping behind her he handed the gun off to another team member, grasped her left hand and handcuffed her behind her back. She didn't struggle. Three other team members entered the department, weapons drawn and ready. One quickly reappeared at the front door holding up the familiar four fingers.

"It's over," said Miller.

He ordered Mrs. Brewster to be brought down and sent paramedics into the apartment. They quickly confirmed that Alex Brewster was dead, so he declared the apartment a crime scene and cleared everyone out.

Mrs. Brewster had been placed in the back seat of Miller's patrol car and a deputy handed him her .38 revolver.

"There's another one just like it next to the body," said Bert Vega. Miller looked up in surprise.

"Two guns?"

"That one's mine," said Alice Brewster from the backseat. "When my son-of-a-bitch husband bought one, I told him I wanted one too. I was trying to keep the playing field as level as possible. He was a mean one. I thought he took it with him, but I recognized it as soon as I saw it in Alex's hand."

"Did he hurt you?"

"Which one?"

"Well, either of them."

"Bobby beat me once or twice a week until he left. Sometimes he'd hit Alex too. Alex never physically hurt me. He just talked down to me and treated me like dirt."

"You've been read your rights, so you don't have to talk to me, but I want to know what happened up there."

"He was losing it. He was getting madder and madder. Finally I just went to my room and shut the door. I could hear him talking to you and it was obvious things weren't going his way. I found my gun in the back of a drawer and stuck in in my waistband and pulled out my blouse to cover it. I went back out to the living room and he was on the phone with you. I heard him say 'I'm done talking,' and then he ended the call. He turned around and saw me. He had his phone in one hand and his gun in the other.

"He said, 'That's it, it's over.' Then he looked me right in the eyes and said, 'I can't get the others in my book, but I can get you.' So I shot him. Once. Right in the middle of his chest. He looked surprised and then he fell down. That's when I came out."

"I'm sorry," said Miller. Tears formed in her eyes but didn't fall.

"Don't be, Sheriff. It was bound to happen sooner or later. His father was all bad and the apple don't fall far from the tree. I brought him into the world, it's probably right that I was the one to take him out of it."

Miller closed the patrol car door and he and Upton climbed the stairs to the apartment. The crime scene technicians waved them in with an admonishment to not touch anything.

Brewster's body was flat on its back in the middle of the living room. A wet red spot the size of a saucer stained the center of his shirt. His eyes were open, his arms by his sides. The .38 lay inches from his right hand.

The position of the body reminded Upton of his final image of Jen. He walked closer and looked down at Brewster.

"My God. He's just a kid. Somehow I forgot how young he was."

Miller put his hand on Upton's shoulder.

"He was full-grown evil, Tommy. He was old enough and smart enough to know what he was doing. Don't lose one minute of your life feeling sorry for him. He left a trail of tragedy behind him. If you're going to feel sorry, feel sorry for Jen and Lisa, Paul and Sandra. And for all the people who loved them.

"Alice Brewster did us all a favor. We can start healing right now. No trials. No reliving the crimes. No plea bargains. It's over. Done and done."

"What's going to happen to her?"

"Probably not much under the circumstances. She'll probably face some charges, but there's a strong case for self-defense and I can't believe the D.A. will have a lot of energy to prosecute her for anything."

Upton continued to stare down at the body. Suddenly his chest heaved and a sob escaped.

"He took her from me, Dave."

"I know, Tommy. But I don't think Jen would want you being angry with him. And I don't think she would want what he did to her to be the memory of her that you carry with you."

Upton took a deep breath. "You're right. I think I need to get out of this room.

CHAPTER
THIRTY-FOUR

Upton gave the orderly three dollars and carried his tray over to where Eddie was staring out the window, his food untouched.

"How're you doing, Eddie"

"Hey, Tommy. Better, man. Better."

"Doesn't look like you're eating much."

"Yeah, well, I'm sober enough to know the food stinks here."

The two sat in silence for a few minutes. Upton picked at his dinner and pushed food around the plate. Mercer's food sat untouched. Upton forked some kind of batter-fried meat into his mouth and agreed with Eddie's assessment of the food.

"I've been eating, Tommy. I just don't have much stomach for it. I'm doing everything they ask. I'm eating, taking my meds, going to meetings; whatever it takes."

"That's good, Eddie. That's really good. And speaking of good, I've got some good news for you.

"We found the guy that killed Jen and the others. He's dead now, but that's not the good news. The good news is that once we knew who the suspect was, the sheriff's department could go looking for evidence. Some of the evidence they reviewed were security tapes from Plumrite. All of those videos show you in the areas where things went missing. But they all show someone else, too. Alex Brewster."

"Alice's son? The nerdy one?"

"That's the guy. He was also our murderer and it turns out that everything that was missing from Plumrite was used in the murders. He wrote it all down in a little book."

Eddie stared at Upton without speaking. His eyes glazed with tears and, when he spoke, his voice quivered with emotion. "So I'm in the clear? Tommy, this means I could get my job back."

"I think it does, Eddie, but you've still got all of this to work out."

"I have a meeting with Shirley Albertson tomorrow."

"The head of Human Resources?"

"Yes. I called her after I sobered up. She didn't sound very promising on the phone, but I think she's willing to listen. Now this. This could change everything."

"I hope it will. But you're going to have to be strong."

As Upton drove home his mood felt lighter than any time in recent memory. He wasn't happy. He wasn't celebrating. But a tremendous weight had been lifted from his spirit.

He turned the key in the front door lock of the condo and wondered how he would feel when he crossed the threshold.

He felt fine. Jen's presence was strong, but Upton could sense a new calm, a peacefulness. And when he looked at the photos of Jen a warmth radiated from her smile.

He set his hat down on the kitchen counter, picked up the phone next to the refrigerator and dialed Vic Yanuzzi's home number.

"Vic, it's Tommy. I've got your story. All of it, and I'm not giving one word of it to Jerry. He wasn't even at the apartment today."

"It's your story, Tommy. Go with it. I still have time to hold tonight's print run. Can you give me something tonight, just four or five inches with the basics?"

"I'll pound it out right now and email it to you. But you won't believe the whole story when you hear it."

"Tell me in the morning. Start writing."

Upton opened up his laptop and quickly wrote the brief story on Brewster's death, but even as he typed he was thinking about the bigger story. He'd write a story for Vic that everyone in town would read, and then he'd try to find a bigger audience. He was back. He could feel it.

———————

He was at his newspaper desk the next morning when his phone rang. It was Eddie. He was being released and needed a ride. Upton pulled up to the curb and could see Eddie sitting in the lobby, just inside the door.

"This is good news, Eddie."

"I told you I've been working hard. They're letting me go home, but I have to come back once a day for a meeting. At least for a while."

"That's great. You can handle that."

"I'm going to, Tommy. I'm changing my life."

Upton threw Eddie's small suitcase into the back of the Jeep. Eddie kept a small plastic bag of personal items on his lap.

"Do you want to stop at the store and pick up some groceries, or just go home?"

"I think I just want to go home."

"I don't blame you."

Eddie climbed the stairs to his apartment a little unsteadily. Upton followed him with the suitcase. Eddie turned the key and stepped inside.

"Thanks, Tommy. The place looks fine."

"It was my pleasure, Eddie. But there's something we need to talk about."

"Booze."

"Yeah. I didn't want to invade your privacy, so I didn't look, but if you've got any liquor stashed, it needs to go."

"It's not stashed. I live here. But there's plenty of it. Most of it is in the cabinet over the refrigerator. There's a bottle in the nightstand by the bed, and one under the sink in the bathroom."

Upton started taking down bottles and lining them up on the kitchen counter. There were six bottles of vodka and one bourbon bottle. All of them had been opened except for one bottle of vodka.

"Is that all of them?"

"It's all of them I remember."

"How about in your car?"

Eddie's shoulders sagged and he heaved a heavy sigh. "Oh, God. I'm sure there's at least one in there too."

"Give me your keys. I'll take these down to the trash and check your car while I'm down there."

Upton found two more vodka bottles in the car. He threw them all in the dumpster, trying very hard to break each bottle. Upstairs, Eddie cringed at each crash.

When Upton got back to the apartment Eddie was sitting on the living room sofa, his hands in his lap.

"I read your article. It's a terrible thing."

"You have no idea. I hate to use the cliché, but that article was just the tip of the iceberg. Wait until you read the whole story."

"Tommy, would you mind turning on the Keurig? I think I could use a cup of coffee."

"I'd be happy to." He turned on the machine and found a supply of the little cups in the cabinet above it. He brought Eddie the steaming mug of coffee.

"You want anything in it?"

"No. This is fine." He took a sip and then said, "Plumrite is going to give me another chance."

"You don't sound very excited."

"I am. It's just that it's going to be really hard. I know people will be looking at me."

Upton sat down next to him and put his hand on Eddie's shoulder.

"I'm sure you're right. Nobody said recovery was going to be easy. You're getting a second chance so of course there are people who will be watching you. Show them you deserve the second chance."

"When am I going to start feeling better?"

Upton knew he wasn't talking about the alcohol.

"It takes a while, Eddie. Like they say, one day at a time. But if you need me—day or night—call me. I'll help you through this. And then, one day, things will seem brighter and it just gets better from there. At least, that's how it worked for me. You want me to go get you some food?"

"I've got some stuff in the freezer. I'll be all right. You got a story to write."

Upton stood and walked to the door.

"Thank you, Tommy."

"You're welcome, Eddie. Call me if you need me."

Before he got into the Jeep he looked around and inhaled deeply. Things did seem brighter.

CHAPTER THIRTY-FIVE

Tommy Upton sat at his desk in front of the window at the *Register* sorting through a large stack of mail. His feature story on the murders was in papers all over the state and was picked up by the national wire services. A lot of the mail was job offers.

Alex Brewster had been buried without ceremony or sympathy. The grave was unmarked, but the brown grass above it was hard to miss in a small-town cemetery. Some people in Los Robles were already saying grass would never grow there. Grass can't grow over evil.

He looked out the window and saw traffic making its way around the circle. The town was trying to get back to normal.

Checking his watch he saw he was due over at the café. He picked up his hat and walked the short distance. Dave Miller was already there and had a cup of coffee waiting for him.

"Still fielding offers?"

"Nope. I've decided."

"Really? Where are you going?"

"I'm not going anywhere. Vic offered me my old job back, and then he surprised me. He said he's getting old and, if I was interested, I could work for a couple of years and then decide if I want to buy the *Register*. I told him I was interested."

"It sounded like some of those other papers were offering good money. You weren't tempted?"

"Sure I was, but when we moved to Los Robles, Jen and I decided that this is where we wanted to build our life. I ruined that. And then Alex Brewster stole *my* dream. Now I feel like I've been given a second chance. I owe her that."

Dave Miller looked better, too. Upton hadn't realized the toll the murders were taking on Miller, he had been too focused on his own issues. But now he could see that Miller looked relaxed and confident.

After the shock of Alice Brewster shooting her own son, the hardest part of the whole ordeal might have been the conversations Miller had with the families of the murder victims and Darrell Bingham. Upton had gone with him on the visits and it seemed to help the families to have him there. They knew he shared their pain.

Ana Espinoza was rarely seen in the sheriff's office any more. She seemed to find enough to do upstairs and, during city council meetings, she wouldn't make eye contact with Miller. Miller and Upton laughed about it. Vic Yanuzzi had told Upton that Espinoza's re-election was anything but certain.

Since its days as an oil boom town Los Robles had always considered itself independent and self-sufficient. Espinoza's persistent calls for outside assistance during the search for Brewster had alienated many long-time residents and had incensed Dave Miller's loyal voter base. Now it appeared Espinoza would run as a virtual outsider and her chances didn't look good.

Overall, things were getting back to normal in Los Robles, except normal felt different, fresher. Like the air after a storm passes through. Upton had gone back to spending part of his mornings on the bench in front of City Hall watching the traffic pass by and reading his copy of the paper. The draw of Louie's was now only an occasional yearning, and he and Eddie spent a lot of time letting Frannie pour them coffee.

After reading his stories online, Jen's parents had called. They spoke for only a few minutes, but Upton could tell their anger had softened. With Jen gone, they no longer had anything in common, but at least there was peace.

Vanity Fair had called and wanted a feature story on the murders and an option on a book. He had a yellow pad about half-full of ideas for the book, but it all seemed too recent to really start writing.

Jerry Morris, relegated to the second string, had left town to take a job with a paper in Fresno. It hadn't been a very good paper to start with.

To write his article, Upton had visited Darrell Bingham. He had made a full recovery. He said that you had to be hard-headed to sell insurance in Los Robles. He had also resigned from the scholarship committee of the Petrolia Club.

Upton looked up and saw Eddie and Mary Ellen Driscoll come through the door. They came to the booth and sat, Eddie next to Miller and Mary Ellen next to Upton. Frannie was walking up to the table with a pot of coffee in one hand and two mugs in the other. When Mary Ellen sat down next to Upton, she shot a glare at her but neither Mary Ellen nor Upton seemed to notice.

Upton could feel warmth coming from Mary Ellen Driscoll, their shoulders almost touching. After she had finished examining Alex Brewster's body, she and Upton had gone for coffee. Miller had been invited, but demurred. Now they had coffee about once a week. Upton thought he might want to buy her dinner sometime soon.

Upton looked down at his empty coffee cup and waived off Frannie's attempt at a refill.

"I'd better get going," he said. "I'm on deadline for a front-page story on Alice Brewster's trial."

"She'll walk," said Miller. "Her name was on the list and she was being held hostage. After what happened, no jury would convict her."

"True enough, but the story will still sell newspapers."

"You're already talking like you own it."

"Are you kidding? I'm just glad I'm not writing obits anymore.

ABOUT THE AUTHOR

Bill Nash is a veteran newspaper columnist, photographer and award-winning writer based in Southern California. He also writes occasional feature stories and has published nearly 50 travel destination pieces on locations around the world. His first novel, *Fog Delay*, was a thriller set at the San Francisco International Airport. As a non-fiction author, his is also known for writing *Oil, Orchards and Flames*, a history of the fire department in Santa Paula, California. He has a background in journalism, public relations and advertising; and has won numerous local, state and national awards for his work.

59179995R00151

Made in the USA
Lexington, KY
26 December 2016